ERRANT ANGELS

By the same author:

Fatal Tears, Book Guild Publishing, 2013

ERRANT ANGELS

An Eccentric in Lucca: Book 1

Stuart Fifield

Book Guild Publishing
Sussex, England

First published in Great Britain in 2013 by
The Book Guild Ltd
The Werks
45 Church Road
Hove, BN3 2BE

Typesetting in Baskerville by
Norman Tilley Graphics Ltd, Northampton

Printed and bound in Great Britain by
CPI Group (UK) Ltd, Croydon, CR0 4YY

A catalogue record for this book is available from
The British Library

ISBN 978 1 84624 970 9

For DJH, who had the vision...

1

'It's getting late and it doesn't look as if she's coming!'
'There's still plenty of time. I'm telling you that she'll be here. Thursday wouldn't be Thursday without a visit from the...'

Their muttered conversation was interrupted by the arrival of yet another group of customers who, like all the others, stared covetously at the display of cakes. It was obvious that they were tourists; not that Gianni Canetti needed any further proof of this simple fact. The dazzling arrangement of delicate pastries, chocolate-dipped dainties and large cream-filled fruit creations displayed in the long, ornate, glass-fronted counter always produced the same effect on tourists. The locals had long ago accepted this mouth-watering Aladdin's cave of wonders as the norm, just like buying tomatoes or peppers at the market. For the army of tourists brought to this deliciously calorific heaven on the advice of all the leading guidebooks, the promise of a few moments of unrivalled pleasure on the taste buds produced a strange, glassy-eyed glaze, which quite literally stopped them in their tracks.

'Hello, we are...' said one of the group, intently studying a thick guidebook he held in both hands. It was opened at the section devoted to a vocabulary list. The man's sentence remained unfinished as he scanned the list of Italian words and useful phrases in his book. Gianni, who thought the man quite thick-set and unusually tall for an oriental, stood patiently behind the counter, a look of mild, amused

1

tolerance on his face, '…visitors,' said the man eventually, a look of triumph on his face.

'Um hum…' replied Gianni softly, his smile unchanging. *Japanese? Or possibly Korean,* he reasoned.

The man was grinning and bowing slightly, which seemed to be part of the ritual of pronouncing the selected words from the guidebook.

'You are visitors to Lucca?' cooed Gianni, grinning at them all in that natural, seductive, everyday way only successfully managed by Italian males.

While the visitor's smile remained fixed to his face his eyes betrayed the truth, which was that he had not understood much of what Gianni had said. He buried his nose in the guidebook once again, desperately trying to remember the sounds he had just heard and to match them to some phonetic translation in the list of phrases. He had not noticed that the rest of his group had abandoned him to his fate, spreading themselves out along the curved glass front of the counter, animatedly engaged in an intensive, yet subdued welter of indecision as to which pastry to select.

'I have only a little understanding,' replied the man with the guidebook, reading out the phonetic translation of the phrase he had found. He looked relieved.

Gianni smiled back warmly, but out of the corner of his eye he had noticed another smaller group, which was congregating outside on the pavement on *Via Fillungo*. They, too, would soon enter the cool atmospheric interior of the *Café Alma Arte* – most visitors to Lucca did – and that would cause a bottleneck at the counter. The café was an Art Nouveau jewel and was one of many such buildings lining *Via Fillungo*. But it had not been built to accommodate the army of tourists that the beginning of the twenty-first century had brought with it. More often than not, the busy little café was bursting at the seams. Confusion over the vocabulary in a guidebook definitely did not help the

2

free flow of customers in and out of the single, bevelled glass door.

'Would you like to speak English?' asked Gianni effortlessly, as he saw the next group about to enter from the pavement. In a perverse sort of way he quite enjoyed the struggle most tourists went through with their attempts to speak Italian – sometimes he found it difficult to control his mirth when what had been said in all good faith would have been enough to cause a diplomatic incident or send the visitor straight to the nearest confessional to do penance.

'Ha... Yes, you speak English,' replied the visitor, who was only too pleased to close the guidebook and put it away. He turned to the rest of his group as he did so, gabbling happily in the knowledge that, for the time being at least his problems with the Italian language were over.

Of course I speak English, thought Gianni, as he quickly and expertly placed the assorted order of dainties on individual white plates, *and so would you, if you had to deal with someone like the Contessa.*

Behind him, his sister, Anna, was manipulating the Gaggia with similar dexterity, churning out all manner of coffee – *espresso, caffé Americano, latte* and *cappuccino*. In fact, the *Café Alma Arte* – the 'nourishing gift' in a mixture of Latin and Italian – positively reeked of coffee. That was a large part of the café's attraction. There were those who said that they always had two cups for the price of one: the first being the inhaled luxury of over a century's accumulated coffee aroma that could be savoured before they imbibed the second one, the one for which they actually paid.

'I told you she's not coming,' repeated Anna, as she distributed the cups of steaming liquid amongst several small trays that lay on the serving shelf. 'She's usually been in and out by now. It's not like her to be this late. You know what the mad English are like; they have clockwork for souls!'

'She'll be here. It is Thursday right up until we close,' replied Gianni, returning a large spatula to a basin of water and wiping his hands on his apron.

'Perhaps she's had a fall... At her age it is possible,' continued Anna, rolling her eyes in mock alarm as the Gaggia spat and fumed away.

'What dark thoughts you entertain, *sorella mia*,' muttered Gianni. 'I hardly think the Contessa would be bothered by a fall. In any case, *if* anything had happened, all of Lucca would have heard of it by now. Have you heard of anything?' he asked, raising his eyebrows to emphasize the ridiculousness of her suggestion.

'At her age she *would* be bothered by a fall,' replied Anna, her gaze firmly fixed on the chrome machine in front of her, 'and you'd be lucky to hear *anything* above this racket,' she said, gesturing into the bowels of the café to where a capacity crowd was happily engaged in the twin delights of the palate and good conversation.

The consumption of the exquisite calorific creations and intoxicating coffees was almost a religious rite and the contented chatter in many tongues made the place sound like the United Nations. In fact, it was a bit like that august institution because any sense of international goodwill was only skin deep. The café's faithful but slightly belligerent locals were obliged to sit cheek-by-jowl with the tourists and were not about to give up their usual tables for anyone.

'And I have to tell you that the Gaggia has decided to play up ... again,' continued Anna, wiping down the front of the coffee-making machine with a damp cloth. The spout, through which scalding steam escaped to froth the milk, sputtered and occasionally spat angrily, allowing some of the leaking steam to condense on the front of the machine. The Gaggia was much older than either Gianni or Anna. Their father seemed to think that it had been there since Mussolini's time and there were many amongst the

4

cognoscenti who claimed that the ancient build-up in its extensive network of pipes was partly the reason why the coffees it produced tasted so memorable. Over the intervening years, regular repairs and threats of replacement seemed to have kept it going. It might not be of quite the same vintage as the Contessa, but then again, she seemed ageless anyway.

'Someone is going to have to look at it; the bloody thing's got a mind of its own at times,' continued Anna, slapping it with the wet cloth. 'It belongs in a museum.'

2

At the same time as the Gaggia was giving vent to its feelings in the café a delivery was being made further along *Via Fillungo.* Midway between *Café Alma Arte* and the old Roman amphitheatre stood *Casa dei Gioielli,* the 'House of Jewels'. It was not a particularly large shop, but it was crammed to the gunwales with antiques. The exquisite items on display were of the utmost quality and none of them had a price ticket displayed. It was the kind of shop where customers knew exactly what they were looking for and did not concern themselves with the cost. Gregorio Marinetti, the much respected proprietor of this grand, if modest, emporium, stood looking at his latest acquisition.

'*Bellissimo,*' he purred in semi-ecstatic enjoyment of the object that stood on the tiled floor in front of him. For just a moment, standing in front of the age-clouded screen, he forgot the grim reality of his situation. In addition to being a well-known connoisseur of fine *objets d'art,* Gregorio Marinetti also harboured a recent secret, the alarming implications of which he had to fight very hard to keep in check. In the few minutes since the arrival of the screen, this secret had come to subconsciously terrify him. He had debts – very serious debts. Business had not been good of late and in a moment of desperation, he had turned to gambling to raise the much-needed finances. It had been a disastrous foray into something about which he knew absolutely nothing. In fact, his huge gambling debts had added to his problems alarmingly and his creditors – his gambling 'associates', all of whom were unpleasant at the best of times – were becoming more and more aggressive due to his inability to settle.

'Are you certain that no one knows?' he whispered. The sound came out like a strangled wheeze. He tried again, taking care to take one or two calming breaths before he did so. 'Are you certain that no one knows ... about the screen? Nobody can trace it ... back to me, I mean ...' He cast a furtive glance over his shoulder and out through the shop window. He was also aware that he was sweating under the expensive cut of his business suit.

'As certain as the Holy Father is a true Catholic,' muttered the smartly dressed man, irreverently. He stood behind Marinetti and spoke with a southern accent, which the antique dealer found hard to understand on certain syllables. Gregorio thought that this man probably came from Naples, or perhaps even further south.

'Of course nobody knows, otherwise we wouldn't last five seconds in this business now would we?' continued the smartly dressed visitor after a short pause. There was a lot of calm sarcasm in his voice and it was obvious that he did not tolerate foolish questions. 'In our business, we just *do*. We do not *explain*.'

He took a cigarette from his gold case and lit it. He didn't offer Marinetti one. As he replaced his lighter in his pocket, he turned his head and glanced casually out of the window. He wore an extremely well-cut suit that had probably cost twice what Marinetti's had. Despite the fine clothes, this man had a dangerous air of menace about him, but without any sign of nervousness. Why should there be? He was used to these sorts of deals; it was an important aspect of his profession. It was obvious to him from just looking at Marinetti's behaviour that *he* was the newcomer to dealing on the dark side of his profession.

'So...' said the man with the Naples accent, turning back

7

to Marinetti now that he had satisfied himself that everything was as it should be outside the shop. He exhaled a fine plume of smoke, '…if you are satisfied, I believe that we agreed a sum … if you please,' he said softly, gesturing towards the screen. Gregorio did not notice. Instead, he focussed perspiring eyes on the two associates his visitor had brought with him to carry the heavy screen into the shop in its protective wrappings. They now stood at the door, one on either side, like two nightclub bouncers. The antiques dealer shivered. These were large, well-built, muscle men under their Armani suits and looked decidedly unfriendly – even more so than the Neapolitan, who now stood waiting for payment of the agreed sum.

'Yes… Yes, of course … the sum agreed…' repeated Marinetti, his baritone voice suddenly pitched unnaturally high. He coughed and his voice returned to something nearer its normal pitch. 'If I may, I would like to have a closer look.'

'If you must,' replied his visitor, making a second irritated sweeping gesture towards the screen, as he shrugged indifferently. 'But I need hardly remind you that my time is extremely limited,' he continued ominously. Gregorio detected the hint of impatience in the man's voice, but as his nerves were severely on edge anyway, he put it down to his own over-active imagination.

The visitor turned and crossed the shop floor to where the other two men were standing. The three of them formed an inverted triangle pointing menacingly into Gregorio's usually placid and ordered world – a world which had started to fall to pieces. The antique dealer's palms were wet, as he expertly cast his gaze over every detail of the screen. It was Venetian, probably late fifteenth century and worth, at a conservative estimate, many times more than what he was going to pay for it. In his business, there were those silent collectors for whom the price of an article they desired was of no consequence. Any illegalities simply disappeared into the anonymous and very isolated safety of their private collections.

'There will be no questions?' asked Gregorio, a faint tremor in his voice; he wasn't sure if it was due to the excitement of being so close to a thing of such value or simple fear. He was still standing in front of the screen and had half-turned towards the door, dividing himself equally between the beautifully dingy object in front of him and the decidedly dodgy reality of his situation. The screen was going to be his salvation, but the human triangle at the door could yet prove to be his undoing. His visitor had almost finished his cigarette and shrugged, raising his eyebrows enquiringly in an unasked question. Gregorio raised his hand feebly towards the screen. 'No questions about the screen?' he repeated.

'How many more times must I say this? I have already told you ... we do not answer questions,' replied his visitor softly, menacingly. 'Besides, if I were to tell you anything...' he paused, placing one hand in his trouser pocket, '...it would almost certainly be a lie. That is the nature of our business,' he concluded, a leer playing on his lips around the smouldering end of his cigarette. He had delivered the whole of the previous speech with the cigarette clamped delicately to his bottom lip. The ash had not even fallen from the end, so practiced was he in this manoeuvre. 'You have *that*, which is what you wanted,' he said, pointing to the screen with his free hand. 'You do not need to ask questions.'

Gregorio attempted a chuckle, but the noise that escaped from his throat sounded more like a phlegm-induced choke than an indication of mirth. His feet had started to sweat. He couldn't remember that happening since the day of his final *viva voce* examination at Pisa University, and that had been all of thirty years before. His nerves really *were* stretched and they had started to buzz.

'The agreed sum?' repeated the visitor, as he plucked the butt end from his mouth, dropped it on the marble floor and ground it out with his shoe. It was a simple, smooth action, but one laced with warning menace. Marinetti suddenly felt an overwhelming urge to get this man and his two acolytes out of his shop before they polluted his environment any further.

'We agreed the sum,' repeated Marinetti, casting a nervous glance out through the shop window. *Via Fillungo* seemed oddly deserted for the time of day. It was as if everyone knew that there was something less than legal going on in *Casa dei Gioielli* and had no wish to become involved. 'Please follow me to the office,' he continued, indicating the two doorways at the rear of the shop. One was his inner sanctum, the other was his stockroom. *Casa dei Gioielli* was, after all, of modest proportions and he couldn't put *all* of his treasures on display at the same time.

Twenty minutes later, the area of *Via Fillungo* outside Gregorio's shop was still almost empty – not that he noticed. He had paid for the screen in cash, which had all but wiped out his remaining cash reserves. Marinetti had let out a deep sigh as his three visitors eventually evaporated into the empty street. He hurriedly threw a large piece of brocade over the screen before anyone out in the street could get a good look at it. Then, as his lip curled up in disgust, he bent down to sweep the crushed butt end into a dust pan. Apart from the brooding presence of the screen, which remained standing in all its faded glory in the middle of the marble floor, the shop looked as it had done when he had opened it that morning. He fussed around, tidying and straightening his treasures. However, the brocade he had flung over the screen did not quite cover the face of the animal on the centre panel. The winged Lion of St Mark – the ancient symbol of the Venetian Republic – seemed to glare at him from underneath the many layers of darkened varnish as it peeped around the hanging swag of fabric. From its position on the central panel of the screen, it seemed to know that its new owner had done something wrong. The noble beast resented being part of the dishonesty of the purchase. For the first time in his life, Gregorio Marinetti had involved himself in a seriously illegal transaction – something which, if it were ever to become common knowledge, would ruin not only his own, but also his family's long-standing reputation within the *Comune di Lucca*. His standing as a respectable antiques dealer would be in tatters.

'Desperate times call for desperate measures,' he hummed to himself nervously. All he needed now was the telephone call from his customer's agent to arrange collection of the screen and he could start to breathe easily again. 'Why doesn't the telephone ring?' he muttered. He found that with a little juggling, the words almost fitted the melody of '*Di Provenza il mar*', Germont's aria from Verdi's *La Traviata*. It was his party piece – one that the Contessa said he sang particularly well. The lion remained oblivious to this fact and the one eye that could see around the end of the brocade swag continued to follow Gregorio with a malevolent glare. 'And let us be quite honest, they couldn't really get much more desperate than they are now.' He stopped suddenly and chuckled. It was no good; there were too many words to continue singing them to Verdi's famous melody. He felt far more relaxed now and, still chuckling, he straightened an ornate mirror and flicked at the gilded frame with his duster. He caught the reflection of the lion in the glass and turned around in surprise, to be met by the accusing glare. 'You have to take risks to restore the balance,' he muttered to the screen, 'and when *you* are collected and paid for, the balance will be fully restored.' He promptly felt foolish for having spoken to an inanimate object. He was on edge and his nerves were still a little raw. They were made even more so by the ringing of the telephone. Although expected, the sudden noise came as a shock and caused him to back into a seventeenth-century *escritoire*, its delicate legs scraping across the marble tiles.

'Yes... Yes, I have it here... Oh... Is it not possible for you to collect it today? Forgive me, but I thought that that was the arrangement and...' There was a note of worried dismay in his voice, as the caller cut across him. 'But of course, any time to suit the *signore*... Indeed, cash would be acceptable... Very well, until next Thursday then, when you will call to make final arrangements for the collection,' continued Marinetti, his mouth now quite dry, 'if it cannot be before...' he added somewhat pathetically, trying to disguise the anxiety in his voice. 'Please use my mobile; you have the number.' There was a curt mumble of acknowledgement on the line. 'I think it is better that we...' but the line had gone dead. As he replaced the handset, he realized that his client was the one who was used to giving orders – people who were that wealthy usually had no problem at all in making the world revolve around their particular needs and arrangements. Whilst still looking absently at the telephone, a new worry suddenly revealed itself to him. The simple fact was that this sudden change of plan had serious ramifications; he would have to find a safe place to hide the screen for a week. His feet were as wet as his mouth was bone dry. For a second, he looked up and stared straight ahead into his shop. The stark reality of the situation was that the *signore's* agent had delivered his client's message and had hung up. There would be no collection of the screen that day, or the next, or the day after. In fact, it would be a full week before he could get rid of the thing – as beautiful as it was – and solve his precarious financial situation. Once the screen had been collected Gregorio would have his money in untraceable cash, but having to find a safe place to hide a stolen artwork for a week had not been part of the equation.

'Yes, you will have to be hidden in the lock-up whether you like it or not!' he snapped at the lion, whose accusing glare scythed through the layers of darkened varnish like a surgical laser, until it fixed itself firmly on Marinetti. He crossed quickly to the screen and adjusted the piece of fabric until it hid the greater part of the lion's face and the accusing eye. Despite this absolving action, he still felt the eye boring into his conscience from under the cloth. The Lion of St Mark was displeased, even if, like Polonius, it had been concealed behind the arras.

Gregorio Marinetti felt a little calmer for not being stared at. Despite that, his feet were now so wet that they squelched in his expensive shoes as he walked across the marble tiles of his shop towards the inner sanctum.

'Yes, it will have to be the lock-up,' he repeated.

3

Meanwhile, back at *Café Alma Arte*, business was as brisk as ever. Gianni picked his way through the tables, his hands full of small round trays bearing the delights on which the establishment's reputation was built.

He reached the far left-hand corner of the café, the place where the Contessa always sat to take her tea – yes, her *tea*. Since before he had been born, she had appeared at the counter every Thursday afternoon, to be ushered to her usual table to drink her afternoon cup of tea. In a country awash with all kinds of coffee this English woman, who was considered by some to be more than just a little eccentric, always had tea. He took a cloth from his apron pocket and wiped the top of the little table. There was no one sitting at it, despite the covetous eyes from the crush of customers who regularly cast questioning and envious glances at its free space. Nobody had been allowed to sit at it since earlier that afternoon, when Gianni had removed the chairs to ensure that it remained available for the Contessa. That was the Italian way – valued customers were always well looked after. For a moment the noise and movement that filled the café vanished and Gianni smiled again as he stood back and looked at the ornate round table. Puccini himself, Robert Graves and a whole host of other luminaries had sat in the café over the years (possibly even at this very table) but from the middle of the afternoon onwards, every Thursday it was *her* table – the English Contessa, to whom the family would be eternally respectful and to whom Gianni would always be grateful.

'I'm telling you, she's not coming,' muttered Anna, as Gianni once again resumed his position behind the ornate mahogany and bevelled glass counter, 'and you've got cream down the front of your apron. Here, use this,' she said, passing him a damp cloth.

As he looked down the burgundy apron to where the name 'Alma Arte' was embroidered in large white letters, he stopped, his hand poised in mid-wipe. Several splatters of cream made a confined, intricate pattern across the upper part of the apron. Some of the letters had been masked so that, as he stared down, what Gianni saw filled him with sudden apprehension. Even looking at the letters upside-down, those which were still clearly legible spelled out most of a word: '- - *M* - - *RTE*'. The second 'A' of Alma had been filled in with cream, so that it resembled the letter 'O'. Suddenly uneasy, Gianni crossed himself quickly with the damp cloth. '*MORTE*' – death. He turned and glanced back down the length of the café to where the solitary, empty table stood lost in a sea of animated and contented faces. The sound of cutlery clashing on crockery and the din of international conversation did nothing to banish Gianni's sudden mood of pending doom. That could also be the Italian way; superstition and reality often walked together as equal partners. He glanced up at the large wall clock. *It is getting late*, he realized as he wiped the cream from his apron.

4

At about the same time as Gianni was looking at the clock and contemplating the possible hidden significance of the word '*MORTE*' on his apron, the 3.50 p.m. train from Pisa was pulling out of Lucca's station and was already disappearing up the track on its way towards the interior. It had deposited an assortment of passengers on the platform, most of whom were locals returning from a day in Pisa; any tourists, who were not part of an organized coach party, would have arrived at the latest by mid-morning. There were several youths – students from the university in Pisa – who had completed their lectures for the week and were returning home with their laundry and to benefit from a couple of days of their mothers' good home cooking. In the middle of the platform, next to the entrance to the station building, a little knot of people were clustered around a young couple, both of whom carried large backpacks.

'We bought the tickets in Pisa ... at the airport ... not an hour ago,' said the young man in a heavy Australian accent.

A flood of Italian washed over him in return, delivered quite loudly by a uniformed official of *Ferrovie dello Stato*, the Italian State Railways. He held the two tickets in his hand and was waving them about, as if conducting an orchestra.

'You have not cancelled them! You must cancel them before you get on the train,' said the official, pointing to the tickets. He was becoming more and more animated.

The young man stared at him for a second and then looked at his companion, a young woman of his own age, which couldn't have been more than twenty-four. She shrugged, not having understood a word the official had said, and attempted to point to the tickets as they scythed through the warm afternoon air. This was a near impossible task, as their movement was unpredictably erratic.

'We don't know what y're saying,' she said calmly, 'but we've done nothing wrong. As Jez told ya, we bought the tickets in Pisa this afternoon before getting on the train.' She smiled rather sweetly at the official, who, for a moment at least, seemed to be taken aback by a pretty face wearing a rather skimpy T-shirt. Then he recovered his officiousness and started waving the tickets about again.

'This is a return ticket from Pisa. You have used the outward part, but have not cancelled it. That is an offence and there is a fine.'

'What do ya think he's on about, Vic?' asked the young man quickly. He spoke out of the corner of his mouth. He also kept his eyes firmly engaged with those of the railway official, who continued to talk and wave his hands about with a look of near exasperation on his face.

'Buggered if I know, Jez,' replied the young woman. 'Did we get into the wrong class carriage or something, d'ya think he means?'

'Excuse me. Can I help at all?' asked a voice from behind them in English. 'Don't mind Alessandro. He quite likes getting on his high horse, but he doesn't usually mean any harm by it.' An elderly lady, short and smartly dressed in a style from an earlier age and wearing a pair of pointed-frame glasses, suddenly appeared at Jez's elbow. 'Alessandro! How are you today? What seems to be the trouble? Have they done something wrong?' she asked in fluent Italian, a disarming smile on her lips.

An instant change came over the railway official, as he bowed slightly towards the newcomer. 'The Contessa is too kind to enquire. I am well, thank you,' he replied politely,

17

'but they have not cancelled the outward part of their tickets...'

'Well, are the tickets valid?' asked the elderly woman. Her voice was also polite but possibly even firmer than Alessandro's – and without the aerobics of the waving arms.

'Yes, Contessa ... issued in Pisa ... today, but they have not cancelled them and...'

'...and I'm sure that you can do that for them, can't you, Alessandro?' she said, smiling in that affectionate way everyone admires in their favourite grandmother. 'We want them to take away many good memories of their visit to our beautiful Lucca, now don't we?'

A few minutes later the four of them – the two tourists, the elderly lady and her small white Maltese poodle – emerged from the railway station into the bright sunshine and walked slowly across the *Piazzale Ricasoli*, the combination of garden and car park in front of the station. The small dog was trotting behind his mistress at the end of his leash. He was happily playing a game of nipping at the flapping hem of her skirt, which had come undone at the back. He growled softly as he did so.

'They do sometimes tend to get a little power-crazy with responsibility, you know,' said the elderly woman. 'It's probably something to do with wearing a uniform. Alessandro is a good sort and doesn't mean anything by it. His bark's usually worse than his bite.'

Victoria, once again a beast of burden to her backpack, eyed the elderly woman's dog, which had been growling almost constantly since the business with the tickets. She wondered if the same could be said of this angry little beast.

'You see, the ticket is valid for several months, but you have to insert it into one of the yellow machines on the station before you board the train; that cancels it, but it's really validating it within its time period. All very confusing, really ... to us foreigners,' she said, smiling. Her two companions nodded, as if reluctant to admit their confusion.

'So we just have to remember to shove the ticket into the yellow machine and that's all there is to it? Not like being back home,' Victoria added.

'And where might *home* be, my dear?'

'Perth ... Western Australia.'

'Do you know, I went to Australia,' said the elderly woman. 'Yes, just once ... to Sydney. But that was *many* years ago.' The elderly lady seemed to lose herself in some fond memory. They walked on in silence, apart from the contented growls from the dog, who continued to chase his mistress's flapping hem, which was now beginning to disintegrate. On reaching the busy *Viale Regina Margherita* they turned left and walked slowly towards the *San Pietro* entrance gate in the massive city walls. Out of thoughtfulness for the elderly woman's age, both Victoria and Jez had kept in their bottom gear, ambling along at a pace that was within her capability, which they thought was probably arthritic.

'Did you enjoy y're day at the museum?' asked Victoria, above the noise of the passing traffic. She pointed to a large bag the elderly woman was carrying, which had 'Pisa Museums' written on it in very large letters and in several languages.

'The museum, my dear?' repeated the elderly woman, smiling back at her. 'Well, you'll find the Puccini one quite interesting, but it needs a bit of a facelift I'm afraid. He was born here, you know. Yes, indeed. It was a very musical family, going back many generations,' she continued, 'right here in Lucca ... on the *Via Calderia.*'

Victoria raised her eyebrows at her companion. 'Who's Puccini?' she mouthed at him silently. Jez shrugged.

'And you can walk around the city walls, which are quite

19

massive, as you can see,' continued the elderly lady. 'You'll enjoy strolling around Lucca because most vehicles, apart from those of the residents, are prohibited. So it's not like London or Pisa.'

The action of turning her head to reply to Victoria's misunderstood question caused an earpiece to fall from the elderly woman's ear. As she made a fumbling grab for it she inadvertently tugged the dog's leash, which was draped over her left wrist. The animal stopped harassing the flapping hem and responded with several loud yaps, which made Victoria jump. Then the animal started to run around his mistress's legs, entwining her in the leash. From the look on the animal's face, Jez got the impression that this was a regular occurrence. With another couple of yaps – a kind of a victory howl – the dog sat down on the pavement. The woman's retro glasses slid off her nose and dangled limply from their chain against her chest as the little procession ground to a halt. With considerable sympathy, Jez looked at what he had mistaken to be one of a pair of hearing-aid earpieces, given this woman's obviously advanced age. Then, as he watched her fumble to catch it, he saw that it had 'Sony' stamped on it in tiny letters. As far as he knew, Sony did not make hearing aids.

'You bad, bad boy!' said the elderly woman, pointing an accusing finger at the animal, which now sat on its hind quarters, despite the insolent smile on his face, every inch the cute model for an animal charity fundraising poster. The growling continued softly. She slid the leash off her wrist, unwound herself with practiced ease and replaced it.

'I'm sorry about that,' she said, as they moved off again to cover the short remaining distance to the gate. 'He can be quite cantankerous at times.'

Victoria and Jez glanced at each other, but said nothing. They just nodded, but more in sympathy than agreement, Jez tapping the side of his head under the cover of shielding his eyes from the afternoon sun.

'I was actually asking about the Pisa Museum,' continued Victoria, pointing to the bag for a second time, as they reached the welcome shade of the gate. 'I assumed y'd been there for the day.'

There was a sudden peal of laughter from the elderly woman, as she moved her left hand to pat the large bag. The dog growled again.

'Good lord no, my dear... Oh, no. This is my general purpose holdall,' she chortled. 'Well, to be more accurate, it is Carlo's general holdall actually.' She gestured towards the little white dog, who seemed to glare resentfully back at her. 'Water bowl, water, of course, a few treats, his ball, just in case he feels like a game; you know what they're like.'

The young Australians smiled tolerantly, but said nothing.

Passing through the *San Pietro* Gate, the small dog and his owner led the visitors up a side street, towards the much larger *Corso Giuseppe Garibaldi*. The conversation, apart from the occasional huffling growl from the dog, had all but dried up.

Jez took this opportunity to look around at the buildings of the town, now that they had come within the embrace of the city walls. With the freshness of youth, he exclaimed, 'Ya know, Vic, we have actually made it into Lucca. At one point, I didn't think we were going to get off the railway station, what with all that shouting and arm waving. If it hadn't been for this lady here ... well I dunno what would have happened to us. It was very good of you to come to our rescue like that. Back there at the railway station, I mean ... all that fuss about the tickets.'

'Yes, I'm afraid it must have sounded more serious than it was... Storm in a tea cup, really.'

The conversation dried up again.

'We're staying at a hostel called...' There was a pause as

Jez slung his backpack around and fished in one of the side pockets. He took out a folded fistful of papers, sorted through them with some difficulty and extracted one. '*Ben-ven-u-to Mon-do* in the *Via dei Fi-ta-ro-li*,' he said with some difficulty. 'I don't suppose you'd happen to know where that is in the town, would ya?' he asked, hopefully.

The only map they had was a very small-scale affair printed inside the back cover of their even more uninformative guidebook to Tuscany.

'First of all, don't let the *Lucchese* hear you referring to their pride and joy as a town,' she replied, a smile on her lips. 'We have a cathedral here, so we are a city.'

'Oh,' replied Jez.

'*Via dei Filatori*... we don't need a "the" before *Via*, my dear. Now let me think...' She paused in thought, but did not stop walking. '*Via dei Filatori*,' she corrected his mispronunciation kindly as she recalled the position of the road. 'I am sure *Via dei Filatori* is on the other side of Lucca. Yes, I remember now; it is near the Guinigi Museum. They were a very important family you know. As I recall, they ruled Lucca in the fifteenth century.' The Contessa's love of history made it easy for her to remember such things. 'Yes, a very powerful family. The museum is full of sculptures and the like. They also have the 1529 inlaid choir stalls from the cathedral... We call it *duomo*. That same family also built the Guinigi Tower with the oak trees growing on the top.'

Victoria looked first at the elderly woman and then at Jez, her eyebrows raised. She wondered how they had drifted on to this topic of conversation and where this woman was getting all this useless information from.

'You get a splendid view of things from the top, under the shade of the trees,' continued the Contessa. 'It's over there. You can see it from anywhere in Lucca.' She stabbed a finger of her leash-entrapped hand in the general direction of the tower. 'Well, maybe not quite from where we are at present, but it is there, nonetheless.'

The dog muttered under its breath as silence once again descended on the little group.

'So, how do we find this *Via dei Filatori*?' asked Jez once again, pronouncing the name correctly. In fact, he was becoming quite adept at pronouncing it, considering the number of times he had just had to repeat it.

'Just keep walking to the east,' replied the Contessa, 'and when you meet the city wall, turn left.' She suddenly stopped. 'I tell you what you should do; after you've made your way to your hotel and settled in, you should take a walk and visit Roberta.'

Victoria chortled at the suggestion that their backpackers' hostel could be as luxurious as this woman's suggestion of a hotel implied.

'Oh, thank you. Who's Roberta?' asked Jez.

'I think it would be easiest for you to simply retrace your steps back here and then go straight back the way we came in, through the *Porta San Pietro*, and make your way back towards the station. Off to the left you will see a white building in the shape of a wedge ... a little like a door stop. That's your best bet,' she concluded.

Jez looked at Victoria with a bemused expression on his face. He still had no idea who Roberta was. The elderly woman was about to turn once again and resume her own progress when Victoria spoke.

'I don't quite follow ya. What about this wedge-shaped building?'

'That's where Roberta works. If you want to know anything about Lucca she's the person you want to ask. She's a mine of information and extremely helpful, too. And she speaks excellent English, you'll be pleased to know.'

'Do we just go in and ask for her? Can we do that if she's at work? Won't her boss mind?' asked Victoria who, like Jez, was starting to become more than a little confused by the direction the conversation had taken.

'Of course you can, my dear,' smiled the elderly woman. 'That's her job. She works in the Tourist Information Office. There are several around the city, but Roberta's is usually the first port of call for any tourists needing help. It's so terribly convenient to the railway station, you see. And I think she has a map of the city that would be of great help to you.'

She smiled at them and turned around to continue forwards. The bells of the city suddenly started to chime.

'Good heavens! Is that the time?' she said, suddenly struggling with some considerable difficulty to bring her wristwatch into view.

Victoria's eyes widened slightly as she saw that it was a Cartier – one of the older, more expensive models; she had made it her business to notice such things, ever since she had been old enough to understand fashion.

'I'm afraid I really do have to fly. I have to get almost to the top end of town before closing. It's been so nice meeting you,' she said, shaking each of them by the hand, 'but I really must be off now. I do hope that you enjoy your stay here in Lucca. And don't forget the Puccini Museum, will you... *Via Calderia* and follow the signs. Oh, and don't forget to tell Roberta that I sent you. Goodbye!'

And with that she marched on up the street towards the *Piazza Napoleone*, in a welter of dog, leash and large 'Pisa Museums' carrier bag.

'For God's sake, look at the old bird go, will ya!' muttered Jez as they watched her diminishing form rapidly disappear. 'And *we* were walking slowly so as not to tire *her* out!' he continued in some disbelief.

'And did ya notice the watch?' asked Victoria. 'Cartier – one of the older models, very retro and highly desirable – costs a bloody fortune, if ya can find one.'

'Can't say that I did notice it,' replied Jez, 'but it certainly seems that she's not quite as ancient as she appears. And aren't we going to look a little stupid telling this Roberta that we've been sent by ... who? She never did tell us who she is!'

5

'You are going to have to pay for that lot,' hissed Anna angrily, in competition with the spluttering steam spout on the Gaggia. 'You really are nothing better than a clumsy idiot!' She was trying to keep her voice down as a steady stream of contented tourists ambled past the ornate counter towards the door. Closing time at the *Café Alma Arte* was drawing ever nearer and the legion of coaches, which waited patiently for their cargoes outside the city walls, would soon ferry the tourists back to their hotels in Pisa or Florence, the lingering pleasure of their short visit to the café clinging to their taste buds.

'It was an accident, for Christ's sake,' replied a tall, sunburnt youth, as he knelt on the tiled floor picking up the smashed pieces of white crockery. Despite his tan, the tell-tale spots and pimples of early manhood were clearly visible. 'And I don't see why I should pay if it was an accident. Such things happen.'

'And they always seem to happen to *you* ... *poverino*,' continued Anna, the anger in her voice suddenly masked by a warm Tuscan smile, as yet another little column of satisfied and revitalised tourists strolled towards the door.

'*Ciao... Arrivederci...* Thank you,' she beamed whilst mentally continuing to berate her unfortunate cousin. 'Poor *clumsy* you,' repeated Anna once their customers had moved on. '*Papà* and your father will have something to say about this,' she hissed at the unfortunate youth, as the

26

bevelled glass door closed, 'and count yourself lucky that the cups were all empty!'

'*Papà* already knows I hate this business,' continued Verriano. 'I'm only here because he made me. I've told you that ... you and Gianni. I'm into computers, not fancy cakes and cups of *cappuccino*.'

Verriano was certainly working at the *Café Alma Arte* under sufferance. Neither he, nor his elder brother, had ever had any interest in their own family's business, which had been one of the most popular restaurants in Viareggio long before the time of Mussolini and even that of *maestro* Puccini himself. The assumption that the elder son would dutifully continue the established tradition and simply allow himself to be subsumed into the family business had been rudely dashed when Andrea had upped sticks and left for London. A long-festering family situation, remembered in the Italian way with deep resentment, had been further compounded when Verriano had announced that he wished to go to the university in Pisa to study computers. Uncle Federico, at his wit's end, determined that Verriano should be removed from the immediate family circle so that he could get some broader life experience working in another, but similar, environment. This would be under the guidance of his cousin, Gianni, whom Verriano had always looked up to. On that basis, Verriano had been despatched from Viareggio to the café in Lucca with instructions to Gianni to knock some sense into the errant youth's head. Seething at the injustice of his current situation, Verriano set about clearing up the mess. Somewhat petulantly, he snapped, 'And why is that machine making so much noise?'

'Don't change the subject and make sure you clean up *all* the pieces and don't try and get away with flicking any under the counter!' replied Anna, picking up a damp cloth and turning to go and clean the tables that now stood empty amongst the thinned-out crush in the café. Once she had turned her back on him and walked out of view, the youth mimicked his cousin's instruction.

'Even if it *was* an accident, such carelessness isn't going to help Uncle Federico change his mind,' whispered Gianni, who had been taking cash from yet another departing group of tourists. 'People like us have no need of computers and we don't have any need of universities either. It is our duty to keep the family business going.'

'That's why, one day soon, this place and the one in Viareggio will have to close ... because there's more to life in the twenty-first century than fancy cakes and noisy Gaggias,' replied Verriano as he stood in front of Gianni. In his hands he held the tray on which rested a pile of assorted crockery fragments resembling something recently recovered from an archaeological excavation. As his hands were full with the results of his recent carelessness, his pent-up, rebellious anger caused him to lash out with his foot and kick the base of the wooden unit on the top of which resided the noisy coffee-making machine.

'Oouw!' he yelled, as the soft toe cap of his designer trainers made no attempt to protect his toes from the force of the kick. 'Bloody thing ...'

The Gaggia continued to splutter and spit, somewhat contentedly.

'Just make sure that you don't drop that lot a second time,' said Gianni, pointing an admonishing finger at the tray and its contents.

'Yeah, yeah!' replied Verriano as he limped off towards the kitchens and the rubbish bin.

'Do you still say that she'll come today?' asked Anna, softly, as she knelt down and started to transfer the cakes remaining in the cabinet to the chilled storage space at the back of the counter. 'It's still not too late to place a small bet ... either way.'

Gianni Canetti smiled down tolerantly at his sister, but

didn't reply; although he had not shared the inverted word of revelation on the front of his apron with anyone, it still lingered faintly in the back of his mind: *MORTE*. He bent into the cavernous space of the large display cabinet and took out the remains of two large cream cakes. Then he turned to pass them down to his sister.

'Of course she'll come. It is Thursday and you know how set the English are when it comes to a routine – they run on clockwork, like I have already said.'

A short walk down the *Via Fillungo*, the lady in question remembered that she had to call in at Barattoni's Pharmacy. Animals were not permitted within the antiseptic confines of Barattoni's, which meant that Carlo would have to be tied to the large metal ring set into the wall and sit patiently on the cobbled street until she re-emerged into the afternoon heat. Being left out in the street was something Carlo did not enjoy, not so much because of any sense of abandonment, but because there were always one or two tourists who could not resist the temptation to talk to him in somewhat childish tones or – the worst affront of all – try to pat him patronisingly on his head. Carlo Quinto, the fifth Charles of Maltese poodle extraction to be owned by the Contessa over the years, had never made friends easily and was a great respecter of his own aloofness, no matter how 'cute' certain gullible tourists to his city – usually Americans – found him.

'Here we are,' said the Contessa, transferring the large 'Pisa Museums' bag from her left to her right arm and securing Carlo's leash through the ring. 'Now, I want you to be a good boy and behave yourself. I'll be back in a minute.' The dog paid no heed to either the Contessa or to the rattle of the bag's contents, as the Contessa deposited it against the wall of the building behind where Carlo was sitting on his haunches. He looked far from pleased. He growled softly.

They were standing opposite the *Torre del Ore*, Lucca's tall

29

fourteenth-century tower, the large clock face of which could be seen from all over the city. The Contessa paused for a moment and looked up at the hands. It was almost a quarter to five. Then she smiled, as she thought how apt it was that Barattoni's, the pharmacy which had been there for nearly a century and a half and which was the necessary key to the prolonged survival of many of Lucca's residents (the ill and the aged), should be located under the enormous shadow of the instrument that measured the remains of their allotted life span. It was not a morbid reflection on her mortality, but rather an ironic observation on the active life she had made it her mission to enjoy to the full. With concerts to organize and charity work to be done, time waited for no man; even Carlo would have to wait for *Signor* Barattoni to dispense her medication.

'I am leaving you in charge of the bag, so stop complaining and keep a watchful eye on it,' said the Contessa as she straightened up, turned and pushed open the pharmacy door.

'Why are you so concerned about this one woman?' asked Anna, looking up from her crouching position. 'Even if she *has* been a great help to the family, she is still a mad old woman and to make matters worse, she is a mad old *English* woman. They are all the same and –'

'What was that? They're all the same? Oh dear! It *is* nearly five o'clock. Have I left it too late to have my usual selection, Gianni?' asked an elderly voice from the customers' side of the counter. 'I didn't quite catch what you said, Anna dear… Still can't. It's these earphone things… I've got them a bit tangled with my glasses, you see. Just a minute and … Carlo, will you stop that this instant! You are a bad boy!'

There was the sound of falling objects as her large shopping bag hit the floor at her feet. It was followed almost immediately by the sudden eruption of loud, strenuous yapping. Even allowing for the bulk of the counter that separated them, the barking seemed to be only marginally removed from the spot where Anna's face was. In fact, so sudden had been its commencement that it had given her quite a start, which caused her to flick the plate she was holding upwards slightly, like a ping-pong bat. A slice of cake toppled majestically over the side and landed in a flattened, creamy heap on the floor between her feet.

Bugger it! Can't blame Verriano for that one, she thought as she stood up to see who had caused the disturbance. As she straightened up, even before her vision cleared the top of the counter, she realized perfectly well who was responsible. In front of her stood an elderly lady, tastefully dressed in the style of, perhaps, forty years before. A large carrier bag, emblazoned with the legend 'Pisa Museums' lay at a crazy angle on the floor at her feet. Around her neck hung a pair of thick-lensed glasses in frames which would not have looked out of place in an optician's catalogue of the 1950s. Between the spectacles, hanging from a fine gold chain, dangled a delicately worked, heart-shaped locket in gold. Tangled up with the glasses and locket was the wire and earpiece of a Walkman. The other earpiece was still firmly plugged into an ear and it was open to debate as to exactly what was making the most noise – Carlo, the belligerent Maltese poodle, or the recording of Elgar's first 'Pomp and Circumstance March', the 'Land of Hope and Glory'. The strains of the famous piece suddenly seemed to fill most of the café with distorted, tinny sound, despite the otherwise perfect performance by the Royal Choral Society and the Royal Philharmonic Orchestra. From the far end of the café Verriano paused in his sweeping and turned to look at the source of the distortion. He was into heavy metal, but even his music didn't distort his iPod to quite the same extent.

'Just a minute, Gianni... Would you hold that for me,

please?' The Contessa passed a small handbag and a paper bag emblazoned with the green cross of *Farmacia Barattoni* over the top of the counter. 'I should be able to sort this out with both hands free.'

At the end of his leash, which was slipped over his mistress's left hand, the Maltese poodle continued to yap at the remaining customers. In truth, it was more of a snarling growl. Carlo Quinto was almost as eccentric as his owner and took to yapping and snarling at anything for no apparent reason. That was why it had been decided that the dog took after his mistress. Although she did not yap or snarl as Carlo did, it was a well-known fact that she was most definitely an eccentric – and an English one at that.

Time seemed to have suddenly stopped as most of the eyes remaining in the *Café Alma Arte* turned to stare, almost disbelievingly, at the short figure at the counter.

'Let me turn this thing off,' she said as she took the Walkman out of her pocket. 'If I can just find the button without my glasses... Nearly there,' she said, her grey-blue eyes sparkling in open defiance of her age. 'I think that I've pressed the right button.'

The café suddenly fell silent. Cups of coffee and cake-laden forks remained suspended in mid-air between the table and the customers' mouths in expectation of what might happen next.

Gianni Canetti watched with compassionate amusement. The Contessa didn't usually get herself into such a muddle. In fact, given her well-known ability to organize her concerts and various other charitable events, he knew her to be capable of a great deal of logical, careful planning. As he watched, he guessed that his own grandmother must be of a similar age to this woman, although she was far less active and not quite of the Contessa's mental capability. *Nonna* was also a lot clumsier and was always dropping things, especially when in the kitchen. Perhaps, he thought, the Contessa was allowed to have the occasional moment of disorganisation. His glance flicked down to the handbag and then to the pharmacy bag he still held in his hand. A shadow of sadness flashed across his mind with the speed of an express train and then it was gone again. Perhaps what he was watching with such compassion was simply part of growing old.

'If I pass this through there ... and put this thing into my shopping bag for the moment...' Her glasses, suspended at the end of their chain, which had become hopelessly tangled with the wire of the earpiece, suddenly fell free against her chest as she bent down to put the Walkman into the 'Pisa Museums' bag. Carlo turned and yapped at her as she did so. 'Sssshh! You are a noisy dog,' she said, reaching out to pat the tussled white curls of the dog's head. There was an instant flash of mutual affection between the two – a confirmation that each had been made for and had found the other. 'Now, where was I?' she asked absently as she straightened up again, putting the pointed glasses on her face. 'Good afternoon, Gianni. How are you today? What was that you said a few moments ago? I didn't quite catch it. Wasn't it something about everything being the same?'

La Contessa Penelope di Capezzani-Batelli (to some the mad Englishwoman of Lucca and to others – those she considered her true friends – simply 'Pen') had kept to her predictable routine after all.

'I hope the Contessa is well?' asked Gianni with genuine interest, relieved that she had restored order about herself.

Even Anna, who had straightened up from behind the counter just in time to be greeted by the Contessa's bird-nest mop of grey-white hair, the crown of which had been presented for inspection as she had bent down to put the Walkman into her bag, involuntarily found herself suddenly under the spell of this elderly lady.

'Contessa,' she said respectfully, taking a step forward,

nearer the counter. She had forgotten the large slice of cream cake on the floor, but was instantly reminded of it as she felt the cream well up through the ornate lattice work of her expensive *Andrea di Favellor* shoes. The smile on her face suddenly became very fixed, as if chiselled on.

'Good afternoon, Anna my dear. I hope you are also well?' she beamed. 'Such a pretty pair of earrings you're wearing.'

Anna, still smiling fixedly, made a mumbled sound in the affirmative, but her mind was firmly focussed on her cream-filled shoes. In Venice, at the *Biennale*, a cream-filled shoe might become a prized exhibit; even in the nearby artistic community of Pietrasanta, which was well known for its sometimes artistic excesses, such a thing might happen. But not here in Lucca – the *Lucchese* were far too level-headed for that. Here, it would simply remain a cream-filled shoe – and a rather expensive one at that. Anna sighed. The Gaggia spat and gurgled in sympathy.

'Excuse me, please,' she said, as she hobbled away towards the kitchen.

'Will the Contessa be taking her usual tea?' asked Gianni as he handed her handbag and medicine back to her. He kept one eye on the Contessa and the other on Carlo, who continued to growl softly, as yet another group of tourists attempted to escape through the main door and seek the security of their luxury coach. The dog's glare followed them as they passed.

'Not today, thank you, Gianni. I've been to Pisa and then I helped a young Australian couple at the station. They had managed to work Alessandro up into such a state over their tickets, but it's all sorted out now. And I have much still to do before this evening.' Although her Italian was fluent, even after nearly sixty years, she spoke with a strong English accent. 'So, if you please, I would like my usual pastries ... and I have to compliment you on last week's Florentines –

delicious, if perhaps just a little sweeter than usual?' Despite the outward appearance of a dithering old woman, she had a relaxed, gracious air about her. 'My regular selection if you please and as a special treat today, a large piece of your famous peach and cream cake. We have our weekly rehearsal this evening and my artistes will appreciate the gesture.'

She smiled contentedly and took the glasses off her nose. They once again dangled free against her chest.

'I trust the Contessa had a pleasant day in Pisa? It is many years since I have been there myself,' he continued as he prepared the Contessa's order, carefully packing the items into a large, white cardboard box. 'Most unfortunate as Pisa is such a short distance away, but there is never the time.'

'You work too hard, Gianni,' replied the Contessa, suddenly looking serious. 'I know how much work goes into maintaining the standards we have come to expect from *Café Alma Arte*. It is those standards that make a visit to this place such a delightful event. Where else in Lucca is it possible to absorb such atmosphere ... such aromas' – she took in a deep breath – 'and to enjoy taking a quiet cup of tea quite so much? Do you know that I have been doing so since before you were born?' She smiled at him, a warm, generous, maternal approval of both himself as a person and of his efforts.

'The Contessa is too kind,' replied Gianni, smiling even more broadly than before.

'Nonsense! It is the simple truth. Good quality requires a lot of effort and hard work. I know how hard it can be.'

For a moment, Gianni wondered how this woman, this Contessa – the present holder of an aristocratic title that went back to the Renaissance – could know about hard work. It occurred to him that, despite the support and help she had given to his family over the years, he knew very little about her.

'Yes Gianni, in answer to your previous question, I had a lovely day in Pisa. I went to see some friends I have there – dear old friends of my poor Giacomo. They are going to help me with my next project: another concert in two months' time to raise money for...' She suddenly stopped, a look of mystification on her face, and removed the other earpiece. 'I thought that this thing was making a hissing noise, but I've just remembered that I turned it off.' She looked around the café, trying to locate the sound of the low noise, which had suddenly become such an irritation to her. 'Is it his growling again or has he turned into a cat and started hissing?' she muttered, more to herself that to Gianni. She bent down to listen closer. As she did so the glasses on the end of their gold chain swung out crazily. 'It is *very* bad manners to make a noise like that in public,' she continued, as if talking to a very young child. That was how she sometimes saw her Carlo, how she had seen all of them over the years, as the next best thing she had to her dear, lost Enrico. Then she would chide herself; such a thought was unseemly and very unfair on darling Luigi. The dear boy always came around for supper on Saturday. That was the occasion on which she would make a fuss over him as a kind of penance for her unappreciative thoughts. Luigi had been a loyal and loving son over the years, even if he was not darling Enrico. But that was hardly his fault.

Gianni craned over the counter and looked down at the dog. Carlo half-turned his head at his mistress and partially opened his right eye to look at her, as if to say, *What are you making a fuss about now?*

'Oh, I say ... how curious,' continued the Contessa, straightening up. 'It's not him after all. So what *is* that hissing noise?'

'The Contessa must not concern herself,' he replied casually, 'it is the Gaggia; the steam pipe for frothing milk is in need of attention, that's all.'

'Oh, I see, but don't you find the noise irritating? All day?' she asked.

'I don't really notice it above all of the other noise,' he replied, 'but we have sent for someone to have a look at it. The Contessa was saying that she is going to organize another concert?'

'Was I?' she replied absently, waiting for her memory to provide the appropriate information. 'Oh yes, of course I was, wasn't I. How silly of me!' She had suddenly lapsed into English. Gianni's English was good and had improved over the years to the point where he was able to converse equally well in either language. 'I will be asking for your help again … for the catering and to display a poster … and possibly some small handbills on the tables.' She gestured around the café. Carlo yawned loudly.

'But of course,' replied Gianni gallantly. 'We are always at the Contessa's disposal. Also, I can assure you that we will be ready with the consumables for next week's concert.'

'How kind. I know I can always rely on you. What a good boy you are, Gianni,' she beamed, picking up her bag as he finished tying up the white cardboard box with some thin pink ribbon.

'The Contessa has still to mention for whom the next concert is to be organized,' he continued, passing the box over the counter. There was no question of payment. Such things were never discussed with long-established and much-valued customers. The amount would be entered in the day book and the account would be promptly settled at the end of the month.

'Didn't I?' she asked as she fought to balance the various items of her load against the handling of Carlo's leash. 'Well, it's something quite new for me, I have to say.'

The dog was sitting up and had once again become his belligerent self, growling *sotto voce* at the few remaining customers. For their parts, they had thought it prudent to delay their departure until after the noisy – and possibly dangerous – dog had left.

'The Contessa's concert?' prompted Gianni, softly. 'Who will be the beneficiary?'

'The concert... Ah yes, the concert,' she replied, suddenly back at a familiar point in the conversation. 'I recently read about this wonderful charity. They work with horses and donkeys ... in poor countries, you know. Teaching the locals how to look after their animals and keep them fit and healthy for work ... that sort of thing. It was all started by one single woman's determination and compassion. Just think of it, Gianni; one person had the vision and the drive to help all of those poor animals...' She seemed to have drifted off somewhere. 'So, I thought to myself, we are going to do our bit and help them too ... from here in Lucca.'

'Ah, I see,' replied Gianni, but he was not sure that he actually did. The English were funny, with their clockwork routines and their obsession with animals.

'But I mustn't keep you any longer. It's already quite late and I'm sure that you will want to be tidying up and going home to your family.' That was a thought generally shared by the other customers remaining in *Café Alma Arte*, who were already preparing to follow the Contessa out of the door once the threat of the little Maltese poodle had been removed. 'Oh, I nearly forgot to ask you – how is Fiorenza? Not many weeks left now and then you'll have a little brother or sister for Virgilo.'

'It would be nice to have a sister for our son, but God will decide,' replied Gianni. 'Both my wife and our expected baby are doing very well and, as always, we thank the Contessa for her many kindnesses.'

The Contessa would never forget the complications that had followed on from the birth of his firstborn. She had been only too glad to help. The memories were of a worrying time, which cut close to her heart. Happily, unlike the memories she held of her own dear Enrico, the memories of the Canetti family's problems had a happy ending.

'Good, good. You will keep me informed? And I'll let you know about the horses and donkeys concert and bring you some posters and things when they are ready,' she continued as she replaced both of the earpieces, fumbled around in her large bag to retrieve the Walkman and pressed the 'play' button. Then, once again the model of her usual composure, she turned and negotiated the door. 'Everything is still at the planning stage and I have a lot of arrangements to work out.' She had started to shout as the Walkman's earpieces shut out the sounds on the border between *Café Alma Arte* and *Via Fillungo*, and replaced them with the last rousing appearance of the choir singing the big tune in Elgar's march. The British presence was very much alive and well in Tuscan Lucca, as the immortal notes of the melody bounced and ricocheted off the tall buildings that lined the ancient road.

'Mind you don't step in the cream,' said Anna, who had reappeared behind the counter carrying a mop and pail.

'She still did not tell me the name of these people who concern themselves with horses and donkeys,' said Gianni.

'What do you expect?' replied Anna as she bent over the bucket to rinse the cream-filled mop. 'She is a mad English-woman.'

6

Despite the lateness of the hour it was still warm. The sun had traversed the canyon of *Via Fillungo* and the tall facades of the buildings that formed the sides now relaxed into the approaching cool of late afternoon. The tinny echoes of 'Rule Britannia', which escaped from the Contessa's earpieces, rebounded robustly off the steep walls of plaster, masonry and decorative architectural relief that made the ancient way such a magnet for tourists. As she walked steadily along, surrounded by the iconic sounds of her homeland, it seemed as if this little elderly woman played the role of a representative of a foreign empire that, together with its considerable power and influence, had long since ceased to exist. Accompanied by the still-grumbling Carlo, and proceeding as stately as Kitchener's gunboat moving up the Nile towards the relief of Khartoum, the Contessa was making her way home to her spacious apartment in the walls of what had once been the town's Roman arena.

'Nearly home, you noisy boy!' she announced over the sound of Thomas Arne's patriotic air. 'Come along now. Keep up.'

Tethered as he was to his mistress by the leather leash, Carlo Quinto didn't have much choice other than to obey. As if to remind her of this fact, he yapped loudly twice then resumed his semi-permanent soft growling.

'Oh, here we are at Gregorio's,' she said, stopping in the middle of the pedestrianized road. The sudden manoeuvre required considerable concentration on her part, laden as she was with her armfuls of bags, the Maltese's leash and the white box with its delicious contents. 'I wonder if he has one?' she muttered to herself as she fought to put her glasses back on her nose. 'Come on, Carlo, let's have a look then, shall we?'

She moved to the side of the street and stood in front of the window of *Casa dei Gioielli.* Again, Carlo had no choice but to accompany her, which annoyed him somewhat. He had noticed an interesting splash up the wall and a corresponding puddle on the pavement and would far rather have investigated that. He was, after all, only a dog. He growled to himself.

'I wonder if he has a screen we could use; we'll need it for the *Marriage of Figaro* excerpt,' she said, talking to the dog as if he were human.

Although the lights were on in the shop, there was no sign of life. So the Contessa took the opportunity to stare intently through her own reflection on the glass and scrutinize the contents of Gregorio Marinetti's antiques emporium. As her eyes adjusted to the light levels, she focussed in on the large object standing in the centre of the shop. From the street it was difficult to work out exactly what it actually was, as it had been placed with its narrow side towards the window and had a length of brocade draped over it. She made a note that the cloth was neither swagged nor generously draped with the usual artistic flair Lucca had come to expect from this flamboyant antiques dealer: she would have to have a word with Gregorio about that. Nevertheless, this object intrigued her and by moving further along to her right she found she could catch the reflection of the back of the screen in the large gilded mirror that hung on the side wall. She was now convinced that this was a screen that would do justice to her staging of the Mozart item in her programme, even if it did have

41

an animal of some description painted on it.

As the Royal Choral Society launched into the third verse of Arne's great song, the Contessa reached out with her free hand and tried the handle of the door. It was locked. Carlo yapped again. Putting her hand up to open the door had jerked his leash and taken him even further away from the alluring puddle, which was destined to remain unexplored by his inquisitive little nose. The Contessa looked down to see what all the noise was about and it was then that she saw the neat handwritten notice propped up in the bottom corner of the window.

'*Ritorno subito*' – 'I'll be back immediately,' it read.

Oh dear, that is a pity! He's gone out, she thought wondering how long Gregorio's 'immediately' might be? Carlo couldn't have cared less if Gregorio Marinetti never returned. He was not sure if he even enjoyed going into the shop in the first place, as he got the feeling the man harboured a permanent suspicion that he was up to no good and might well either chew something to unsellable oblivion or leave a calling card somewhere on the marble tiles. Furthermore, the man always seemed to be on edge and nervous, and there had been instances during the Contessa's regular rehearsals when he, Carlo Quinto, had had to get up from his cushion and leave the room, almost suffocated by the stench of cologne which emanated from the man. His eyes narrowed as he remembered the worst incident three weeks ago, when the cologne had been so liberally applied that he had started to sneeze and had only managed to stop the irritation in his delicate little nose by submerging it in the cleansing coolness of his water bowl.

'Come along, you noisy boy, we won't wait. It's time to go home,' she declared as her little caravan resumed its progress up the nearly deserted *Via Fillungo* towards the Roman arena.

The Contessa resolved to speak to Gregorio about

borrowing this screen and about the gilt chair he had already promised. In her mind's eye, she was already seeing the tableau of singers involved in this excerpt using the chair in some dramatic way, with the screen in the background draped with some pale-blue damask to brighten the setting. *It will be the highlight of the concert,* she thought.

The Royal Choral Society had reached the end of their performance and the machine had clicked itself off at the end of the tape – not that she'd noticed at all. Still with her earpieces in her ears, the Contessa walked on, listening to a silent Walkman. *I wouldn't be at all surprised if it's not to everyone's taste, so it is possible there will be no interest in it before next week … not until after the concert… Let's hope that nobody else has seen it yet.*

But she was wrong. There *had* been someone who, a few minutes before, had stood almost exactly where she had just been standing. This someone, who had been walking up *Via Fillungo* and had seen Marinetti disappearing in the opposite direction as furtively as one of the guiltier characters in an opera plot, had also peered through his own reflection and into the *Casa dei Gioielli,* with a pair of eyes in far better working order than the Contessa's. Those eagle eyes had also seen the dark bulk of what looked like a screen, decorated as it was with the doleful expression of what he knew to be a lion – not just any lion, but the winged Lion of Saint Mark.

7

The vestibule outside the reception rooms in the Contessa's apartment positively reverberated with the sound of the emotionally charged duet, *'Verranno a te sull'aure'* from *Lucia di Lammermoor*. The rehearsal for next week's concert was underway and, by the sound of it, Renata di Senno and Riccardo Fossi were running through one of the items on the programme. Their considerable vocal talents were doing justice to this passionate operatic farewell.

Standing outside the music room, Gregorio Marinetti paused to listen to his fellow artistes and to catch his breath. He had been let into the apartment, on its lower level, by the Contessa's faithful retainer and personal maid, Elizabeth McGraunch, who had greeted him with the sharp side of her tongue for being late. He chose to ignore her and swept in up the stairs: after the difficult day he had just endured, he was in no mood to explain anything to the domestic member of this household.

In the later part of that afternoon, Marinetti had telephoned the Contessa in a very flustered state, to offer his profuse apologies that he would be running late as he had an urgent delivery to make, but that he would attend the rehearsal as soon as possible. The Contessa thanked him for his politeness in advising her and mentioned that she had something to speak to him about after the rehearsal. Safe in the knowledge that the screen was out of his shop and was secured in his lockup away from prying eyes, he could now look forward to singing at this evening's rehearsal; this was his comfort blanket and it was very much needed after a stressful afternoon dealing with what amounted to a stolen antique.

As Donizetti's music permeated his brain, he truly started to relax as the duet drew to its conclusion. *I'll stay here until they finish, before entering the room*, he decided. *It would be impolite to do otherwise.*

Elizabeth was heard puffing up the stairs to this level of the apartment muttering under her breath. Marinetti had left her at the entrance door engaged in some dispute with two children who were playing outside the apartment. From this viewpoint, he could see the strange, flattened cloth-cap affair she wore on the top of her head. It was held in place by two ribbons, which met in a mangled bow under her chin. She had never been seen by visitors to the apartment without this curious piece of headgear. At first glance it resembled the little white lace cloth worn by the aging Queen Victoria, but on closer inspection, which was rather dangerous and always best carried out surreptitiously, it was a formless piece of material, which had long since lost the identifiable structure of its original construction. It was also more grey than white.

Arriving on the top step, and still wheezing from the climb, she motioned Marinetti towards the music room and gasped, 'Herself was beginning to think you weren't going to appear, so she was.'

They spoke English – she in her fractured and often tortuously distorted brand of Irish–English and he in his considerably more fluent Italian–English: Miss McGraunch had never concerned herself with learning Italian, despite having lived in Italy for over fifty years. Elzeebit, as she pronounced her own name, held the belief that anything worth saying should only be said in English – Irish–English at that.

'I prefer to wait,' replied Marinetti, wanting to remain where he was so that he might hear how Renata and Riccardo would manage their respective top Cs in the *cadenza* towards the end of the duet.

'Nonsense,' Elizabeth said dismissively as she shot past him. Grasping the handles of the music room doors, she flung them open with a crash and with her usual acerbic turn of phrase, brought the rehearsal to a standstill by announcing, 'Him what wasn't here is here now and he's saying he is putting on *weight*, but I told him that's not an excuse.'

Riccardo and Renata, who had been on the cusp of climaxing, musically, whilst '*proclaiming their sorrow at their impending parting*' now floundered to a halt. The resultant sound of gasps, flat notes and expletives, certainly never envisaged by Donizetti, now echoed around the room. The other artistes in the room had been gathered in an informal laager around the Steinway grand piano and, as true musicians, had been totally immersed in the music that was being performed. Awakened from that spell, they now all gazed in astonishment at the scene enacted before them in the doorway.

'Weight?' repeated the Contessa from her position at the piano's keyboard. 'What weight?'

'Contessa, I merely said I wanted to wait until the duet had finished … I am mortified by the interruption, my apologies to you all,' Marinetti babbled. 'Riccardo, … what can I say … Renata, … I'm sure that top note would have been … won…derful… It must have been a misunderstanding, but I spoke English to…' He gestured discreetly with his chin to the right, to where Elizabeth was standing.

'I'll be putting on the kettle for tea,' continued Elizabeth, oblivious to the mayhem she had caused.

'Thank you, Elizabeth,' said the Contessa, still not totally clear as to the significance of what either her faithful retainer or Marinetti had said. 'I think we need to do some work first, so we'll have our tea a little later.'

The others drew closer to the piano, laying their music scores on top of it.

'We've a little bit of the cake you brought back from *Almartyr's*. And there might be some of those nut *briskets*, too. Will that do?' asked Elizabeth, pausing in the still-opened doorway, eyeing the Contessa with a pained look of tolerance. ''Tis all that's left from the box. He had a good mouthful of it before I was stoppin' him,' she said, pointing an arthritic finger at Carlo, who was seated on one of the Louis Quatorze chairs close to the fireplace. Carlo snarled back at her quietly. 'I told him he was *disbehavus*, but he's not after listening to Elzeebit ... never has.'

There were those who could be forgiven for thinking that Elizabeth was a direct descendant of Mrs Malaprop: so obtuse was the meaning behind her pronouncements at times. Over the years, the Contessa had become acclimatized to this and paid little heed, accepting it as normal *lingua franca* between them. For others, particularly those with English not as their first language, Elizabeth's way of talking was unfathomable.

Renata di Senno, the leading soprano of the Chamber Opera Group of Lucca – or COGOL as the Contessa affectionately referred to her pride and joy – suddenly caught a whiff of something that offended her finely shaped Tuscan nose. She leaned forward, picked up her score from the piano and moved from her position near the fireplace to one further away from the source of the sudden stench of rotten eggs.

'The bloody dog's farted again,' she mouthed as she walked behind Gregorio Marinetti. Protected by his customary screen of cologne, he had not noticed. He had calmed down a little since the episode with Elizabeth, but his feet were still a little moist with the nerves he was experiencing since he had taken delivery of the screen. 'It is always the same,' she continued, speaking *sotto voce*, with exaggerated mouth movement; 'you don't have to wait for the break for the little rat to make a good fart.'

'What was that, Renata?' asked the Contessa, who had seen her mouth moving but had not actually heard anything.

'Contessa, I was simply saying that we are ready to make a good start ... with our next piece.'

'*Brava*, Renata. You are absolutely correct. We should always maintain a positive attitude. That's what my dear Giacomo used to say.' She paused and touched the small, engraved locket, which hung around her neck. 'So, now that Gregorio is with us, let us commence,' she continued, suddenly once again in charge of the rehearsal from her position at the keyboard. 'Let us begin exactly at the intro-duction... Two bars and then ...' She nodded her head to indicate the entry point of the vocal lines. The members of COGOL drew closer to the Steinway, focussed on their scores and mentally prepared themselves to tackle the sextet from Donizetti's *Lucia di Lammermoor.* 'As you might remember, our new member, Yvonne Buckingham, will be joining us for her first COGOL concert next Friday evening. This evening, however, she's going to be a little late, as she has to attend a parents' evening at the International School in Pisa. She will join us as soon as she can.'

Yvonne Buckingham, a petite, delicate English Rose, had only been in Italy for ten months. She had heard of the Contessa from her sister, who had recently graduated as a violinist from the Royal Academy, where the memory of Professor Giacomo di Capezzani-Batelli was still very much alive in the Department of Vocal Studies. Unlike her sister, Yvonne had no formal musical training; she was just blessed with the gift of a glorious soprano voice. She had attended teacher training college and was a holder of the TEFL qualification, which allowed her to teach English as a Foreign Language in Pisa.

'In the meantime, let us commence. I will fill in Yvonne's part,' said the Contessa.

The room filled again with music made by aged fingers tripping lightly across the ivory keys and the subsequent singing from the opera group rising to match the magnificent, but faded, glory of the room itself. Although the combined talents of the pianist and of the singers now splendidly filled the space with sound, the focus of the music room remained on the Steinway grand piano that represented the undying love of a husband and wife. *Il Conte* had given the piano to his wife when they arrived in Italy and had taken up residence in the *Villa Batelli*. Since then it had been moved to various homes they had shared until it had accompanied her to the apartment when she had been widowed. It was now carefully positioned between two large, luxuriously curtained French windows and was a constant reminder of a wonderful and loving musical partnership. Accordingly, it was polished daily by the Contessa in homage to its beauty and its memories. In contrast, close inspection of the windows' formal decoration revealed that the generous swags and tails were laced with what looked suspiciously like cobwebs. Instead of detracting from the setting they somehow managed to add to the patina and stability of the Contessa's home.

A large portrait in oils, encased in the confines of an ornate and heavily gilded frame, beamed down approvingly from its place above the mantelpiece. *Il Conte Professore* Giacomo di Capezzani-Batelli, the Contessa's late, much-loved husband and one-time Professor of Voice at both the *Istituto Musicale Luigi Boccherini* in Lucca and London's Royal Academy of Music, watched with varnished satisfaction as the music flowed. Like almost everything else in the apartment he was a lingering relic of an earlier time and, like the heavy brocade that grandly draped and swaged the windows, he too was gently encased in a filigree of cobwebs. Elizabeth had never taken positively to the skills of wielding a feather duster – or any duster, for that matter. A cursory flick with a cloth and the occasional wheezy blow, ineffectual at best, was as good as things got. Over the passing years, her already short stature had become even shorter due to the curvature of her spine. As a result, anything above head height stood very little chance of being assessed as a job opportunity. For his part, suspended in semi-majesty against the wall, high above the large marble fireplace, *Il Conte* had long ago resigned himself to never being freed from the gentle spidery embrace that enfolded his upper regions.

The room fell silent as the last notes of the sextet died away into the late afternoon. The Contessa's music room became, once again, an oasis of calm and serenity; a monument to the cultural passion she and her husband had shared. The position of the apartment ensured that the bright Tuscan sunlight never reached the sacred confines of the Steinway and it was only at this time of day, when the subdued tinges of the fading light reflected off the buildings opposite, that the colours of the floor rugs began to glow.

'*Bravi, angeli miei* ... that was beautiful,' said the Contessa, beaming with enjoyment. 'Such phrasing and breath control. You have remembered what we practised at our last rehearsal very well.' She always referred to her singers as her angels. It was a sincerely meant, warm term of deep affection. 'Did I tell you about my plans for our next project?' she said suddenly.

Carlo shifted his position, snorted and let out a couple of growls. Renata di Senno, who had removed herself to a

50

safer distance on the other side of the piano to Carlo, glared at him.

'Fart?' she mouthed to Riccardo Fossi, who stood opposite her, perilously close to the chair and belligerent canine.

'What?' he mouthed back, his brow furrowed.

'The dog; has it farted again?' She tried to communicate her question through a combination of exaggerated mouth movements and glaring eyes, which bulged in the dog's direction.

Riccardo shook his head – he couldn't smell anything.

'My poor Renata,' said the Contessa, who had changed her score to Flotow's opera *Martha*. She had caught sight of the end of Renata's mouth aerobics as she did so. 'Is your jaw no better? You sang "Lucia" most beautifully just now, my dear. I do hope your jaw problem isn't about to return, not with our concert so close.'

For a moment, Renata completely lost the thread of the Contessa's question, as her attention was still divided between Riccardo and the dog. 'Pardon, Contessa?' she asked.

'Your jaw; is it starting to trouble you again?' asked the Contessa, her face clouded with concern. The next COGOL concert was in just eight days' time and as usual, the ticket sales had been brisk. She could not afford to have any of her angels fall out at this late stage.

'Oh... I see... No, not at all. I was simply performing a few stretching exercises. The Contessa is most kind for asking.'

On the other side of the Steinway, Riccardo Fossi smiled to himself with a knowing glow as he turned the pages in his score. He could tell them a thing or two about Renata and her accommodating stretching exercises.

'Oh, that *is* good news, my dear,' said the Contessa, pressing the pages of her score firmly open on the piano's music stand. 'I can't have my star soprano in any discomfort.'

51

Riccardo Fossi snorted out aloud and then attempted to disguise his unplanned outburst behind a mini fit of coughing. Julietta Camore, who also sang soprano, smiled what could best be described as a tolerant grimace. There were rivers of jealous rivalry running not too deep beneath the surface of COGOL, something the lovely Yvonne still had to discover.

'Are you alright, Riccardo?' asked the Contessa, turning her gaze from Renata to look at him. 'Would you like some water?'

'Thank you, no. It is simply a tickle on the vocal folds, nothing more. It has already passed,' he said, smiling broadly. No one caught the quick wink he flashed at Renata as he threw her a knowing glance that explained everything. She caught it and threw it back with her eyes. Between them, they knew things which did not have to be said.

'Bravo! Then let us encourage the approaching evening with the Nocturne. You already know who will be performing this piece in our concert. Everyone else, please either follow the music or just relax for a few minutes.'

Those COGOL members who were not involved in the quartet-nocturne dispersed themselves to the various chairs that were dotted around the large room. All were still within easy range of the Steinway and the knack was to make sure that the two chairs nearest to the fireplace and Carlo Quinto were left vacant. For his part, the dog growled along more or less in time with the bouncy piano introduction to the Nocturne.

'Sssshh! Carlo, that is quite enough!' snapped the Contessa without missing a note, as her fingers wound themselves easily around the notes of the keyboard. 'I know you like this piece, but will you please stop that noise!'

Predictably, there was no response from the dog, who continued as before.

'It is one of his favourites,' continued the Contessa as she played. It was rather a long introduction.

The others regarded Carlo suspiciously as they waited for their entrance cues. They had long ago formed the opinion that the bad-tempered little beast had no favourites of any kind, other than itself. The Contessa suddenly stopped mid-bar, just as chests had been expanded in preparation for first entries.

'Did I tell you about our next project … for our concert in two months' time?' she asked, smiling at the group. Several confused expressions were raised from the printed pages of music to focus on her. 'When we take tea… Oh, Gregorio, I must talk to you, too… Where was I? Oh yes – the new project. You must not forget to remind me to tell you all about it. As usual it will be a fundraising event, but this time the charity we will be helping is completely different to the usual. It is really quite exciting.' Immediately, her fingers resumed their intimate contact with the keyboard, picking up the accompaniment at the exact spot where she had suddenly stopped. Not a beat had been lost; her questioning outburst had simply put the notes into temporary suspended animation. Indeed, it had been such a fluid motion that the singers, who had only just released their lungs of un-needed air, were taken completely by surprise. Gregorio Marinetti's normally warm baritone was the first voice to be heard. However, on this occasion, he valiantly tried to sing the smooth vocal line on little more than a quarter of a lungful of air. It was a technique the members of COGOL had all learned to do, as the Contessa's behaviour grew more and more erratic with the passing years.

As the rooftops of Lucca became engulfed by the warm embrace of the evening, the music room continued to fill with the melodies of Verdi, Puccini, Mozart and Humperdinck as, under the Contessa's direction, COGOL continued to work through the programme for their approaching concert. *Il Conte* continued to look down appreciatively from behind his gossamer net and Carlo continued to growl softly to himself on his chair. And then, without any warning, the doors to the music room suddenly burst open to reveal Elizabeth. She was struggling with a large tray, on which was an assortment of tea things arranged in a haphazard fashion.

''Twas sounding most *malodourous*, to be sure,' she said as she strode purposefully across the room in the direction of the piano. '*Maladies* of the great masters, so they are. But 'tis getting late and you need to have this, if you're after having it at all. Herself knows Elzeebit can't be doing well when it gets too dark,' she said as she hefted the heavy tray and its clinking, quivering contents up to the piano and onto the heavy fringed cloth that covered the bottom half of it. 'Herself might remember 'tis because of the *contracts* I'll be having,' she continued, ignoring everyone in the room and, once relieved of the burden of the tray, pointing towards her eyes, her fingers in a 'V' shape.

'Yes ... how thoughtful. Thank you, Elizabeth. That will be all,' said the Contessa, resigned to the interruption. They had almost finished, anyway. 'Surely the electric light must be of some help to you, Elizabeth?' she added. Even if she had felt any irritation at the sudden, unannounced arrival of the tea things, she had learned from long experience that she was totally powerless to do anything about Elizabeth's perception of things. '*Angeli miei*, let us stop there and take some tea,' she continued, without giving Elizabeth an opportunity to respond. '*Bravi*. You have all worked so hard tonight.'

The Contessa's singers closed in about the tea tray and proceeded to impose some form of order on the jumbled contents. They had all developed a taste for tea over the years of their involvement with COGOL, which was just as well, as coffee was never on the menu. Elizabeth had retreated back across the room and was about to close the doors behind her, when she stopped in mid-action and glared at the group around the piano.

'And there's none of them *briskets*, you'll be noting ... only what's left of the cake.' She grabbed the handles of the doors. 'The bit *he* didn't get!' she muttered, thrusting her chin out in Carlo's direction. Then she closed the doors with a bang.

At the foot of the piano, where Elizabeth had unceremoniously deposited her burden of the large tea tray, Renata di Senno suddenly caught a whiff of the rotten eggs again. With a flash of diamonds she raised her hand to her nose in an attempt to block the smell. Something was going to have to be done about the little beast. Things had gone on for quite long enough. Assuming the role of the perfect hostess, she poured a cup of tea for the Contessa and moved towards the keyboard to put the hot drink on a cork mat, which the Contessa kept next to the piano's music stand; it would not do to leave a ring on such an expensive instrument. As she did so, she walked past the chair on which Carlo lay snoring, undisturbed by Elizabeth's interruption. Renata was somewhat surprised and more than a little perplexed to find that the air in the immediate vicinity of Carlo Quinto lacked the unpleasant hint of the sewers she had detected at the foot of the piano. In fact, apart from the gentle sound of grumbling, the air around the little beast was filled with nothing more unpleasant than that which is associated with the freshness of a pleasant summer's day out in the countryside. Renata turned and retraced her steps to the foot of the piano to collect her tea, which Julietta Camore, with artificial generosity, had poured for her. As she stood stirring her tea, it suddenly occurred to her that perhaps it wasn't the unpleasant little dog that was sharing the results of its internal gaseous problems with everyone within reach. Perhaps it was the equally unpleasant maid. Of course, nothing could be said in the Contessa's presence. In any case, whilst this trivial little conundrum had occupied Renata's mind, or more correctly her nostrils, the Contessa was explaining her latest idea for their next fundraising project. It was something to do with horses and donkeys in Egypt.

No sooner had the Contessa finished than the doors burst open once again to reveal an angry-looking Elizabeth, her face a picture of atmospheric disturbance, her chest heaving with the effort of having had to negotiate the stairs once again, so soon after bringing up the tea tray.

'The new one's here now!' she snapped between wheezes. 'Elzeebit has brought her straight up to yourself, as *instraticted...*' The last word was lost in a fit of coughing, as she waved a hand in the air as if to dismiss the entire company, turned on her heel and lurched away. Her place in the doorway was taken by the quintessential concept of the fair English Rose.

'Good evening, Contessa.'

'Welcome. Yvonne, my dear, do come in and meet everyone,' said the Contessa, advancing from behind the piano. '*Angeli miei,* let us welcome Yvonne Buckingham. I am sure that our new member's musical ability will enable her to rise to any future challenges.'

Riccardo Fossi felt his member tingle at the thought. A new object for his insatiable appetite had crossed his sights.

8

The Contessa's rehearsal had gone well and she was confident that, with another rehearsal still in hand, COGOL would be well and truly prepared for their forthcoming gala concert. The singers had left the Contessa's spacious apartment and had gone their separate ways, returning to the reality of their everyday lives in the world beyond the music room and the escapism of opera. In *Via Antonio Mordini*, close by the old Roman amphitheatre, Riccardo Fossi sat in the semi-gloom of the street lights. He was nervously tapping the varnished wooden steering wheel of his new Alfa Romeo, as he glanced repeatedly in its wing mirrors. Suddenly, the catch on the passenger door clicked, the door swung open and the car was immediately filled with the subtly heady fragrance of Renata di Senno's very expensive perfume.

'I thought you weren't coming,' he hissed as he turned to kiss her passionately.

'Riccardo!' she replied, fighting him off, but only after she had enjoyed the thrill of his mouth touching hers, 'can I at least get in and put the seatbelt on?' She closed the door and clicked the seatbelt into position. 'Okay ... let's go,' she said as he turned the ignition key and the car purred into powerful, expectant life – very much as he had become aroused and full of expectation at her appearance. 'Benito has had to go away. He phoned me this afternoon just after lunch and said he was leaving for Montecatini and would be back tomorrow. That's a stroke of luck, isn't it?'

she said, placing her hand on the inside of his thigh.

'You mean to say that the assistant state prosecutor has the time to go to Montecatini and take the baths?' asked Fossi, laughing.

'No, it is something to do with the two murders in Lucca, you might remember, a couple of months back. Anyway, it does not concern us,' she said lightly, as she brushed her fingers over his arousal, before returning her hand to his inner thigh. '*That* is of far more interest to us wouldn't you say, *amore*?'

Renata di Senno had been married to her husband for nearly twenty years. As his star had steadily risen within the justice department, her sense of fulfilment with their union had diminished. She still felt great affection for him, but affection given and received was not enough for this hot-blooded COGOL diva. It was the sense of incomplete physical fulfilment which had eventually driven her to wander beyond the spacious confines of the grandiose *Villa Legge*, perched on the hills to the north of the city. The name of the marital home said it all – the Villa of the Law. Physical relations had become as routine and boring as a predictable court case.

Riccardo Fossi took his eyes off the road and flashed a broad grin at her. He was reminded of their unspoken conversation around the Steinway – the talk involving Renata's stretching exercises – and that boost to his ego pleased him enormously. So much so that he had to squirm in his seat to ease the pressure in his trousers. The other element that pleased him was derived from the potential danger of having a protracted affair with the wife of the assistant state prosecutor. This added frisson brought both physical and vocal heights to their energetic passion. If Assistant Prosecutor di Senno found out that his wife was having it off with one of Lucca's most highly respected accountants that would be bad enough. What would make it even worse – or more exciting, depending on your point of view – would be for him to discover that his wife's lover was also discreetly involved in highly organized crime – lucrative, financial crime of the most subtle kind. Fossi found sailing *that* close to the strong arm of the law a big turn-on.

'Keep your eyes on the road, *amore*,' cooed Renata as the car sped through the northern city gate, 'we don't want to waste this opportunity by ending up at the hospital, do we?'

9

Saturday dawned clear and bright. Nearly every morning in Lucca dawned clear and bright – even in the winter months. The flood of tourists had quickly choked *Via Fillungo* and would do so for the greater part of the day. In *Café Alma Arte* the Gaggia had been looked at yet again, but still managed the occasional spit and splutter in protest of its workload. Verriano had managed to navigate the early part of the morning without any further accidents and Gregorio Marinetti counted off another day on the calendar; only five days remaining before the screen would be collected and his financial status would improve.

Outside Lucca, up in the hills, Assistant State Prosecutor di Senno had returned from Montecatini to find his wife dutifully supervising the activities of the cook in the kitchen of the *Villa Legge*. He had spent the whole of Friday in Montecatini, reviewing the details of certain cases and had become somewhat apprehensive when he had learned of Rome's growing interest.

'Benito, *caro*,' she said, kissing him lightly on the mouth, 'come... Let me fix you a glass of something.'

He followed her as she walked through the kitchen and out onto the broad terrace that ran along the south side of the villa. The views out and over Lucca were almost as splendid as were the diamonds on her fingers.

'A glass of wine, beer ... or perhaps something stronger?' she asked, crossing to a small bar at the far end of the terrace. 'Did it go well?' she asked over her shoulder. 'You were gone for a long time.'

She did not mention that it would have been helpful for her to have known the previous day that business would be keeping him in Montecatini for another night. As it was, she had not been able to capitalize on the opportunity.

'No, I do not think it did,' he said. 'It is all too uncomfortably similar to the cases we had here in Lucca two months ago.'

He had removed his tie and jacket, which he flung casually onto one of the cane chairs, before flopping wearily down into one of the others. One thing Benito di Senno could not be accused of within his marriage was keeping his wife out of the picture. Of course, he was far too discreet a professional to tell her everything, but what he felt he could tell her was more than enough to make her feel something special, someone important.

'You mean those two murdered women?' she asked, passing him a glass of ice-cold beer.

He nodded once and took the glass from her. 'There is no proof as yet, but yes; there was another young woman who had been strangled. But this time she had been raped first. That is what is different from the two women who were strangled here in Lucca. This recent victim was an innocent tourist who was presumably visiting the Baths … from Germany. Thanks for this, *cara*,' he paused and took a long draught of the beer. He looked tired. 'Rome has become involved. *"Potentially diplomatically embarrassing"* was how they put it this morning.' He took another mouthful of the cold beer. 'The *Carabinieri* are going to be looking into this latest case as well. The diplomatic element makes it far too serious to leave it to the *polizia* to get to the bottom of … apparently. That is Rome's opinion, not mine.'

Renata looked at her husband with mild curiosity.

Although she benefited materially from his hard work and position, she had never understood what made a person spend their life working with something like the law, which was a concept she found lifeless and impersonal. She had always been excited by the enjoyment of her singing – not to mention the recent enjoyment of Riccardo's regular, throbbing arousal, which was even more memorable than hitting a brilliant high C at the end of an aria. All poor Benito had to contend with was one boring criminal case after another and a large criminal element that seemed to have learned nothing from past police successes.

'So, now I think I should go into town and file some reports about Montecatini and see if anything else has come in.'

'Must you?' whined Renata. 'How long will you be gone? I have prepared a meal for us,' she said, wondering how far the cook had got with it. 'It is such a beautiful day and I thought it would be nice to go for a stroll.'

Riccardo Fossi had told her that he had to go to Torre del Lago for the day to visit his aged aunt, so there was no chance of a repeat matinee performance of Thursday night's frolic.

'I am sorry, *tesoro*,' he said, picking up his jacket and tie before bending down and kissing her, 'but you know what they say about time and crime waiting for no man. I'll take a quick shower and then I'll be off.'

'Do you need any help?' asked Renata seductively. 'I could wash your back for you … or anything else that might need a tickle.'

He smiled apologetically at her and shrugged. Then he put down his glass, turned and walked into the house.

Twenty minutes later, Renata di Senno stood on the terrace watching her husband drive away in the direction of the city. Behind her, she heard a cough, followed by the cook's voice.

'Does the *signora* wish me to make the lunch into dinner?' she asked.

As Assistant State Prosecutor di Senno parked his car in the yard of the prosecutor's office, the bells of the *duomo* sounded out across the city. It was lunchtime and the business community would soon be shutting down for the afternoon's heat-escaping siesta. That was the way it had always been in hot Mediterranean countries, as far back as anyone could remember.

Further along *Via Fillungo*, Gregorio Marinetti heard the distant sound of one o'clock fade through the streets outside the air-conditioned tranquillity of his shop. He dunked yet another *biscotto* – the seventh so far – into his *latte*, as he continued to battle with a quandary.

He dunked his eighth *biscotto* as he surveyed his domain. What concerned him was the question of the Venetian screen, which he had just 'acquired' and now resided in secret in his lock-up out in the country. In his mind's eye he saw once again, strategically placed on the central panel, the winged Lion of St Mark. He also recalled that the beast looked more malevolent than perhaps such a noble symbol of a great city should. He ascribed that to the circumstances under which the lion had found itself in his shop in the first place, circumstances under which he had been obliged – for the first time in his life – to cross the fine borderline from respectability into the shady region of illegality. He dunked a ninth *biscotto*. They were only small and besides, he wasn't counting.

He had hoped that no one had noticed the screen in his shop that previous Thursday, but such a hope had been shattered at the Contessa's rehearsal that same evening, when she had asked him if it had perhaps been a screen she had seen in his shop. He had nearly choked on his tea, but had managed to recover his composure before dropping the cup loudly back onto its saucer.

'Screen?' he had asked feebly. 'Alas, no, the Contessa is mistaken. I haven't had a screen in my shop for a very long time. They are rather rare at the moment.'

'But then what was that I saw through the window? It looked like a dog or something painted on it. It was very dark and depressing ... in the centre of your shop.'

'*Scusi*, Contessa, but what is "*depressing*"?' he asked. They were speaking English.

'Gloomy and drab,' she replied.

Gregorio understood gloomy, but was not sure he fully understood drab. He nodded anyway, whilst thinking furiously for a way around this unexpected problem.

'The Contessa must have seen the panel I recently acquired on behalf of an esteemed client in Florence,' he replied smiling, his voice teetering on the brink of betraying it for the lie that it was. 'Sadly, it was in a state of very poor repair and was only a single panel, but my client had his mind set on it, even allowing for the poor condition. The Contessa could not have seen the chair behind it, which was propping it up.'

'Oh ... that's a pity. You say that you have a chair for us, which is good. And I have that table over there. It's quite light and easy to get down the stairs. But we still need a screen for our *Figaro*,' continued the Contessa. 'It is an important prop and we can't really do without it.'

Gregorio Marinetti had put his cup back on the tray. His hand shook and the crockery rattled as he did so. The others had been looking enquiringly at him ever since he had dropped the cup onto the saucer.

'Are you quite alright, Gregorio?' the Contessa asked, fixing him with her gaze. 'You seem to be perspiring rather a lot.'

Even the expensive cologne he usually floated about in

could not disguise the wet patches that had appeared on his otherwise immaculate white shirt. He had removed a large white handkerchief from his trouser pocket and mopped at his brow.

'It is just the tea,' he replied, his mouth parched absolutely dry, despite having just drunk most of the contents of the cup. 'And is that not why we drink tea?' he continued, replacing the handkerchief. 'Did not the Contessa herself inform us that in India tea is drunk to encourage perspiration, in order to cool the individual down?' He bowed graciously in the Contessa's direction and as she smiled back in acknowledgement, he breathed an internal sigh of considerable relief.

Alone in the tiny office at the back of his shop, Gregorio's normally placid appearance was as ruffled and unsettled as it had been that Thursday evening at the COGOL rehearsal. Safely hidden behind the closed sign on the front door, he absently dunked a tenth *biscotto* in his *latte*, which, by now, was lukewarm.

10

'Make sure that you keep your phone switched on; there might be something I need you to do ... and don't spend all evening fiddling around with your wires and things. By the way, I didn't have a chance to do the kitchen floor this afternoon,' she said, admiring her finely manicured fingernails before gazing into the mirror and attending to an errant curl of her thick auburn hair.

'Alright, Letizia, I'll try and do it. What time do you think you'll be home?'

She cast him a sideways glance in the mirror, as she adjusted her blouse so that her cleavage was displayed to advantage. It was a look devoid of any affection or warmth.

'Whenever the girls think we've had enough,' she replied, a little brutally, 'which could be any time at all. Tomorrow's Sunday, so I can lie in. Don't forget that you have to take the children to see your parents first thing in the morning. Make sure you're back here in time for Mass. We don't want the neighbours gossiping again like they did the last time...'

Tito Viale was only allowed part of his wife's voice; the rest of it had gone through the front door with her and like Letizia herself, was now lost to him. The reality of his situation was that she had been lost to him for years, but he tried hard to grin and bear it for the sake of the children – the two girls, both now in primary school, and little Paolo, not yet three. Tito stood in the passageway staring hopelessly at the bulk of the stout front door with its heavy, almost industrial quality locks. Letizia was obsessed with the threat of burglary and had nagged and nagged – more so than usual – until he had fitted the multi-tumbler security locks on the front and back doors of their apartment. As he stood looking down the empty passageway, he thought the large locks were the encapsulated metaphor for almost the entire twelve-year span of his married life. The locks didn't keep burglars out as much as keep him in; they also kept him apart from Letizia. He sighed heavily, turned and walked back into the kitchen to finish clearing up the dinner things. He slowly stacked the dishwasher that he had purchased for Letizia a couple of years earlier, thinking that it would make her housework easier. He need not have bothered; it made absolutely no difference whatsoever, because he still did most of it. He sighed. At least he had the kids and his music. He consoled himself with the thought that things could be worse.

'*Papà*, can I have a glass of juice please?'

His younger daughter's voice was melodiously sweet and in direct contrast to the acerbic tones of her mother.

'Of course you can, *tesoro*. Help yourself from the fridge. Has your programme finished on the television?'

'Yes,' nodded the nine-year-old girl, filling her glass. 'It was funny, *Papà*. We all laughed a lot, but Paolo fell asleep.'

Paolo had been the result of one of the rare occasions that Letizia had permitted Tito any kind of intimacy. Once she had found out that she was pregnant again, further opportunities had been withdrawn.

'And I am not at all surprised he did. Look at the time – it's late. You should all be in bed by now. We have to go and visit *nonna* and *nonno* early tomorrow.'

Within a quarter of an hour, teeth had been brushed, bladders emptied and prayers said. The usual feeling he experienced when he returned home from his job at the electricity planning department of the *Comune di Lucca* had melted away. He fought constantly to ignore and deny the feeling of hopelessness he felt from being trapped in a union with an unloving partner and not being able to see a future for them. Now, as he bent over the sleeping forms of his three children, Tito Viale smiled down lovingly at their peaceful faces before kissing them tenderly in turn on their foreheads.

'Sleep well *tesori miei,*' he whispered as he put the light out. He was fully mindful that his three treasures were his future and they were *all* that he had to show for twelve hard years of trying to make his marriage work. He left the passage light on and walked slowly back to the sitting room. It was not a large apartment – the children all slept in one room – but it was all they could afford on his salary from the *comune.* Things had become difficult after Letizia stopped working. She was a qualified beautician, but one day had suddenly decided to exercise all of her considerable skills on a single client – herself. The resulting drop in their monthly income had proved to be a huge millstone around Tito's neck. It didn't seem to bother Letizia at all; she carried on as she always had done.

He tidied up the sitting room and put the girls' colouring books back in the basket that served as their toy box. Then he sat down in his own chair and for the first time that busy Saturday, slowly felt himself start to relax. He picked up the TV remote control and scrolled through the programme listings. Nothing really took his fancy, so he settled for an American crime film on one of the movie channels. It was abysmal, but there was no alternative, as the video player had not functioned since Paolo decided to share his honey yoghurt with it, by force-feeding the slot where the video cassette usually went. They had only discovered the sabotage later in the evening, by which time the honey yoghurt had dribbled over the vital internal parts of the machine, rendering it useless and in need of repair. As usual, Letizia had managed to blame Tito for this, even though he had been at his desk on the other side of the city at the time. An argument had ensued, as there was no money for either a new video machine or a DVD player, which was even more out of the question. Letizia's constant demands for things – cosmetics and new dresses – made a sizeable hole in the family's limited finances; not that she ever seemed to acknowledge this.

Tito had been watching the film for half an hour and was starting to feel his eyelids grow heavy, when he became aware of a scratching at the back door.

'All right, Brutus. I'm coming. Calm down,' he muttered to himself sleepily, as he got to his feet and walked slowly to the kitchen. He let out a long yawn as he reached the back door and opened it, but he stifled the end of it as a mongrel came bounding through. 'Hello, Brutus, you sloppy dog,' he said, cupping the smiling face in both of his hands. 'Have you been out on the town again?'

As if to reply in the affirmative, Brutus opened his mouth and let out a low whine, his wet tongue protruding from his pink lips and his tail thrashing the air like a propeller. But Brutus did not bark as a reflection of his excitement at being home. Instead, there were just a couple of subdued yaps – nothing more, despite the dog's obvious pleasure. Although Letizia had insisted that they got a dog, she had not liked his barking. In fact, Letizia did not like the dog at all. Being rather clever, Brutus had quickly learned that it was only safe to bark or yap on the regular occurrences when Letizia was out. Tito soon realized that Brutus seemed to be scared of his wife and the dog made hardly any effort to get too close to her.

'Come on, boy, it's just you and me again. Look what I've got for you. I've saved you the bones.'

The dog seemed to understand his master perfectly and forgetting himself for an instant let out a peal of excited barks.

'Shush! You'll wake the kids if you carry on like that,' said Tito good-naturedly, as he put the bones in the dog's food bowl.

Later, with a second large glass of red wine in his hand and Brutus smiling contentedly on the sofa next to him – something which Letizia *never* allowed – Tito returned his attention to the film. Having missed so much of it, he now found it difficult to work out what was actually happening. Despite the shallow characterisations, which he regarded as usual in American films of this type, it became apparent that the female partner of the gang boss was planning to get rid of him and take over the gang herself.

'What a genius,' muttered Tito, as he drained the wine glass and put it on the floor next to the sofa. 'She knows all about electricity and wiring and such ... and is able to work out a schematic diagram ... and plan the circuitry.' He felt his concentration slowly fade as the flickering image of the television and the sound of the dubbed actors' voices merged into a kaleidoscope of nothingness and he became lost to a half-sleep; one ear fixed on the kids' room, the other on the now-distant television. As he fell deeper into his sleep, a carousel of images revolved through his brain; the gang leader seemed to be in the room with him – the man was trying to use the same video machine that Paolo had made inoperable – the movement on the sofa next to him must be the gang leader sitting down; he seemed to be reaching for the remote control to start the tape – nothing happened. Tito thought he heard a sigh as the man got up and crossed to the video machine. As the man bent down and pressed the play button, there was a blinding flash and lots of sparks. Tito flinched. He then became aware that on the television, the gang leader's girl – the electronic genius – was unplugging the still-smouldering video machine from the wall socket. Then she seemed to rip out several wires from its mangled rear, laughing amateurishly as she did so.

Tito thought that the acting was appalling.

'That's the problem with B movies,' he muttered through his closed, sleep-heavy mouth, 'far too corny to be at all believable!' Then he suddenly felt a cold, wet sensation on his left hand, which was accompanied by a rough, rasping feeling. One of the other gang members was saying something about the gang leader having been electrocuted by a faulty video machine. He pointed to the charred and twisted shape of what was left of it.

It was shortly before midnight when Tito Viale, with Brutus' head resting contentedly on his leg, suddenly opened his eyes with a start. The dog sat up, let out a soft yap and licked the back of Tito's hand again.

'What happened to the film?' asked Tito, yawning and stretching.

Brutus did not answer, but just looked expectantly at his master, his head cocked to one side.

'Oh well, boy, time for bed I suppose,' he said, scratching the dog under the chin. Then he rose stiffly to his feet and yawned. He should have gone to bed hours ago, instead of watching that stupid film. He and the kids had an early start in the morning. 'Come on,' he said to Brutus. 'Two biscuits and then out you go.'

As he turned to walk to the kitchen, he suddenly stopped. Turning his head slightly, just enough to allow him to see the television and the useless video machine underneath it, he stared through sleep-laden eyes. *It's neither charred nor twisted. It must have been the video machine in the film that blew up.*

Then he stumbled off to bed, innocently unaware that in his subliminal consciousness a thought had been planted.

71

11

Comfortably surrounded by the splendour of her apartment the Contessa once again felt that certain tranquillity from which, over the years, she had drawn her inner strength. Life was good, but she would never forget that it had not always been so. She sat in her boudoir, relaxed in her favourite chair, looking out over the railings of the small balcony. Beneath her in the space that had once been the Roman arena, the lights of the restaurants and other apartments that had long ago been fashioned from the former amphitheatre twinkled. Several hundred years earlier, when the arena had been little more than a ruinous pile of ancient rubble, expensive and highly desirable apartments had been created where once the hungry population of ancient Roman Lucca had satiated their blood-lust. From her boudoir, which occupied a position on the north-eastern wall, she enjoyed a panoramic view of the entire structure.

'Himself will be late, so he will. 'Twas what he said into the *trellifoam.*'

There was a clattering of claws on the highly polished marble floor, as Carlo trotted into the boudoir, nearly tripping up Elizabeth as he did so.

'Saints preserve us!' she said, tottering slightly in mid-stride. 'Where is the blasted, cursed beast?'

She cast around trying to locate the dog, but Carlo had already reached the safety of the Contessa's lap. He seemed to be grinning up at the maid as if to say, *nearly got you that time!*

'He's here, Elizabeth,' said the Contessa, transferring her attention from the activity in the brightly lit arena below to the tangled curls on top of Carlo's head. 'What has mummy's darling been up to? Who's been a good boy, then?'

'Twill be a fine day when you can honistelly *say that,* thought Elizabeth, eyeing the dog with a strange mixture of tolerant affection and outright, distrusting dislike.

'He's got them *cryptics* up his rear again,' she announced flatly. 'Yourself isn't to think that all of the marks out on the sitting room floral *crepit* are part of the pattern, neither,' she continued, crossing in front of the Contessa to the large window and closing it with a bang. 'Elzeebit saw him pulling himself along across it, so she did. That's a sure sign of the *cryptics* up the –'

'Yes, thank you, Elizabeth,' interrupted the Contessa.

Carlo growled softly, but he still seemed to be smirking at the maid.

'Poor Carlo,' continued the Contessa. 'You do seem to be having problems at that end, don't you? We'll have to take you to the… Well, we'll have to sort out the crystals.' Everyone avoided the use of the *vet* word, as any mention of it usually sent the unpredictable little dog into fits of hysteria barely matched by most humans. The Contessa patted him on his head. 'The design on the carpet in the sitting room is quite busy enough already, without you adding anything to it.'

Elizabeth had made no mention of having cleaned off the undesirable addition to the design of the seventeenth-century Aubusson carpet, so the Contessa did not enquire. Such things were always best left to Elizabeth.

'You said that Luigi telephoned? Did he say that he'll be late?'

The question went unanswered as Elizabeth wrestled with the internal shutters on the window. In doing so, she caught her foot in the generous length of curtain that flowed onto the floor. The result was that her foot suddenly started to slide ahead of her. She lashed out with her hand to steady herself and grabbed the nearest thing, which was the bulk of the hanging drape, held back regally by a heavy, fringed tassel tie-back. For a split second it looked as if Elizabeth McGraunch was about to descend gracefully to the hard floor, but the fabric proved more substantial than she was and she simply gave a couple of small semi-twists, until she had regained control of her balance.

'You'll be making do with the shutters, so ye will,' she said as she stopped vibrating and released the drape. 'The *cretins* will do just nicely hanging where they're at for tonight.' As she spoke, a delicate frosting of un-removed dust gradually descended over her from the upper reaches of the swag, which had been manipulated into unaccustomed swinging life by the semi-frantic movement of the drape underneath it.

'Luigi?' repeated the Contessa, who had missed most of Elizabeth's performance as she had been deep in conversation with Carlo, who still sat on her lap looking up at her. 'What did Luigi have to say?' She had raised her voice at the further repetition of her question. Recently, she had begun to wonder if Elizabeth's hearing was starting to deteriorate.

'Yes, himself was speaking into the *trellifoam* and he'll be a bit behind himself. So he said.' Elizabeth had regained what passed for her usual demeanour, following the near disaster with the puddle of heavy curtain. She turned to walk back towards the door. The Contessa inhaled and was about to speak, when Elizabeth – never pausing in her progress out of the room – cut across her.

'Elzeebit was after telling her highness in the kitchen to not be so punctual with the food … unless she wants it all

stuck to the pans and spoiled by the time himself arrives.'
'Thank you, Elizabeth. Perhaps you could ask –'
The loud click of the door lock stopped the Contessa
in mid-sentence, as the door closed behind the retreating
maid.

'But, then again, perhaps not,' the Contessa continued to
the now-empty room.

Carlo jumped down and trotted off to sit on the sofa,
which stood diagonally opposite the Contessa's chair.

'Luigi works far too hard, bless him,' she said, looking at
Carlo, who had suddenly sat up, raised one of his back legs
in the cello-playing position and turned his attention to the
irritating matter of his anal crystals. 'Still, I suppose that's
what he wanted when he started his career. And he has
done very well for himself at the hospital.'

Carlo paid her no attention, but continued his licking. In
the distance, the bells of the *duomo* chimed the hour, the
sound of which carried easily on the balmy evening air.

'Seven o'clock,' said the Contessa, getting up out of her
chair. 'Let's see what has happened today in the wide world,
shall we?'

Carlo kept licking. As she walked past the window where
Elizabeth had performed her choreographic routine with
the heavy drape, she looked down at the little Maltese.

'Oh dear! Mummy's little boy isn't well at all, is he?' she
said, pausing at the sofa to tickle behind the dog's left ear.

Carlo, who had stopped his licking, looked back at the
Contessa with that specific look of intolerance, which said
simply: *What on earth are you on about? I have a small problem,
that's all.*

'We'll have to have something looked at, won't we?'

She gave Carlo another tickle and then walked to a sleek,
modern-looking laptop that stood on a small, marble-
topped, round table in the corner of the room. Luigi had
bought the computer for her last Christmas and Tito Viale

had wired it up after an extra rehearsal one Saturday afternoon. Luigi, who was a brilliant pathologist by career, might have known all about the wiring of the human body, but he was woefully ignorant as to the mysteries of electronics. Familiar only with the basic uses of such electronic equipment, he had tried to show his mother how to send emails, but to no avail. Although impressed with her son's prowess in such matters, the Contessa could not be convinced that she would ever need to use such facilities. Instead, she had once again counted herself very fortunate that her little band of singers – her COGOL, her angels – contained splendidly fine people with a wide-ranging collection of skills, some of whom would know considerably more about computers than she, herself, was ever likely to know.

Tito had tried to explain how the signal came into the apartment through a satellite dish, mounted discreetly on the side of the chimney. The well-meant attempt at broadening her understanding of the twenty-first century had been a total flop as, like Luigi's attempted explanation about emails, she had understood practically nothing of what Tito said. In fact, Tito had been obliged to revise his approach and had confined himself to showing her how to switch the thing on and off and which icon on the desktop she had to click to access BBC News 24 or BBC Radio 3 and Classic FM.

It's marvellous, when you think of what's going on inside of this thing. That had been her reaction as she watched the screen glow and the image of her desktop fade up and into life for the first time. Tito had also borrowed an old photograph of the Contessa's, which he had scanned onto a memory stick and which now resided proudly as her desktop background image. He had tried to explain how he had used a scanner to copy the picture, but she had thought that was what Luigi sometimes used in his work up at the hospital to see the inside of bodies, which didn't make much sense to her at all. The modern world could be so uncomfortably confusing. The image was an old faded photograph of the Count, taken just before the war, during happy days at the Royal Academy of Music in London. He was standing at the head of a phalanx of students, who were grouped around a large grand piano. Seated behind the keyboard was a young girl of, perhaps, no more than eighteen or nineteen. Penelope Strachan was her name and she was an outstanding student pianist.

'This is the Six O'clock News,' said the voice of the BBC newsreader.

And it will be the usual round of depressing revelations, contemplated the Contessa as she walked back towards her chair, patting Carlo once again as she passed the sofa. As she sat down, she drew a footstool nearer to her and rested her feet on it. Her prediction about the contents of the news had not been far off the mark, as one item after another reported doom, gloom, corruption or outright mayhem. As she sat in the gently lit room listening to the news (she hardly ever watched the pictures on the laptop's screen, as she thought that they flickered too much and gave her a headache), she felt her eyes grow heavier and heavier; she had not had her afternoon nap and now felt that she was paying for failing to recharge her batteries.

'...main line and Eurostar trains are worst affected. It is not clear how long it will be before the Eurostar service returns to normal. This will depend on how long it is before the damaged length of track is repaired. A company official said that further breakdowns could not be ruled out, given the age of some of the signalling equipment and track. Questions have been raised in Parliament about this accident. Passengers planning to travel to France should ma...'

The Contessa's eyes became even heavier. Carlo had started to snore softly.

'...it is anticipated that the worst passenger congestion will be at Waterloo Station.'

The news changed to another item, but the Contessa was no longer listening...

'There you are dearie. That'll be tuppence, please.' The severe-looking waitress in the tearoom on Waterloo Station stood behind the counter holding out her hand for the required payment.

'Oh ... yes ... right. I'll just get my purse out and ...'

In the sudden confusion that resulted from changing bags and raincoat from one hand to another, the bulging leather bag fell to the floor with a dull thump, spilling its contents all over the floor at the young woman's feet.

'Oh dear, dearie,' offered the waitress dispassionately. There was a war on and she had seen far worse over the last couple of years than this gangling, clumsy girl. 'That's a bit of a pickle, isn't it? That'll be tuppence,' she repeated, her voice carrying a steely edge as she eyed the queue that was building up.

'Yes, I'll just get my purse out... It's in my coat pocket... No, it's in my bag ... I think.'

The waitress stared at the younger woman with some-thing bordering on thinly disguised contempt. She reached up and adjusted the white, triangular cloth she wore on her head, the two ends of which were tied neatly into a knot just above her forehead. She craned forward slightly to see what it was that had fallen out of the case.

'Them's funny books, dearie.'

She was looking at the pile of books on the floor, several of which had fallen open to reveal pages of music. Some were manuscript sheets, on which music notes had been written in black ink in a very neat, flowing hand; some were printed scores and some were music for piano.

'Yes, they're music books. I'm a student at the Royal

Academy,' replied the young woman as she bent down to collect the books and replace them in her music bag.

'Oh yes?' replied the waitress, folding her arms across her chest, putting her head to one side and trying to adopt a superior expression. 'Royal Academy, is it? And them's music books ... with all them dots and things?'

The young woman nodded up at her. 'Yes, I play the piano and this is the music I have to prepare over the holiday ... at home.'

With the help of the man behind her, most of the books and manuscript sheets had been quickly returned to the secure captivity of the music bag. Only the score for *Lucia di Lammermoor*, which had fallen open at the beginning of the famous sextet, still lay on the floor awaiting recovery.

'Thank you ever so much,' said the young woman as she stood up again.

The young man behind her, who was dressed in army uniform, smiled and nodded his head.

'Right then ... tuppence you said, wasn't it?' she said, holding out two copper pennies.

She had found her purse at the bottom of the music bag which, together with the coat, was now securely held in check under her left arm, leaving her right hand free to proffer the two coins.

High up on the wall behind the waitress was a large poster issued by the War Ministry. *LET US GO FORWARD TOGETHER*, it proclaimed, repeating Winston Churchill's recent exhortation to the war-weary British public. From the look on the waitress's face, it seemed to be precisely what she was about to do. She saw herself as a guardian of state security and was prepared to report anything unusual that came within her sights in order to help Mr Churchill win the war. The waitress took the money and stared long and hard at the fresh young face, as if she was trying to impress the features indelibly into her memory. She had heard about suspicious happenings before. The war gave rise to all sorts of unusual stories and rumours. The lines and dots on those pages, at least the ones she had seen before they had been hastily retrieved could be more than just music. What if they were some sort of secret code? Music books, indeed! *If this slip of a girl turns out to be an enemy agent,* thought the waitress, *I need to be able to identify her to the authorities. Winston would expect nothing less of me. We all have to do our patriotic duty.* 'Ta, I'm sure,' the waitress grunted, her gaze never wavering from the face of her customer. Even after the young woman had picked up her cup of tea and turned away from the counter, she stared after her, wondering...

The tearoom was crowded, almost drowned out under a sea of khaki and blue. At some tables, couples sat talking or sat in tearful silence. Soon they would make their farewells amongst clouds of steam and the desperate noise of departure; farewells in a war that would separate husbands and wives, mothers and sons, fathers and daughters, perhaps for ever. At other tables, groups of service men and women sat smoking, chatting loudly, playing cards or just staring pensively ahead. The odd one here and there was writing a letter or reading one, recently received.

Balancing the cup of tea, the music bag and her coat, the young woman traversed almost the entire length of the large, crowded room, before she caught sight of a man who was making ready to leave his seat at one of the two-seater tables. Several of these lined the walls of the furthest perimeter of the room and because of their position, were not as well lit as the mass of tables filling the main seating area. For an instant it occurred to her to speculate as to where the young man might be going. He wore pilot's wings on his Royal Air Force uniform and was probably not much older than she was. He looked so handsome in his uniform – they all did. The compassion inside her wanted to ask him where he was going and to wish him luck and for him to have a safe journey, but it could not be done. During the war, thousands of people moved about constantly. Posters and propaganda films at the cinema warned everyone about the folly of speculation and careless talk. After nearly two years of grim conflict, it seemed to have become second nature to most people not to do either.

'Are you off?' she asked brightly and with an encouraging smile.

'Afraid so, dear lady,' he replied, flashing a friendly smile in return. 'Can't stop. I've finished with this, by the way. You're quite welcome to it,' he said, offering her a folded copy of that morning's *The Times* newspaper.

'That's very kind of you,' she replied, suddenly struck by the realisation that she had no hands free with which to accept his generosity.

'Don't mention it. Here, I'll put it on the table for you.'

A couple of minutes later, once she had stowed the music bag and her folded coat between the wall and her chair, she picked up the cup and took a mouthful of tea. There was no sugar – again – but she had grown used to not putting it in her tea and now she hardly missed the comforting sweetness. She replaced the cup in its saucer and picked up the still-folded newspaper. It was only then that she became really aware of the huddled form seated on the chair opposite her. It was a young woman, obviously slightly built, who had slumped down so low in the chair that she resembled nothing more than a bundle of clothes. She sat staring blankly at the empty cup in her lap. She held it in both of her hands, as if to hide the fact that it was empty. People became very heated when chairs were not vacated as soon as anything purchased at the counter had been consumed. This woman's cup had not held anything for some time and she was lucky not to have been evicted from the chair.

'Oh, excuse me. I didn't really notice you sitting there,' said the young woman with the music bag. It sounded ridiculous, but in the crush of the crowded room, it was the truth. The other woman said nothing. 'The news is getting a little better, isn't it?' Still, there was no response. She tried for a third time. 'Do you have long to wait for your train? I've got about forty minutes –'

'I'll not be going anywhere,' replied the other woman, suddenly interrupting in a strong Irish accent, 'and I'll not be going back there neither, so I won't.'

'Oh, I see,' replied the young woman, not quite sure that she had fully understood what the other had said, 'and where would that be ... the place you're not going back to?'

'Carlow, I'll not be going back ... not now.'

'Is Carlow near London?'

'Near London? Saints preserve us, no! 'Tis in County Carlow. That much they taught us in the convent.' There was no humour in the voice, only a heaviness, which indicated a serious internal struggle for a future direction. 'On the other side of the water ... in Éire.' She fell silent once more.

'I'm Penelope,' said the woman with the music bag. She couldn't think of anything else to say, 'Penelope Strachan. I'm studying music.'

For a few seconds there was no response from the other woman. She had a shock of thick auburn hair, which she had crammed into a cheap hat, the likes of which could be bought anywhere for no more than a couple of shillings. In fact, the more Penelope looked at her, the more it became apparent that the rest of her clothing was also far from new. She had the look of the poor about her.

'Elzeebit,' said the Irish girl eventually, almost reluctant to give anything away.

'Pardon?' asked Penelope.

'Elzeebit,' she repeated, slightly louder than before.

'Is that a place near ... er ... Carlow?' asked Penelope, taking another mouthful of her tea, which was now barely lukewarm.

'No! 'Tis me own name, to be sure. ELZEEBIT, like the princess.'

'Oh, you mean Elizabeth,' said Penelope, laughing softly.

'That's what I'm telling you. 'Tis Elzeebit, Elzeebit McGraunch.'

Having decided to reveal her identity, it was as if a barrier had been lifted from her shoulders. Within a few minutes, she had told Penelope that she had been sent across from the convent near Carlow to a good position as maid to a wealthy Catholic family in Liverpool. The nuns had arranged it all and, despite her initial misgivings, she had quickly adapted to her new life, free from the shackles of the convent school back in Carlow. That had been three years ago, on her fifteenth birthday. Then things had started to go wrong. Her employer, a highly respected businessman, had suddenly taken more than just a passing interest in her and had gradually become more assertive in his advances. His wife had noticed and quite often the two of them could be heard arguing violently. Apparently, Elizabeth had not been the first. Out of the blue, the mistress had then announced that she would be visiting London and that Elizabeth was to accompany her. On the platform of Liverpool Street Station, the young girl had been given two ten shilling notes, absolved of any guilt concerning the master's behaviour and then abandoned, as her now former mistress prepared to catch the next train back to Liverpool.

'This has happened before,' she had said, staring Elizabeth straight in the eyes, 'and I know of no other way to resolve things. We do not want any breath of scandal and if I were to ask the nuns to take you back or move you, there would be embarrassing and awkward questions. You're a good worker, Elizabeth, and this way at least I can give you the chance of starting again.' The public-address system suddenly announced the departure of the Liverpool train. 'Now I must go. I do not blame you. God go with you,' she had said. Then she was gone.

Penelope sat dumbfounded, staring in disbelief.

'God...! GOD? What had he to do with it all is what I'm after asking?' There was real bitterness in her voice. The fingers clenched the cup even tighter than before.

'Then what did you do?' asked Penelope.

'Do? 'Tis like dropping a tadpole in the mighty ocean. Do? I don't know what to do, other than move from station to station; at least you can eat and drink there and they have the *faculties*.' Her voice had risen in its intensity of bitter realization to the point where others at the nearby tables were casting furtive glances in their direction. Elizabeth McGraunch lowered her head and stared back from beneath hooded eyes.

'The what?' Penelope asked.

'You know; the...' she made the action of flushing a lavatory chain.

'Oh ... I see. You mean facilities.'

Elizabeth did not respond. Her features had become very set, like one of the wax figures Penelope had seen years ago on a trip to Madame Tussauds.

'I don't know where I am or what 'tis I should be doing,' said Elizabeth, suddenly looking very fragile and helpless, 'and there's nobody I can ask for help.'

There was a slight pause, during which she looked Penelope in the face for the first time. It was then that Penelope suddenly realized that the girl must be of her own age, although she had a look of weariness about her.

'But what about the Church? You said you came from a convent school. Can't the Church help you?'

'And send me back to himself in Liverpool? I'll not be doing with the Church any more. They know how to look after themselves first, to be sure. Someone like me counts for little. Even less if 'tis I who is after being seen as a problem.'

'But then what are you going to do?'

Elizabeth did not answer, but simply sat staring at Penelope with unblinking eyes.

Out in the cavernous hanger of Waterloo Station, announcements were being made about train departures. Time had passed very quickly and Penelope's cup was now cold and empty.

'I'm sorry, but I have to go and catch my train,' she said, starting to retrieve her belongings, 'but I'll be back in a couple of weeks. As I said, I'm studying music … at the Royal Academy. You can come and visit me there when I return, if you like.'

Elizabeth made no response, but continued to stare hard at Penelope, who had started to look for something in her music bag.

'Are you going, Miss?' asked a masculine voice behind her. It was a sailor, his hat band bearing the anonymous letters *HMS*, instead of the name of his ship.

'Er, yes I am … in a moment,' replied Penelope, half turning to look at him. 'I want to do this first,' she said, turning back to face Elizabeth. 'I made this to take on the train with me. It's nothing special, I'm afraid, just a plain sandwich with the suggestion of some cheese; my ration ran out. You are very welcome to it,' she said and put the little wrapped bundle on the table and pushed it towards the other woman. 'Well, good luck. I hope to see you when I get back.'

Penelope turned and made her way out onto the concourse to check the departure notice for her train to Winchester. She had some ten minutes in hand and decided to visit the ladies, as the provision of a corridor train could not be relied upon in these turbulent times.

Some minutes later, as she emerged from the ladies back into the crush of the concourse, she suddenly saw the almost Dickensian form of Elizabeth McGraunch standing in front of her, clutching the little bundle of a sandwich.

'You were kind to me, to be sure,' she said softly. 'No one else has been. Can Elzeebit come with you? She has nowhere else to be going.'

'Well, I don't know what –'

'I could work for you … or your family. I've got my papers; they made sure of that when they sent me to himself in Liverpool.' There was an equal measure of pleading and desperation in her voice. Behind her, the large station clock showed nine minutes before the train's departure.

'But I don't think that we need any –'

'And I've me own money to buy me own ticket … to wherever that might be.'

12

'...and it is all very interesting. I just hope that I can remember how to do it all,' said Luigi di Capezzani-Batelli, as he picked up his cut crystal wine glass and took a mouthful of the red *Barolo* it contained. 'Some of the procedures are quite complex and the software controlling everything is even more so. Thank goodness the technician is at hand for the next few weeks. He will keep an eye on me and operate everything if I make a total mess of things. I just hope I can eventually understand all of it.'

'I'm sure that you will, my dear. Someone as clever as you will have no problem with learning how to use a new machine,' replied the Contessa, beaming with pride, but she was of an earlier age and had little real understanding of modern technology or of the wonders of modern medical imaging software.

Mother and son were seated at the large dining table and had just finished the *secondo piatto* of their Saturday evening meal together. This was a ritual that had gone unbroken – except for the occasional illness or distant conference – for nearly twenty years, since shortly after Luigi had been appointed to the post of state pathologist and later, senior state pathologist at the hospital.

'Apart from the excitement of the new equipment, it has been rather a quiet week, *cara*,' he continued, smiling at her through his round spectacles with his steel-blue eyes.

Of course, he bore no resemblance to the Contessa, a fact which, in the early days, had prompted some interested speculation amongst the chattering classes of the society in which the family moved. Any thoughts of the young lad's parentage – or rather the fact that he did not seem to resemble either of his parents in any noticeable way – were kept to the level of interested gossip, well out of earshot of *Il Conte* and his wife. After all, such situations were not uncommon amongst the upper levels of Italian Society – even without the upheaval of the recent war – and the blind eye, which was usually turned towards cases of this sort, could well have taught Admiral Lord Nelson a thing or two.

'We have been busy with our rehearsals for the concert next Friday. I hope you haven't forgotten about it.'

'Not at all; I am looking forward to it. Are all the usual old favourites in the programme? And is everyone prepared?'

'Oh yes, they all are.' She paused. 'Although Gregorio did seem a little preoccupied at last Thursday's rehearsal. Maybe he had something on his mind. I do hope he's not coming down with something … not before the concert.'

'That is an occupational hazard, is it not, *cara*?' replied Luigi. 'Coughs, colds and snivels.' He smiled broadly. He could not remember a time when he had not heard tales of the apprehensions of his mother's prima donnas – male and female.

'It is always *such* a worrying time … leading up to a performance,' continued the Contessa, 'but we must think only of the positive … and we do have a good programme. Let them perform the pieces of music they know well; that's partly the key to a successful event. It is also important to maintain interest, so there must always be one or two new pieces. For this concert we are doing for the first time a section from the first act of *Hansel and Gretel.* Do you remember it? We saw it at La Scala … when you were a strapping boy of eleven. It is the part where the mother and then the father return to the cottage to find Hansel and

Gretel have broken the milk jug ... so there is nothing for supper. We will stage it with a chair and a table. I have an old jug for the milk ... a broom, of course' – she paused – 'and the backdrop will be a screen. But we haven't found a screen yet and we will also need it for *Figaro*. Tell me, my dear, you don't perhaps have a screen we could borrow for the evening, do you? That's the one piece of furniture I do not seem to possess.'

Luigi raised his eyebrows above the top of his spectacles. His tastes were very modern and almost minimalist – totally the opposite of his mother's.

'*Cara*, you know that I have modern tastes,' he said kindly, as if replying to a question asked in all seriousness by a young child, 'so, I am afraid that the only screens I have are those of the computer and the television. But I have an idea,' he continued, wiping the corner of his mouth with his napkin.

It was a generous square of linen, but, in the reflected light of the candelabra that blazed in the centre of the large table, it seemed to have the faintest hint of pink about it. Elizabeth had probably managed to get a coloured item muddled up with the whites again when she loaded the washing machine. The Contessa had not noticed it before, but she would now have to enquire of her irascible house-keeper if that had, indeed, been the case.

'I might be able to borrow a screen from the hospital for you, provided it goes back the very next day,' continued Luigi. 'We are not that full at the moment, so I'm sure that it should be possible. You could always drape one of your pieces of damask or brocade over it in an operatically artistic fashion. Nobody would notice it is really a screen from the hospital.'

'That's very generous of you, my dear,' replied the Contessa, who didn't think much of the suggestion at all. COGOL always presented operatic events of the highest artistic and musical standard and she was not at all convinced that the presence of a hospital screen on the stage would serve to perpetuate this tradition, even if it was suitably draped to hide its origins. She suddenly sat up. And what if it came to the concert refusing to leave the smell of stringent hospital antiseptic behind? That would never do. 'Can I let you know about that?' she added.

Luigi nodded and shrugged in the Italian manner, which encompasses everything from acceptance to outright disapproval.

The doors to the dining room opened and Elizabeth shuffled in to clear the plates, which she stacked onto her tray. She returned almost as soon as she had left and cut right across the conversation.

'Last course – 'tis perfectly good eating pears boiled in wine ... again,' she muttered as she placed the two plates in front of the diners. She did not go much with this fancy cooking business.

'I like a pear steeped in wine,' said the Contessa, picking up her spoon and fork.

'To yourself be your taste,' muttered Elizabeth, as she shuffled on around the end of the table and headed once again for the doors.

'Thank you, Elizabeth,' Luigi called out after her. She had been part of the family for as far back as he could remember.

'Welcome you are, to be sure,' she replied without turning her head to address him. 'Myself will be back to me own *plain* pear with her majesty in the kitchen.'

The doors closed with a loud bang, which was nothing to do with anger on Elizabeth's part, but rather more to do with the increasing inability of her arthritic hands to successfully control items such as doorknobs.

'She's getting worse,' said Luigi, as a plainly stated matter of fact. He sat looking at the door, his voice tinged with a hint of sadness. He was used to the decay and collapse produced in humans by the passing of time – it was his job. But *this* gradual decline was personal. It was within his family circle and that made it harder to accept.

'As are we all, my dear,' said the Contessa, her spoon full of succulent pear and sweet red-wine syrup. 'It is the certain inevitability of the uncertainty we call life.'

'That is a philosophic pronouncement,' said Luigi, looking at his mother.

'It is a simple statement of the truth, my dear, and the truth is something that we should never be frightened of.'

They continued in companionable silence, the room echoing to the clink of their cutlery against the fine china of the dessert plates. Somewhere further off in the distance, the faintest rumble of the city by night lingered.

'What was it you were telling me before the pears interrupted us?' asked the Contessa. She patted her mouth with her napkin. Viewed up close, it definitely did have a faint pink tinge in places. She sighed. They had been in Giacomo's family for years and were even older than she was.

'Uhm ... I was telling you about an interesting case we had yesterday; quite late it was, too. They brought a person over from Montecatini.' Luigi used this terminology when talking to his mother about his work; he had always thought that she would find the blunt use of the word 'corpse' rather distressing. 'A young foreign woman; it was all rather unpleasant. Strangled and...' he paused, sanitising the more unpleasant aspects of the case. 'Well, there were other things done to her as well.'

'Luigi, dear, if this lady was visiting your department at the hospital, she must have been dead,' said the Contessa with sudden frankness. She did not look at her son as she spoke, but kept her gaze fixed on her half-eaten pear. 'Poor girl,' she continued, with genuine remorse. 'A stranger in a strange land.'

'Yes ... and there are other considerations about the case, because what happened seems to be very similar, if not identical, to two similar cases here in Lucca a few months back. Identical that is except for the ... interference.'

'What is the difference between violation and murder?' muttered the Contessa. 'They are as heinous as each other. Were the two poor souls found in Lucca foreigners, too?' she asked, an absent look on her face.

'No, they were both local,' he replied, 'and there were no other complications, other than the strangulation.'

'Well, at least they were not strangers in a strange land,' she continued softly. 'When I first came here with *Il Conte*, I felt like that for a little while. I used to feel really lost when we lived out at the villa: that huge house surrounded by acres of vineyards, stuck way out in the hills. That was before you were born. *Il Conte, La Contessa* and En...' There was a pause, during which a look of profound sadness and longing flashed across her face and was gone again. 'And energetic servants, of course. It must have been the same for *Il Conte...* He was a stranger in a strange land when he went to live in London. But that was many years ago, even before you were born, my dear,' she said kindly, repeating herself and reaching out a hand to pat him on the arm, 'so you wouldn't remember any of that, naturally.'

The Contessa had subconsciously avoided the use of the word 'father' when speaking to Luigi about her husband. He thought nothing of it, as he had been brought up to address the person he regarded as his father as *Babbo* – the Tuscan term of endearment. The fact that his mother did not use the same terminology did not strike him as unusual. There were formal as well as informal forms of address used in Italian.

'I do remember going to the villa when I was a small boy,' replied Luigi, 'but only just, and it seemed such a rare occurrence. How often was it that we went to look at the villa and the vineyards?'

The Contessa smiled at him. 'We used to go once a year … just before the grapes were picked,' she said. 'Do you need to go out there very often these days?' she asked, changing the subject slightly.

'Occasionally, *cara*, but I can usually talk to the estate manager by email. The wine continues to do well and I am pleased to say we are in the running for a medal at the next Merano International Wine Festival.'

They sat in contented silence for a few moments. The Contessa beamed proudly at her son, her expression hiding the confusion she was experiencing over what he had just said. Even her extremely limited grasp of the technology of the twenty-first century was sufficient to know that you couldn't talk to anyone using an email.

'Do you know a funny thing about the villa?' continued Luigi. 'Despite all of our guests there and the staff who look after them, to me the place is so big that I find it hard to believe it was ever actually a home.'

'The guests continue to visit, which is excellent news,' said the Contessa, looking at the remains of the pear on her plate, 'and you have told me that we are fully booked up to February of next year,' she added, a sense of triumph in her voice masking the flood of sad memories of her dear Enrico and of her last year at the *Villa Batelli*. 'You were telling me about your latest case,' she said, suddenly changing the subject.

'I was, indeed, *cara*. This case from Montecatini is so serious that I have had a meeting with Assistant State Prosecutor di Senno – you know, Renata's husband,' he continued.

'Oh, but surely you've met him before … at one of our concerts?' she asked, the empty expression of sadness now gone from her face.

'Certainly I have,' he replied, 'and very occasionally I also meet him through my work at the hospital … through the more rare and serious of cases. I mention this latest instance to show just how serious the Montecatini case is. Apparently the Department of Foreign Affairs in Rome has asked to be kept informed of the investigation because of the diplomatic complications of the girl being a foreigner – a German.'

'Yes, so you said, my dear; the poor soul who was a foreigner in a foreign place.'

'Coffee?' asked Luigi softly.

The expression on his mother's face was an indication that in the fields of her memory, she had left her seat at the head of the dining table to wander through the years of her past…

A young Penelope Strachan stood at the tall window and gazed out over the street below her, out across to the Royal Albert Hall and the spacious Victorian apartment blocks, which were a landmark of the well-heeled in South Kensington. It was a perfect summer's day. In the large room behind her were several rows of chairs and a Steinway grand piano. On the wall were pictures of the great composers and on the top of a tall wooden filing cabinet was a plaster bust of Giacomo Puccini, who stared down into the empty room with the superiority born of the inner knowledge of self-worth.

'I am very sorry that I am a few minutes late,' said a deep, well-focussed voice behind her. The sudden pronouncement made her start with surprise. 'And I apologize a second time for making you jump,' continued the voice, as its owner crossed to the piano. He deposited the pile of papers he was carrying onto its closed lid. On the top of the pile was a folded copy of that morning's *Daily Telegraph* – Thursday 15th June 1939.

'That's all right,' replied Penelope, turning around as she

regained her composure. What she saw took her breath away. For a moment, she thought that Rudolf Valentino or Douglas Fairbanks had entered the room.

'Firstly, I must thank you for coming to see me after a tiring day of study. I must also assume that my request has been favourably received by the powers that be in this place and that they have sent me one of their most outstanding pianists as a result. Please, do sit down,' he said, indicating a chair in the front row.

'Oh ... thank you,' she said, settling onto the indicated chair and dropping two of her books in the process.

'Allow me,' he said gallantly, bending down to retrieve them for her. 'Chopin and Bach. What a good combination. One for the heart and one for the brain, would you not agree? I'll leave you to decide which is which.'

He smiled and revealed even, white teeth, which seemed to glow like lights against the olive tan of his skin. Penelope Strachan's head was spinning as she suffered the onset of juvenile infatuation. The man must have been a good fifteen years older than she was and he was absolutely charming.

'I have been asked to come to your room, Professor, because I was told that you wished me to play for you.' She smiled embarrassedly and felt a little stupid for having told him what he obviously already knew.

'Indeed, you did ... and I do,' he continued, smiling. His command of English was excellent, even if there was the slightest deeply buried hint of a foreign accent. She thought that was proof that this man was a foreigner – with the name of Professor Giacomo Capezzani-Batelli, he could hardly have been anything else. She giggled softly at her own silliness, as if to hide her embarrassment.

'Is that such an amusing thing to request?' he asked, still smiling.

'Not at all; I was just trying to match Chopin to the heart

and Bach to the brain. Wouldn't you agree?' she asked as her giggles turned into a smile almost as broad as his.

'Most certainly I would. But when it comes to the deepest emotions of the heart, there is nothing to beat the music of Verdi or the great Puccini. What skill they both had in being able to play with their characters' emotions right in front of your very eyes and your ears. Do you know their work at all? Very often, pianists do not have the opportunity to ... shall we say *stray* beyond the considerable limits of their own extensive repertoire.' The statement was without prejudice and was simply a revelation of what he had found to be the truth over his years of coaching singers, who were accompanied by pianists more at home with the piano repertoire than with the operatic one.

'My parents took me to see *La Traviata* at the Royal Opera House a couple of seasons ago and I have also been to Glyndebourne, to hear Mozart. I am not sure if I have ever heard a Puccini opera. My father is very fond of the sextet from *Lucia di Lammermoor*. I made a piano reduction of it for his birthday earlier this year... I didn't write it down or anything... I just play it from the score...'

'You have the score for *Lucia?*' he asked, impressed. Scores were expensive things to buy.

'Yes. I also have *Le Nozze di Figaro,*' she continued, pronouncing the name of Mozart's masterpiece in rather quixotic Italian.

'Ah ha ... *si parla Italiano, Signorina? Sono impressionato che si prova.*'

Penelope Strachan sat perfectly still, the smile still on her face. She looked as if she had been caught in the headlights of an oncoming car.

'Do you speak Italian?' repeated the professor softly, encouragingly.

'Oh ... I see,' she replied, giggling. 'Goodness me, no ... not at all, I'm afraid.'

'Then that does not matter. I will teach you as we work through the great works of the operatic repertoire. Would you like a little coffee?' he asked, suddenly changing the subject. 'I have my own Thermos flask and bring some in with me every day. I have just enough left for a small cup each.'

'Er ... yes ... thank you, Professor. That would be very nice.'

'Excellent! Then I will pour it for us in the twinkling of an eye.' He got up and crossed to the filing cabinet. Then he bent down, opened the bottom drawer, removed his flask and stood up again, closing the drawer as he did so. 'There are those who might think that such a useful storage place is full of reports, forms, music, scores and all of the other paperwork associated with working in an academy as august as this one. But there are often far more important things to find a hiding place for, like a good cup of coffee, for instance,' he laughed as he regained his chair.

For Penelope Strachan, that cup of coffee was to create an enduring memory. They continued in polite conversation, the Professor outlining her duties as accompanist for his numerous master classes and at the individual lessons of his more outstanding students.

'I play myself, of course, but I find having my concentration divided between the voice and the keyboard is not that conducive to a successful lesson. It is far better to rely on the skills of someone as competent as you.'

He smiled warmly once again and she felt herself sinking even further down into the impenetrably hard surface of the chair.

13

Julietta Camore felt herself to be very much the second fiddle of the two sopranos in COGOL. As a result, despite superficial pleasantries, she had become somewhat of an arch-rival to Renata di Senno. In fact, rivalry was not a concept of Julietta's life that was confined solely to her participation in COGOL; she maintained further rivalry with her sister. As is often usual between family members, a routine of telephone calls 'just to catch up' had evolved and over time had become almost a chore that was neither looked forward to, nor relished during the transmission of the call. It being Sunday morning, she found herself sitting at the kitchen table with a steaming cup of frothy *cappuccino* in front of her and the kitchen timer ticking silently away next to it; she had recently taken to timing and thereby limiting the weekly telephone calls with her sister.

'...but of course, *cara*, we have the villa for two weeks,' cooed Mirella down the line from distant Rome. 'It's Libero's place down on the Amalfi Coast. They're off to some festival or other in Switzerland and then they plan to do Vienna and then Paris. You know how opera-mad they are – a little like you.'

Julietta had never actually met Libero and his family although, lately, as Mirella had spent so much of her time talking about them, Julietta felt that she had. On reflection, she didn't really want to meet the Libero clan anyway. They sounded as flash and gauche as her sister had become. Listening to the weekly dose of what her beloved sister had done was just about all Julietta could cope with.

'Oh well,' continued Mirella indifferently, 'there's plenty of room; why don't you and Fabio come down for a couple of days? You're probably not doing anything, are you?'

There was more than a suggestion of mockery in her sister's voice. Ever since they had been young children, Mirella had always been the one to have the better opinion of her own worth, often to the detriment of her sister's self-confidence. This attitude seemed to have been amplified by their father, who almost always made his preference for his firstborn perfectly obvious, albeit in a not unkind way – or so it had seemed to Julietta at the time. Now, despite having charted a path through life that had seen her become a capable hand at many things, and yet never a master hand at any single one, Julietta Camore had increasingly begun to feel the weight of insecurity tighten its insidious grip on her. She glanced at the timer – four and a half minutes so far – then swallowed a mouthful of *cappuccino* before returning her concentration to her sister's tedious conversation.

'I have a concert to sing,' she replied, 'and Fabio is very busy with the business,' she continued, replacing the cup in its saucer. 'He has a new client, a company from Bologna who want him to re-invent their Internet presence, so he will be busy with that contract for the next couple of months. Then, he's had another enqui –'

'I suppose the concert is with that little opera group you belong to? Still going, is it? I must try to get up to Lucca one day and hear you all.'

Julietta flushed at the barely hidden provocation in her sister's voice. There had been a time when she had given Mirella the benefit of the doubt and had put such remarks down to her sister's clumsy way of expressing her thoughts. After many years, however, she had now made a different and less generous assessment of her relationship with her only sister. She knew perfectly well that Mirella had

99

absolutely no intention of making the trip to Lucca to hear her sing. Mirella had never put herself out for anybody or for anything, unless Mirella benefited directly from that action. She had not changed.

'Yes, but we are not just a "little opera group", as you put it. We are the Chamber Opera Group of Lucca.' Julietta spoke with some force and then, in response to the conditioning of years, immediately regretted having given her sister a possible excuse to retaliate. Mirella was far better at handling such situations, which only made Julietta feel even more insecure and in the shadows.

'And I'm sure that you are all very good,' Mirella replied in her irritating, almost dismissive way, 'and Aldo sends you his regards,' she added, almost as an afterthought. 'Did I tell you that he will be in Abu Dhabi for a week? Bank business, you know. He said that I should join him. The shopping is very good out there – gold and diamonds, that sort of thing. Aldo said that he would buy me something nice if I was there so that I could try it on and see if it suited. He's such an angel … just like your Fabio.'

There was another pause, during which Julietta took another mouthful of *cappuccino*. Six minutes twenty seconds. Then she gritted her teeth against her sister's none-too-subtle dig at the fact that her husband Fabio's income was simply not in the same league as Aldo's and banged the cup back into its saucer. Was it *that* hard to think up an excuse to avoid having to sit and listen to her sister's endless opinions of her own self-importance? It had always been 'Aldo sends you his *regards*' and never 'Aldo sends you his *love*'. Julietta liked her sister's husband and, on the occasional holiday when they had all managed to get together, they had all got along extremely well. In fact, Julietta harboured many affectionate memories of just how well she and Aldo had passed their time together. They were memories which, of necessity, she had been extremely careful to keep to herself, as they were of an intimate nature. Julietta sometimes wondered if her sister had a suspicion or two. That would be one explanation for why Mirella's passed-on greetings were always so formal. Julietta often wondered what the revelation of these secrets would do to her sister's control over Aldo; she reasoned that it would be weakened if she passed on what she really felt for her brother-in-law. She had always seen Mirella as a person who insisted on being in control of the situation and of the people around her.

'I had better go now,' said Julietta, a little lamely. 'I have some practising to do; I am working on my favourite aria "*O don fatale*" from Verdi's *Don Ca...*'

'Aldo is taking me out to dinner tonight ... that new restaurant in *Piazza Cavour*,' Mirella cut in abruptly. 'It's *very* exclusive and *very* expensive. Their speciality is something to kill for, so I'm told. They start by lightly braising veal in...'

Julietta had stopped listening to the endless ramble of one expensive delight after another and emptied the remains of her *cappuccino*. She didn't know anything about any of the restaurants where her sister lived. It irritated her that Mirella should even think that she did. Perhaps that was not the important point; perhaps what her sister wanted her to pay attention to was the drawn-out word 'very' and the emphasized word 'expensive'.

'So I must go now. Speak to you soon,' Julietta interrupted, 'and give love ... from both of us ... to Aldo.' She knew that that was one message that would not be passed on; at least not in the form she had given it. Sometimes she really despised her sister.

'Have a good concert then, *cara...* Sing like an angel... *Ciao*,' replied Mirella emptily.

Julietta was about to hang up when she heard her sister's voice shouting through the tiny earpiece of the telephone.

She put it back to her ear. Eight minutes forty-three seconds. 'Yes, I'm still here,' she said with a sigh. *Why doesn't she just hang up?* 'Yes, what is it? I'm still here.'

'What with all our goings-on at this end, I almost forgot to tell you something important,' Mirella continued.

If you could just develop the idea that there are other people on this earth besides yourself, you might well become aware of the lives of others, thought Julietta, realising, predictably, that her sister would not allow *her* to be the one to end the conversation.

'*Cara* ... I have some exciting news for you,' continued Mirella. 'Do you remember my friend Carlotta?'

There was an expectant pause, during which it felt as if Mirella was waiting for her sister to say that she did. Julietta vaguely remembered someone called Carlotta, but she couldn't place her. Mirella's list of 'friends' would half fill the Rome telephone directory, so it was quite possible that Carlotta had been mentioned on a previous occasion.

'I think so,' answered Julietta lamely. She had become more tired than usual with this particular conversation and had started to bitterly regret not having allowed gravity to finish its work and draw the handset safely back to its cradle.

'Well, Carlotta's cousin has a son going up to university in Pisa. Very bright ... He's going to study aeronautical engineering ... or was it physics?'

Julietta couldn't have cared less if he were to study the menu outside his local *pizzeria*. 'I'm very pleased for him, but I really must go now. I have practising to do.'

'But, *cara*, you don't understand. He has a voice ... such a beautiful voice. In fact, there was some debate in his family as to whether he should study music or one of the sciences. Anyway, I happened to mention your little singing group to him and his mother and she was very keen for him to join

102

you. Lucca isn't *that* far from Pisa is it?'

Julietta immediately sensed Mirella's interfering hand. She had refrained from voicing her opinion and had been about to tell her sister that the journey was only twenty minutes, but she got no further than an intake of breath.

'So I've given him your telephone number and he said that he'll be phoning you, once he's settled in at the university. So, what do you think of that?'

Julietta had not thought much of it at all. She was used to her sister's grandiose schemes and the way she thought that everything she organized would be met by all and sundry with unbridled gratitude. She resisted any inclination to answer. Nine minutes and five seconds.

'I had better go now, *cara*, I have an "eleven o'clock" at the health spa with Ferruccio. Did I tell you about my personal trainer? He's quite something.'

That was the first that Julietta had heard of Ferruccio, but she seized the opportunity to escape from the irritation of the telephone call. 'Of course you did,' she lied, cutting across her sister, 'and I hope you have a good work out, but now I really must go.' She had no idea what it was that prompted her next question. 'What is this singing angel's name?'

'Er ... Ruggiero,' Mirella replied, momentarily knocked off course by the sudden interruption to her train of thought. She seemed to hesitate, presumably as the athletic shape of Ferruccio dissolved in her mind's eye. 'Ruggiero Mondini... He said that he'll call you.'

'Fine, now I must go. Enjoy your gym. *Ciao, ciao,*' Julietta repeated as the receiver descended to the welcoming grasp of its cradle. She had only just made her self-imposed limit of no more than ten minutes for a single call with her sister and sat looking at the telephone. On the table in front of her the empty *cappuccino* cup that had long since said farewell to the last lingering wisps of steam, stood as a record of the time spent speaking to her sister. She reached out and switched off the kitchen timer, got up and carried the cold cup over to the dishwasher. She would immerse herself in her scores and put in a good hour of concentrated practice. As far as she was concerned, at least *her* existence had a purpose in it, even if, in her opinion, that of her beloved sister did not.

Walking into her music room, she picked up her diary from the top of the piano, opened it to one of the pages reserved for making notes and wrote down the name of Ruggiero Mondini. She would tell the Contessa about this young man with the outstanding voice, but only if the singing angel ever actually telephoned her from Pisa.

14

The average Monday morning was not generally a busy one for Riccardo Fossi. Shortly before ten he had descended the stairs to his small, but tastefully decorated office. He strode through the modest outer office, acknowledging the greetings of his small team of employees, but saving his cheeriest greeting for *Signora* Litelli. She was busy at her desk, typing her way through the correspondence he had left the previous Friday. She was a mature woman, well past the age of presenting any danger of physical attraction to a passion as potentially volatile as Riccardo's. Besides which, his intentions were firmly fixed on Renata di Senno and had been for some considerable time. *Signora* Litelli's attraction for the eminent Luccan accountant was the fact that she saw little and said even less. That was important for a man like Fossi.

It had been the same for his father, who had first employed the young slip of a girl many years before – except that then there had been the small matter of a sexual spark, which his mother had moved swiftly to extinguish. The young *Signorina* Litelli had survived the resulting hostile scrutiny from Riccardo's mother and had matured into the elderly woman she was today. In fact, so secure had her tenure behind the desk in the inner office become over the years, that to dispense with her services had long ago become unthinkable. That had not been the case in the past.

'Get rid of that seducing witch!' Riccardo's mother had

wheezed at him, through pain-racked eyes heavy with the languid ambrosia of diamorphine, as he sat at her bedside in the hospital. 'Your father never listened to me ... God rest his soul.' There had been a rattling pause. 'Get rid of her before she brings down ruin on your head.'

'I cannot, *Mamma*,' he had whispered softly in reply. 'You know that. She has given us many years of loyal service and what reason would I have to do such a thing?' His mother had made a spluttering sound of vehement disagreement as he wiped the spittle from her mouth. 'Besides which, she has seen things and knows of things ... many things over the years.'

And that was why the now elderly *Signora* Litelli was such a valued inhabitant of Riccardo Fossi's world. She knew a lot about it and to keep her within it, ensuring that such information would remain unspoken, was his only sensible option.

'*Buongiorno, signore*,' she said maternally as he walked up to her desk. She smiled at him, but did not take her eyes off the screen in front of her.

'*Signora*, you are well?' asked Riccardo. It was the same question he asked every morning.

'Thank you, I am. May the Blessed Virgin be praised.' That was the standard reply given each morning as well. Riccardo had lost all but the shallowest of connections to the Church years ago and now any active participation in what he regarded as the nonsensical mumbo-jumbo of the whole thing was purely as circumstances dictated, for the maintenance of his position in society. It amused him that what he had lost over the years seemed to have been added to this woman's portion of belief and faith. He also thought it a contradiction in terms that she could be so devoutly religious when she knew so much about things that were better not to know. Perhaps that was why she was so devoted; she was seeking absolution in the next life.

'Good ... good. Then let us proceed with the day, shall we?' he said, concluding the morning ritual of their greeting.

Signora Litelli clicked the 'print' icon on her screen and a printer to the side of her desk twitched into life.

'No mail yet... No faxes either,' she said very matter-of-factly, as she picked up her notepad and flipped back to the previous page, 'but you have two telephone messages,' she said. 'The Contessa says that you are not to forget to ask your clients if any of them have a screen they would be willing to lend the opera group for the performance on Friday.' She took her pencil and drew a tick through the message, writing the date and time at the bottom of it. She was extremely methodical.

'The Contessa and her screen,' Riccardo chuckled as he lit a cigarette.

'Cannot *Signor* Marinetti provide one ... from the *Casa dei Gioielli*?' she asked, looking up at him for the first time. Her face was lined, but the eyes burned with a steely determination.

'I think that the Contessa has already spoken to *Signor* Marinetti,' he replied.

Signora Litelli knew all the members of COGOL. In fact, she seemed to know just about everything about everybody in Lucca.

'You said that there were two messages?' he asked encouragingly.

'I did,' she replied, looking back at the pad, 'and there are. The second one was from *Signor* di Leone; he requests that you meet him this morning at eleven to discuss the matter he briefly mentioned to you last week over the telephone – last Thursday at...' she flipped back another page, '...at four thirty-seven.'

'Ah, yes ... I remember,' said Fossi. That had been before

the rehearsal and the resulting night of passion with Renata di Senno at the *Villa Legge*. *Ah*, he thought, inhaling the warm cigarette smoke, *but that memory has nothing to do with you, Signora Litelli.*

She continued to look at him, as if awaiting her instructions.

'You say he will be here at eleven?' he asked.

'No, *Signor* Fossi. You are to *meet* him at eleven. He will wait for you at *del Mostro's* – the café on the *Piazza Napoleone.*' She ticked the message, made the usual notation next to it, turned to a blank page and put the pad back on the desk.

'*Del Mostro's?*' he asked in irritation. 'Their *espresso* is awful. Why does he want to meet there, for God's sake?'

Signora Litelli did not approve of blasphemy. She looked up at him over the top of her glasses, reprovingly. 'I would suspect that *Signor* di Leone has little interest in their *espresso* and is possibly more concerned with a discreet meeting venue, disguised by the presence of several tourists staring at the statue of the *Francese* and at all the trees. The trees are not as green as they should be. The summer has not been kind.'

The *Piazza Napoleone* contained a statue of Napoleon's sister, Elisa Baciocchi, the *Francese*, who had ruled Lucca under the protection of her brother for a few years in the tumult of the early nineteenth century.

'You could possibly be quite correct, *Signora*,' responded Fossi as he walked on into his spacious office, with its view out across *Via del Giardino Botanico* to the gardens beyond.

His father had bought the villa for next to nothing shortly after the Nazis had left, at a time when the country was convulsed by civil war and everything was in a state of almost total chaos. He had turned the ground floor into his offices and had moved his wife and son into the other accommodation offered on the remaining floors. Tucked away in the south-eastern corner of the city, almost on top of the massive defensive walls, Riccardo had enjoyed a blissfully happy childhood, being doted upon and basically spoilt rotten. He had shown an early aptitude for singing and music in general and had sung in the cathedral choir. He had even asked if it would be possible, when he was old enough, to attend the *istituto* in Lucca. That question had not been favourable received, as it had always been understood that he would follow his father into the accountancy business and perpetuate the good name of Fossi, which his father had worked so hard to establish.

'Music does not make you rich,' his father had told him, 'not unless you are a Puccini, a Verdi, a di Stefano or a Gobbi. You have a God-given voice, and God has smiled on you, Riccardo, but not to the same extent as He did with these others. You are none of these people, I am sad to say, so you had best take what fortune has placed on your plate and learn to be an accountant, just like your *papà*, and follow in his footsteps. That has always been our Italian way.'

And so it had come about, but with one single exception. Riccardo was far more of a lad-about-town than his father could ever have hoped to be. His more outgoing nature, the absolute opposite to the widely held perception that accountants were boring men in grey suits, had allowed Riccardo to make certain contacts over the years – contacts that were very lucrative and also potentially rather dangerous.

'It is nearly ten thirty-five,' called a voice from the outer office. '*Signor* di Leone probably would not like to be kept waiting, especially if the *espresso* is not very good.'

'Yes, thank you, *Signora* Litelli,' he replied. 'I am on my way.'

Riccardo strolled the short distance to the awful *del Mostro's* in the balmy warmth of mid-morning, humming his way through '*E lucevan le stelle*' – the famous tenor aria from Puccini's *Tosca*. As he did so he smiled to himself at the thought that his stars were, indeed, brightly shining. This aria was his party piece and was guaranteed to bring the house down at the concert on Friday.

'...so, that is why I have asked to meet you,' said Daniele di Leone as he picked up his cup of *espresso* and raised it to his lips.

Riccardo looked on in near disbelief; he couldn't believe that this man was actually going to drink such foul liquid. He had opted for a sparkling water – at least that came in a sealed bottle, which meant that there was nothing *del Mostro's* could do to adulterate it, which, in his opinion, was exactly what they did to their coffee.

'Although I am, of course, flattered, I do not quite see why you have come to me specifically. There must be any number of highly respectable accountants to whom you could turn for their services.'

'As I briefly explained to you, *Signor* Fossi, my family have always had extensive involvement in olives and their oil. We have recently purchased extensive groves in Umbria, around Lake Trasimeno. We also have a sweeter interest and produce candied fruits in our factory in Genoa. These are just a few of our business involvements, you understand.'

Riccardo was intrigued by the mention of these being just the tip of this man's empire.

'Obviously, the greater our business activities become, the more will be lost to ... shall we say, lost to the tithes modern business is expected to pay over as a measure – a punishment almost – for their hard work and success,' di Leone continued. 'I have contacted you because of Don Amico Forno's personal recommendation.'

Riccardo Fossi took a long drink of his mineral water and then he reached for a cigarette.

'You will excuse me asking, but di Leone is a southern name, is it not … from Sicily?'

'Yes, from the Trapani region at the western end of the island. That is where the best olives are grown. My family have farmed there since before the time of the Kingdom of Naples. We are well placed and have many contacts … many *important* contacts.'

In the silence that followed, the two men sat at the little round table casually glancing out in to the *Piazza Napoleone* and at the throng of tourists who meandered through it like a steadily flowing stream.

'I am told that you are acquainted with certain ways that payments to the State could be, shall we say, *reduced*,' said di Leone softly, so that his voice barely carried to the other side of the table. 'It is appreciated that these ways can be expensive due to the certain level of risk involved, although they would not be as expensive as the taxes themselves.'

Riccardo Fossi said nothing in reply, but the smile that now covered his face confirmed that what the other man had just said was, indeed, a distinct possibility.

Di Leone relaxed and seemed to settle more comfortably into his chair. 'Don Amico Forno's confidence has obviously not been misplaced,' di Leone whispered as he emptied his *espresso*. 'I am very pleased to have made your acquaintance, *Signor* Fossi. Are you certain I cannot tempt you to have an *espresso*?'

15

What Fossi had no way of knowing was that significant events were unfolding not far from *Café del Mostro*. Although they would not involve him directly, these events were connected to the Contessa's forthcoming concert – albeit in a somewhat tenuous way. In the best operatic tradition, jealousy and intense rivalry had reared their heads in the form of a certain Alonzo Adriani, renowned dealer in antiques and mortal rival of Gregorio Marinetti. He had stood at the window of *Casa dei Gioielli* the previous Thursday and peered open-mouthed through his reflection at what looked very much like a Venetian screen. Not just any Venetian screen, but *the* Venetian screen – the one belonging to the von Hohenwald family and the one which had not been seen since the collapse of the Third Reich at the end of 1945.

Questore Bramanti, the senior officer in charge of the *Questura* – the outpost of the *Polizia*, or civil police, not far from the statue in the *Piazza Napoleone* – had enjoyed yet another bad weekend of over-indulgence and was now paying the price. His stomach felt like a tumble dryer with its control set to maximum, as his ever-growing ulcer fought valiantly to stave off the effects of the excess of garlic, oil and assorted fats his weekend of culinary abandonment had thrown at it.

'What do you make of this?' he barked at his chief inspector, flinging a small sheet of paper across the desk at him, the discomfort of his gut clearly etched on his face.

Michele Conti caught it and looked at it.

'Obviously written with the wrong hand to try and disguise the handwriting... Good quality paper, which could be significant... Written with a fountain pen, which might also be significant... Unsigned, which could indicate a vendetta or someone trying to just waste police time ... and what is the von Hohenwald screen, anyway?' Conti looked up from the paper in his hand. 'Is that a new cinema complex?'

Questore Bramanti groaned, but not in reaction to anything his junior had just said. His ulcer was now in open revolt.

'The *questore* made a comment?' asked Conti, trying not to smirk.

They had all become used to their commander's regular culinary excesses, the results of which were always best observed on a Monday morning. *Signora* Bramanti, not to mention the *questore's* mother, saw it as her duty to feed him with the best traditional Tuscan cooking possible; neither of them had made the slightest attempt to understand what effect their well-meant culinary efforts were having on his stomach and its unhappy ulcer. Bramanti winced and then glared at Conti.

'Go and see what it's about,' Bramanti sighed. 'Pascoli has already looked it up on the computer. He'll fill you in.'

The *questore* was near retirement and wasn't quite a full member of the new technological age; computers were something of a closed book to him.

'Pascoli! Get in here!' he shouted.

The door opened and Sergeant Pascoli entered.

'Tell him what you found out about this screen,' he barked, before relaxing back into his well-padded chair. He had effectively washed his hands of the matter for the next few minutes. Instead of having to tell his junior what to do next, he could now concentrate on the misery he felt in his stomach.

'This von Hohenwald screen was stolen from the family of the same name, who were bankers and representatives of the Austrians in Venice since way back before the time of Napoleon.' It was in a very matter-of-fact way that Sergeant Pascoli made his feelings known about the wrongs done to Italy during its historic past. 'They had no right to be there and who knows, they had probably stolen the thing from its rightful owners in the first place.'

'And how do we know all of this, on the strength of this largely uninformative little note?' asked Conti, holding it up.

'From that we do not know anything,' replied the sergeant, making it obvious from his expression that he was about to launch into a detailed explanation of how he knew what he was about to reveal. 'I have a friend in Geneva.'

Conti raised his eyebrows. It was a widely held belief that the sergeant was so wrapped up in his work that he didn't have time for any friends – or partners, for that matter.

'In Geneva,' he repeated determinedly, 'who works through the Council for Looted Art in Europe. The council is referred to as CLAE and they are affiliated with similar bodies throughout the world. So you have HARP, which is the Holocaust Art Restitution Project in the United States and also the IFAR, which is the International Foundation for Art Research in New York. Then there is –'

'Just get on with it, Pascoli!' snapped Bramanti. 'We all know that you are very thorough and have all the time in the world to play at finding things on your computer at the department's expense!'

For a moment, Sergeant Pascoli stood stock-still glaring at his superior, his mouth still opened at the point in his unfinished sentence where he had been abruptly cut off. It occurred to Inspector Conti that, in the unfortunate event of the *questore's* ulcer finally getting the better of him, there was a certain sergeant who would definitely not be giving a donation to the resulting collection.

'The von Hohenwald family is Jewish. They lost their entire art collection when the Nazis took over in Vienna. This screen is listed in the databases of all the organisations I have already mentioned and it has not been seen since the middle of 1940,' Pascoli concluded with a look of superior triumph on his face.

'And now we have an anonymous, even childish, note telling us that it is here in Lucca?' continued Conti, his disbelief sounding in his voice. 'And why would a stolen, highly valuable art treasure of international significance end up in a little shop in Lucca?'

Sergeant Pascoli was about to say that he had absolutely no idea when he was cut off for the second time in as many minutes.

'How should I know?' barked a very irritated Bramanti from behind his desk. 'I suppose that just to be certain, you had better go and see if there is any truth in this allegation. And don't take all day. We have other pressing matters to continue with.'

'Have any of these agencies of Pascoli's been informed that we might have one of their stolen artworks here in Lucca?' asked Conti.

The *questore*, who was now in considerable discomfort and couldn't have cared less either way, looked enquiringly at Pascoli.

'My friend in Geneva,' Pascoli turned to look at both of his colleagues in turn, 'advised me to inform you that we should make sure of the facts of the allegation before we say anything to anyone. Stolen artworks are a highly sensitive issue and are very emotionally charged. If we say anything first and then, on investigation, the allegation turns out to be a blind lead or hoax, we will not only upset a great many people, but we will also look incredibly stupid.'

The sergeant glowed with a sense of a job well done and a message successfully delivered. The *questore* looked very uncomfortable, a victim of his internal struggle. Inspector Conti felt as if he was about to embark on a wild goose chase.

Some twenty minutes later, Michele Conti stood in *Casa dei Gioielli*. Gregorio Marinetti was being his usual charming self, shrouded in the omnipresent cloud of expensive cologne, as he concluded a transaction with a Swiss couple – regular customers of his – for a miniature chest delicately inlaid with mother of pearl.

'Neapolitan, late seventeenth century and in excellent condition,' he gushed, 'and, if I might be permitted to say, a very wise investment. My able assistant, Nicola, will have the item securely packaged and I will have it delivered directly to you in Lausanne, as per usual.' He nodded to his assistant, who set about preparing the materials necessary to package the chest securely. 'How nice to have seen you again,' he beamed as he held open the door and the couple left the shop. He waved them away down *Via Fillungo* and smiled broadly to himself at the thought that he really did have an international clientele for his business. It was just a pity that there weren't a few more of them, particularly during these hard economic times. '*Buongiorno,*' he half sang as he turned back into the shop and approached what he thought was his next customer. 'Can I help the *Signore* in any way?'

'*Buongiorno,* perhaps you can. Michele Conti … *Polizia,*' replied the policeman.

Although the smile on Gregorio Marinetti's face never faltered for an instant, it suddenly developed the ice-cold attributes of the marble bust of the Emperor Septimus

Severus, which stood on a column in the centre of the window.

'*Polizia?*' he repeated, trying to keep his voice natural and only just managing to avoid an embarrassing swoop up into the falsetto register. 'How can I assist the *Polizia?*' he continued, but the underlying tone was one of immediately suppressed panic.

'*Signor* Marinetti, we were wondering if you could tell us anything about an item – a very valuable item – known as the von Hohenwald screen, from Venice originally.'

Conti was watching Marinetti intently as he spoke, ready to register any flick or twitch of reaction. Gregorio was giving the performance of his life – quite literally. He gave nothing away.

'The von Hohenwald screen... The *Signore* knows about the von Hohenwald screen? Ah yes...' he said, turning away from the policeman to break any remaining eye contact. This action also masked the beads of perspiration which had suddenly appeared on the antique dealer's brow. 'Let us go into the office,' he continued, walking ahead of Conti and past where Nicola was busy with the bubble wrap and cardboard. Such matters were best discussed discreetly. His brain was almost as active as *Questore* Bramanti's stomach as he fought hard to control the sudden panic that this policeman had so unexpectedly caused him. 'How can anyone know?' He blurted out suddenly, giving voice to his thoughts.

'Know what?' asked Conti, alert.

Gregorio Marinetti had realized his unintentional slip even before he had finished making it. He desperately tried to recover. 'Er, know about the screen, *Signore*. It is of great value and importance to the artistic heritage of our country and to Venice in particular,' he continued rambling, 'but it has not been seen since the Nazi collapse. The family lost many of their other art treasures to the Nazis as well, all of

which have long since disappeared. They were Jewish...'
Marinetti shrugged in that uniquely Italian way.

'And do you think that such an important treasure might,
shall we say, "turn-up" here in Lucca?' asked Conti, waving
his arm around the expanse of the shop.

'Good Lord, no!' replied Marinetti, attempting a laugh.
The first word started in the falsetto register and he had to
consciously bring his voice back to its normal level by the
end of the third one. He coughed, discreetly. The panic
continued to rise within him. Were his answers convincing
this policeman? It was hard to tell. In any case, who could
possibly have seen the screen in his shop? It had been there
for less than an hour, in the dead quiet of the mid-
afternoon, before he had fetched the van and spirited it
away to its hiding place. 'Such an event would be the talk of
the antiques world. Lucca would be the unfortunate centre
of attention, I can assure you of that,' he continued.

'So you have not seen this item?' asked Conti. He
preferred a direct approach to his enquiries.

'Me?' replied Marinetti, his voice now firmly under
control. 'But where would I see this precious object? There
is a black and white photograph of it on the Internet... Very
old, from before the war ... but that is the only image I have
seen.' He smiled at the policeman, wondering if he had
given too much away. 'I fear that nobody will see it ever
again, until the police and other agencies have better
fortune in their attempts to locate it,' he continued, his
confidence growing as the panic receded. 'It has been missing for nearly sixty years now, but the police might meet
with ultimate success and trace it... Who is to say?' he
concluded raising his eyebrows.

Michele Conti wasn't sure, but had the feeling that this
man had just delivered a non-too-subtle dig at the police.
'That is always possible,' he replied as he turned to face the
window and the street. 'You are remarkably well informed

about this specific object, *Signor* Marinetti, when I consider the coincidence of my walking in out of the blue and asking you about it, and you being such a veritable mine of information about that same object...' The inspector paused to allow what he had just said to sink in. 'Especially when I am told by Sergeant Pascoli that there are perhaps in excess of 150,000 stolen artworks still to be found and returned to their legal owners; the von Hohenwald screen is but one of very many.' The inspector did not turn around, but addressed Marinetti over his shoulder. For his part, Marinetti continued without a pause.

'It is, indeed, a coincidence that I should recently have read about that very same treasure, but that is part of my job ... to be *au courant* with what is going on in the world of antiques. I am very highly thought of in my profession,' he replied immodestly. He laughed with considerably more success than before, but his feet were swimming in his shoes. The smile on his face was also, possibly, a little too jovial to be convincing. Conti observed none of this.

'I am impressed that you find the time in your busy career to consult the databases of HARP or IFAR or even our very own CLAE.'

'Oh yes ... indeed ... that is where I have seen the photograph I spoke of, but I cannot remember which website specifically,' muttered Marinetti, truthfully. He had searched the Internet for details of the screen when he had first heard of the collector who was interested in acquiring it. It had been quite by accident that he had discovered a less than reputable agent to supply him with it – no questions asked. Risky as it was, the transaction was well worth the gamble as it would resolve his financial nightmare once and for all. 'What on earth makes you think that such a priceless, looted object might turn up in an establishment as humble as mine?' he asked with exaggerated surprise. This policeman and his questions had become somewhat annoying.

There was a momentary pause before Conti replied. 'We have received a note to that effect.'

'Saying that the object is *here* ... in Lucca?'

'Not only that, *Signor* Marinetti, but the note also claims that the object is here in this very shop,' replied the inspector without turning around.

That unexpected revelation caused Nicola Dolci, who had been listening to the conversation, to look up and pause in her task of packing the Neapolitan chest.

'But that is ridiculous,' exclaimed Marinetti, careful to keep himself calm.

'Be that as it may, we are obliged to investigate. That is the nature of our profession,' replied Conti. 'What of your staff? Could they possibly know something about the whereabouts of this object, something that is unknown to you?'

Gregorio Marinetti had reached the stage where he did not know whether to throw himself on the dubious mercy of the authorities or pick up a heavy black marble obelisk and bring it down smartly over the inspector's head.

Conti spared him having to make such a decision by suddenly turning to face him.

'I do have an assistant – Nicola Dolci,' said Marinetti. 'As you can see, she is presently busy packing the small chest I have just sold. Please ... feel free to question her. Nicola! A moment of your time if you please,' called Marinetti.

He was certain that she would know nothing. He had given her the afternoon off the day the screen had been delivered. He had made sure of that – the fewer people who knew about the screen, the better.

'I doubt if she will be able to help us at all,' he whispered, smiling, as Nicola Dolci appeared at the office door.

That, indeed, proved to be the case.

'Hmm...' mumbled the inspector in a non-committal manner, once the two of them were alone again in the little office. 'Do you have any storage space?' he asked, emerging once again into the display area of the shop. He cast his eyes around the crowded contents as he spoke. 'Do you have any other items ... safely in store, perhaps ... which are not on show?'

Through a well-hidden superhuman effort, Marinetti appeared to be calm and totally unflustered, despite the wet feet, which had now been joined by wet armpits.

'I do,' replied Gregorio, a little over-eagerly. 'I have a small storeroom. Over here... Please take a look, if you wish.'

The inspector crossed to the door of the storeroom and opened it, but he knew he would find nothing. In Conti's opinion, this man was far too calm to be hiding anything. Possibly, he was a little nervous, but the appearance of an inspector of the *Polizia* often had that effect on people. He closed the door and turned back into the shop again.

'Do you have any enemies, *Signor* Marinetti?' he asked abruptly. 'Do you know of anyone who might be jealous of your standing in the antiques world, or even of your position here in *Via Fillungo*? Is there someone who might bear you a grudge for, well ... for anything?'

'My dear Inspector, despite any outward appearance of elegance or placidity, the antiques business is rather cut-throat. There are fewer quality articles than there are dealers who wish to deal in them. That adds a degree of danger to any transaction. But to even suggest that this...' He paused for a moment, appearing to search for his next word, but actually marvelling at where the strength for the counter attack to the inspector's questioning had come from... 'Shall we say business rivalry might become violent or sink to the level of a *vendetta* is more than just a little melodramatic. We might deal with things from a past age, but we do not conduct ourselves as if we are *in* that past age.'

The inspector studied Marinetti's face for some moments, but it gave nothing away.

'If, by some quirk of fate, such an item were to come within your reach, *Signor* Mar –'

'Then it would be my duty as an upstanding citizen and thoroughly respectable antiques dealer of many years outstanding reputation to immediately report such knowledge to you, Inspector,' cut in Marinetti. On his face was an expression of total sincerity and earnestness, which would not have gone amiss on the face of any leading politician.

'As, indeed, you should,' concluded Conti, who found himself being considerably impressed by the earnestness of this man. He possibly had an over-inflated opinion of his own worth, but he also seemed to be quite genuine. 'As a well-respected citizen of Lucca and a leader in your profession, we would expect nothing less.'

The two men stood and faced each other, looking firmly into each other's eyes. Then the inspector nodded, shook the antiques dealer by the hand and turned to leave the shop. By doing so, he did not see Marinetti wipe his brow quickly. Another second locked into the inspector's gaze and Gregorio's nerve would have given way. This irritating policeman would then have known the truth. Marinetti shut his eyes tightly, trying to blot out any further thought of the consequences of such a slip.

Inspector Michele Conti was almost at the door when he suddenly turned around to once again face the antiques dealer. Marinetti's heart suddenly plummeted and splashed around in his wet shoes. Despite this, he managed a beaming smile and raised his eyebrows enquiringly in preparation for the next onslaught of questioning.

'You sing in the Chamber Opera Group of Lucca, don't you?' asked the inspector.

'Well, yes... Indeed I do,' replied Gregorio, beaming.

'I have tickets for your concert this Friday evening. What can we look forward to hearing?'

On his way back to the *Questura,* Michele Conti made a detour into the *Café Alma Arte.* He would take some time out and enjoy the pastry delights and delicious coffee the place was famous for.

16

Maria Santini sat at the table on her balcony. From her vantage point on the top floor of the building, a panoramic view of the city of Lucca spread out before her. On the chair to her right was a small pile of vocal scores, from the pages of which protruded bright pink slips of paper indicating the arias and ensembles she would be performing at Friday's concert. On the table in front of her stood a large cup of *cappuccino* and a box of *Carezze*, 'Caresses' – a distinctive Italian chocolate speciality, each of which was crowned by a whole Brazil nut. They were Maria's favourite. Not that she would admit it to anyone, but they, like most kinds of better quality chocolate, were her principal addiction – chocolate and singing. Chocolate, singing and then caffeine; that was probably the most accurate ranking.

She had recently emerged from her morning shower and was still clad in her silken dressing gown. It was a kimono-like garment that she had bought many years before when, as a young singer, she had been offered the role of the maid Suzuki in *Madama Butterfly* at La Fenice in Venice. In those days, when she had first worn the dressing gown, the herons, intertwined with the buds of spring blossom, curved their long necks in graceful arabesques to almost touch their beaks in discreet conversation under her breasts. Time and chocolate had not been kind to her and due to the gradual and seemingly unstoppable expansion of her proportions, the two herons, now faded through a great many washings, had not spoken to each other in years.

124

Suzuki was also supposed to have been the beginning of a brilliant operatic career. Everyone had voiced their opinion that she was destined for great things – La Scala, San Carlo, Paris, Covent Garden...

'Hmm...' she sighed as she popped yet another *Carezze* into her mouth. The screwed-up silver wrapper landed in the saucer where it fought for a tiny part of the ever-decreasing space with all of the others that had preceded it. Maria no longer bothered to count them. What else did she have in her life these days, apart from chocolate, singing and caffeine?

Life has to have something in it, to make it worth living, she thought as she rinsed the cloyed chocolate off her teeth with a mouthful of frothy *cappuccino.* Then she leant across to the pile of music and picked up the first score. It was Verdi's *Il Trovatore,* 'The Troubadour'. Balancing her spectacles on her ample cheeks, she turned to Act II and the gypsy camp. '*Stride la vampa,*' she sang to herself in what was left of her deep mezzo-soprano, but not sufficiently loudly so as to carry over the handrail of the balcony. It was a technique she had perfected for herself – an exercise in placing her voice correctly and focussing it in a confined space without using too much volume. Maria claimed it worked wonders for her vocal production, but there were very few who agreed with her. On the contrary, there were many who muttered that this was just the outward manifestation of a totally neurotic has-been. '*Stride la vampa*' – 'The flames are roaring,' she continued as she ran through Azucena's aria, stopping only once to disturb the pile of crumpled wrappers by removing the cup for another mouthful of *cappuccino.* She had not quite made up her mind whether she would sing that old chestnut or opt for '*Mon coeur s'ouvre à ta voix*', Dalila's seductive aria from *Samson et Dalila.* With three days to go before the concert she was still undecided, not that that was anything to be concerned about. The Contessa was always very good about things like that. She always chose the ensemble pieces, but let her angels decide for themselves which arias they would perform at her concerts. Maria Santini finished Verdi's aria and took another *Carezze* out of the box. She always bought the large size, but even that never seemed to last long. There were so many gaps amongst the remnants of the assembled *Carezze* that she could already see patches of white on the bottom of the box glaring up at her. She could hardly believe what she saw. The box had only been opened the previous evening.

'Hrumph!' she snorted, as if to put the box in its place. *And what business is it of yours? I shall not be made to feel guilty,* she determined. That was the argument she usually put forward for her addiction. She took another chocolate to emphasize her point; they were, after all, only bite-sized. She aimed the crumpled wrapper at all the others, but it hit the side of the almost empty cup, which now stood at a crazy angle on the saucer, balancing on the sea of crumpled silver. Somewhere in the distance, the sound of a siren wafted up on the early morning heat. At the same time, a telephone suddenly started to ring somewhere in the build-ing. That was more than hers usually did. These days it was really only the Contessa who phoned her in connection with some aspect of a concert. On the very rare occasions when it was not the Contessa, she was so far down the track towards becoming a recluse that she found it difficult to have a meaningful conversation with anyone. In fact, Maria had even contemplated having the telephone removed – why should she keep it when hardly anyone called her? But then she had thought twice and decided against it; she had to keep her contact with COGOL open at all times. Take that away – she shook her head slightly. Take COGOL away and there was *nothing*.

In addition to her addictions, Maria was also a slave to

her nerves; no longer because of her singing, but now for life in general. Her nerves had never been the same since that night of the oranges in the Teatro di San Bonifacio in Barga. In fact, her *life* had never been the same since then, either.

The sun was beginning to creep slowly across the balcony floor, as the morning steadily progressed. Maria reached for a second score – a book of mezzo-soprano operatic arias. Then she took one more of her chocolate delights out of the box before, with an almost superhuman effort, she rammed the lid back on the pitifully few *Carezze* refugees left.

That will be a reward, she reasoned, placing the one chocolate on the table beside her saucer, *I had best save a few for later*.

She turned in her chair, slid the box across the floor into the cool interior of her apartment, and then turned back to her operatic arias score and repeated her previous exercise, this time with Dalila's aria.

'That's a good one,' she said to herself as she finished, 'and, I think, worthy of a reward.'

The *Carezze* wrapper joined all the others on the table. She had just bitten into its contents when she suddenly became aware of an irritation between two of her teeth.

'Oh no!' she muttered through the remains of the chocolate in her mouth. 'Please! Not the filling again. Not three days before the concert!'

She had had similar experiences before, when her chocolate enjoyment had been temporarily interrupted by the discovery of a tiny portion of hard nut shell that had managed to escape the refinement of the manufacturing process and lodge itself, uncomfortably, as an unwelcome guest in her mouth. It was an extremely rare occurrence and it could happen to anyone, but Maria was distressed that it had happened to her; she had to be so careful of such things upsetting her fillings. She had accumulated four – not bad for a person of her age and palate, particularly with her penchant for chocolate. Over the years she had also become over-concerned with the notion that each addition to the natural topography of her mouth might affect the quality of her voice. The rest of COGOL, worn down by her unfounded anxiety on these occasions, had agreed that the only thing to have been affected by the introduction of the amalgam was Maria Santini's already overworked nerves.

Despite her ample proportions, Maria Santini had extremely delicate, almost tiny hands, the fingernails of which were always beautifully manicured and maintained. They bore deep-red varnish, which she would replace with a colour more suited to the gown she would wear for the concert. However, at that moment, any consideration of her concert outfit was the last thing on her mind, as first her tongue and then her index finger located the source of the irritation between two teeth in her upper jaw. She had broken out in a mild sweat – what if that blasted filling was playing up again? She wouldn't be able to do anything about it until after Friday, at the earliest. And then what if she had to wait for an appointment at the dentist? She felt herself subsiding into a spiral of panic. With practiced movements, she deftly manipulated her finger and withdrew it from her mouth. With great relief she stared at the tiny piece of nut shell, which was safely lodged under her red talon.

'Thank heavens for that!' she said out loud, running her tongue over the filling. 'Safe and sound,' she muttered, extending her other hand to take another *Carezze*. Remembering that the box was now out of reach, Maria sighed heavily and picked up the large *cappuccino* cup instead. The little cairn of silver wrappers fell off the saucer as she did so. The cup was empty.

'Oh, for goodness' sake,' she said, ramming the cup back down onto the saucer, in the process flattening those wrappers that had not managed to escape. 'Dalila it will be!' she announced suddenly in a fit of pique, as she closed the score and threw it, together with *Il Trovatore*, back onto the chair next to her.

She seemed to have momentarily forgotten that Dalila's aria – that famous example of operatic seduction – usually had a somewhat maudlin effect on her, which could linger on for days after a concert. The depression would worsen with her eventual realisation that, unlike Dalila, she had never managed to entrap or, for that matter, even seduce anyone. This stark fact, which usually overrode the beauty of the vocal line, would depress her for days. That was the time when she would turn once again to her addictions to find solace. In extreme occurrences of this phenomenon, she would also relive that dreadful night with the oranges and, when that happened, the others at COGOL had learned to leave her well alone. Then, it would be only the Contessa – the caring, concerned Contessa – who would know how to get through to her and calm her down quite literally with tea and sympathy.

None of these thoughts entered her mind as she flicked the offending particle of nut shell over the balcony and slowly relaxed into the relief of knowing her filling was safe.

'Let us see what we have in the "New Releases" section for this month,' she said, suddenly feeling quite cheery, as she once again leant over to the chair, this time pulling out the current copy of *The Gramophone* magazine from under the scores. This was another of Maria Santini's little vices. Her financial independence – oddly as a result of the sudden loss of her career – allowed her many luxuries in addition to her comfortable apartment. A subscription to this magazine, which was the ultimate guide to what was brand new from the recording studios of the world of classical music, was just one of them. 'Here we are…' she continued. '"New Releases".'

She scanned through the introductory reports on what was new and forthcoming, before turning the page to the alphabetical listings. She read through the different categories until she turned the page to the section headed 'Opera'. As she did so, she flinched at the reappearance of her nerves. In front of her – taunting, almost mocking – was the review of a new recording of Bizet's *Carmen* – the opera with those blasted oranges! As she read further, she felt her head tighten, as familiar names revealed themselves in many of the roles: names which were of her generation – names which belonged to former colleagues who had gone on to fulfil their earlier promise, and from whom she had heard almost nothing since the flood of sympathy cards and notes of commiseration, years before. What depressed her most was the total absence of her own name from the cast list.

She removed her spectacles and threw them onto the table. The lenses glistened as they reflected the increasing brightness of the morning light. She suddenly stood up, the chair legs scraping loudly across the marble floor of the balcony. The pool of calm, into which she had managed to submerge herself, had dried up like the Etosha Pan in the heat of mid summer. In the cool shade of her spacious apartment, to where she had hastily retreated, Maria Santini bent down in her protesting dressing gown, on which the two herons maintained their enforced and distant silence, picked up the almost empty box of *Carezze* from the floor, removed the lid and selected yet another one.

17

'Can it be done, what do you think?'

There was a moment of expectant silence, as the question hung floating on the rising heat escaping from the rear of the monitor screen.

'Well? What do you think?'

There was another moment of silence.

'Tito...? Hello?' whispered the voice with some urgency. 'Are you going to join us today? Sometime?'

Tito Viale sat in front of his monitor, staring blankly at the flickering screen.

'What's the matter with you this morning? You're on another planet!' continued his colleague, prodding him gently in the ribs.

'Yes... Er... No. What was that, Piero? I didn't quite catch it.'

'Too true, my friend; you missed it by a kilometre.' Piero pulled a tolerant face and sat back in his chair. He sighed. Tito seemed to be doing this a lot these days. 'They want to know if Section 201 can be serviced by the end of next month without too much disruption to the other sectors of the network fed by that sub-station,' he repeated, leaning forward to point at a part of the schematic diagram on the screen which was labelled '201'. It was a part of Lucca's extensive electricity network and like the famous map of London's Underground, had been reduced to a simplified mass of coloured straight lines and right angles. The similarity of this complex pattern of lines to a bowl of spaghetti had not been lost on most of the employees of Lucca's Municipal Electricity Department. They referred to it simply as 'The Buitone', after a well-known brand of Italian pasta.

'Yes… I do not see any reason why not,' replied Tito, the semi-glazed expression in his eyes an indication that he was still not totally at his desk. A large part of his mind was still elsewhere, 'Section 210 can be isolated easily enough with sufficient warning. It just depends on –'

'I said Section 201, not 210! For goodness' sake, concentrate before you plunge half of Lucca into darkness and we have to explain things!' Piero turned his head to look at his friend. 'Trouble at home … again?' he asked, more out of genuine concern than pure curiosity.

The two had been friends even before they started working together at the municipality. Piero knew only too well of the increasingly frosty relationship between his friend and his domineering wife. He had never really liked her, but, then again, he had not married her. There had been that occasion when she had phoned him at well past midnight to enquire in a rather off-hand way if he knew where Tito was. Despite the lateness of the hour, Piero had gone around to his friend's apartment. Forty minutes later, Tito had found his way home, looking much the worse for the emotional strain. Piero had then found himself caught in the middle of several hours of acrimonious exchanges between husband and wife; his attempts to placate both parties or – more correctly – to placate Letizia Viale had proved totally fruitless. She could see nothing good whatsoever about her husband, who, by that stage, had been reduced to a gibbering wreck.

It was quite obvious that the marriage, at least from Letizia's point of view, was over. Indeed, it had only been through subsequent counselling over the water cooler in the office that Piero had managed to convince Tito of the importance of hanging on to the one thing which was his. That was why Tito was still an active member of COGOL.

'Perhaps you should both establish clear boundaries for your lives ... to allow each of you to do your own things; you know, compromise,' Piero had advised. 'Letizia can pursue her own interests whilst you mind the kids and then you can do the same whilst she does her bit. Split the time fifty-fifty. They are, after all, half hers as well.'

Since then, although Tito had continued to attend COGOL, Piero had no real idea if things were any better on the home front. In fact, it was as if Tito had withdrawn into a secure state of denial about everything and had entered a world of his own, where disconnection gave him the tranquillity and comfort that his home life seemingly could no longer offer.

'Well? Trouble at home?' repeated Piero softly.

'I'm sorry,' said Tito. 'My mind was on other things... Sorry,' he repeated, adjusting his position in his chair, awkwardly.

At a desk much further down the long expanse of the office, a large man suddenly got up from his monitor and turned to walk up the central aisle between the rows of desks.

'Shit!' whispered Piero, suddenly stabbing a finger meaninglessly at the screen. 'He's coming over to us. Don't worry I'll deal with Section 201's maintenance schedule. You go off and get yourself a coffee. Oh, by the way. Elimena and I are coming to the concert on Friday. We are really looking forward to it; Elimena wants to make it a proper night out. Hope it is a good show?' Then with a note of genuine friendship, he added, 'I was wondering if you wanted a hand with setting up the lights after work. I reckon it must be quite tiring doing all that on your own and then having to perform afterwards. I wouldn't mind learning what to do. You can order me around ... I won't complain.'

There was a pause as Tito processed the offer that was being made to him. During the time his home life had deteriorated, he had sub-consciously built boundaries around himself, as a means of self-protection from the feelings of isolation and of not belonging. By being unloved and worn down by his domineering life-partner, he had become self-critical to the point that he believed he was unlikeable and no longer fitted into society. He knew he wasn't functioning properly at work and even his interaction with the other members of COGOL was no longer the same. Now, suddenly, this simple gesture of help from a long-term friend, who he had known since before he had embarked on what had become a miserable chapter in his life, came like a bolt out of the blue. In a flash Tito saw this well-placed offer of help to be a lifeline; it was a signal that he had some self-worth; that he could do something that would not be picked on and denigrated and that he should accept this offer as a means of starting to clear his mind over what to do next. Perhaps he could get through his misery by owning up to his problem of denial and by starting to do something about it. But one step at a time...

'Thanks Piero. Yes, I would really like that ... Thanks ... I truly appreciate... I'll bring two coffees back with me,' he whispered with a glimmer of renewed confidence.

18

Inspector Michele Conti returned to the *Questura* shortly before 4.00 p.m. He had been to Pisa to give his evidence in a trial concerning a jewellery robbery, which had ended in bloody violence, but he had found the case boring because the evidence against the accused had been irrefutable and so presented very little challenge. The lunch he had enjoyed and the pleasant train trip there and back had more than made up for the cut-and-dried nature of the case. Back in his office, he had no sooner taken his jacket off than he was summoned to his commanding officer's inner sanctum, where he found himself standing in front of *Questore* Bramanti's desk.

'Well? How did it go? Did you get your convictions?'

'It was an open and shut case. Fifteen years each,' replied Conti.

'They should have been given twice that,' grunted Bramanti, shuffling a file of papers around on his desk. 'And what about that screen … the anonymous accusation?'

'I have recorded my findings in my report,' replied Conti, indicating the pile of folders on Bramanti's desk.

'Before I read it, I want you to tell me about it. Is it your opinion that there is any truth in this allegation … about the screen at the Marinetti shop?'

His superior grunted a second time and seemed to be in considerable discomfort, so the prolonged reading of a police report was probably beyond him. Conti had been unable to make his report the previous day. When he had returned to the *Questura* after his very enjoyable interlude in the *Café Alma Arte*, he had been told by the desk sergeant that *Questore* Bramanti had had to go home, as he continued to feel unwell. That had been yesterday. Apparently this morning, in response to an urgent summons from his superior, the *questore* had gone straight to police headquarters in Florence for an important meeting. He had not returned to Lucca until shortly before 3.45 p.m., looking harassed and a little the worse for wear for presumably having indulged in an excellent luncheon with the *commissario*. The desk sergeant had found it rather difficult to maintain the appropriate degree of respectful decorum when relating this last point. Conti, whilst seeing the more amusing side of what an excellent luncheon with the *commissario* implied for the perilous state of Bramanti's stomach, had, nevertheless, reproached the man for his lack of respect. Even if *Questore* Bramanti was a far from popular man with his underlings, a certain degree of deference was due to his position.

'Well?' growled Bramanti. 'I'm waiting!'

The expression on the elder man's face seemed almost unchanged from what it had been the previous morning, following the usual weekend of culinary over-indulgence.

Perhaps it is not the food and he's been on the pills again. That's a bad sign, reasoned Conti as he scanned his superior's face before noticing the half-empty pill bottle standing in front of a framed picture of Bramanti's family. Inspector Conti was particularly observant and his superior's attempt at hiding the bottle had been pathetically amateurish. Conti had also noticed the tell-tale white flecks of chewed pills in the corners of the elder man's mouth – visible evidence of the prescription stomach pills Bramanti had recently taken to chewing like sweets. Conti cleared his throat and began.

'*Signor* Marinetti knew about the von Hohenwald screen,

but I could not see anything on display that matched the photo Pascoli had found on the Internet. Marinetti seemed able to answer my questions satisfactorily and offered no objection to me inspecting his storeroom. In fact, he seemed a little shocked at the very suggestion that he might even consider giving floor space to anything that was not lawfully purchased. He became really rather angry,' continued Conti, embroidering the truth a little, 'and it was only my diplomacy that succeeded in placating him.'

The self-congratulatory comment flew over the *questore's* head unnoticed. He winced slightly and grunted softly. Conti continued.

'After all, *Signor* Marinetti assured me that he enjoys a very distinguished career and is highly thought of in the international antiques trade. He also informed me, with some authority, that he resented any suggestion that he would ever even consider compromising his professional standing ... not even for a single second.'

'Did Marinetti offer any suggestion as to who might have written the note?' asked Bramanti, who seemed to be growing increasingly irritated.

'I did not tell Marinetti about the note. It would have served no purpose other than to cloud his responses to my questions. I have, however, checked with my contacts at Interpol and, as Pascoli has already informed us, there really is a von Hohenwald screen, but it doesn't appear to have turned up here in Lucca,' continued Conti. He enjoyed making the reference to his Interpol colleagues. From past experience, he found it didn't hurt to name-drop when talking to his superior.

'So, it is your opinion that the note was nothing more than a prank ... a malicious joke on *Signor* Marinetti?' asked Bramanti. He eyed the little bottle hidden in front of the picture frame and had to stop himself from involuntarily reaching out for it. A disdainful expression crossed his face, the downward twist of his mouth revealing yet more of the white residue in its corners.

'Or a joke on the police,' replied Conti, 'or on a frustrated lover, or on a rival dealer. Who is to say, sir? Although any of these options could be possible, I think it all highly improbable,' suggested Conti. 'Although, of course, there does remain the question of who wrote it ... and why. I did ask Marinetti if he had any enemies, professional or otherwise.'

Questore Bramanti gave yet another grunt and shifted his position once more. Conti's report served to confirm what, in his mind, he had already decided: the entire affair of the note could be dismissed. Besides, his mind was already firmly centred on other more important internal matters of his own wellbeing.

Conti waited respectfully for a few seconds, but when it became obvious that there were no comments forthcoming, he continued. 'It would seem from what Marinetti said that there is no love lost between antiques dealers generally. He referred to the profession as being a rather cut-throat one. In light of his statement, I could suggest a possible suspect although it would, perhaps, seem a little too obvious.'

Conti was about to suggest the name of Alonzo Adriani, the other principal antiques dealer in Lucca, but he left the sentence unfinished. He stood waiting for a response from his superior. When it became perfectly obvious that the *questore* had lost all interest in the matter, Conti followed suit.

'We have far more important things to deal with at the moment,' continued Bramanti. 'At headquarters in Florence this morning...' A sudden grimace of pain, as momentary as it was obviously intense, caused him to stop in mid-sentence, an action that was not lost on Inspector Conti.

'Sergeant Pascoli!' he bellowed over Conti's head. Almost

immediately, a harassed-looking man appeared expectantly at the office door. 'Pascoli, go down to the canteen and bring me a glass of cold milk – a large one!'

Inspector Conti was about to ask if there was anything he could do to help, but his superior pressed on before he could do so.

'They want us to concentrate on these murders, so just file the report on this antique screen under "Anonymous – unsolved" and get on with solving real crime. Assistant State Prosecutor di Senno has been given overall command of the local investigation: both of the cases here in Lucca and of the murder over in Montecatini of that German woman. The Foreign Ministry in Rome has now become involved and I fully expect that we'll have the *Carabinieri* around here shortly, telling us how to do our job.'

'That's everyone except the Finance Police and the Swiss Guard,' quipped Conti. Bramanti failed to see the funny side and glared at him frostily, as if to cool the uncomfortable heat within his own stomach.

'What?' he asked impatiently. Whether this was as a result of headquarters in Florence meddling in his area or from his internal disturbances, it was impossible for Conti to tell.

'*Sí, signore,*' said the inspector, deciding that there was no real point in continuing with the business of the anonymous note. Everything was dutifully written up in his report, anyway. Given the total lack of evidence, the least said about the von Hohenwald screen under the present circumstances, the better. 'We shall turn all of our attention to solving the murders, as instructed by Florence.'

'That will be all!' snapped the *questore,* waving the inspector out of his office with an irritated flick of his hand. 'I want you to prepare me a detailed report on all three cases – the similarities, method, clinical implications … everything. You know the routine. Have it on my desk not later than ten thirty tomorrow morning, if you please.'

As Inspector Michele Conti reached the office doorway, he turned. 'There is one other thing. *Signore* Marinetti sings in a chamber opera group. They have a concert this coming Friday. The group is under the direction of the Contessa di Capezzani-Batelli –'

'And is there any significance attached to this information?' asked the *questore*, his earlier expression of discomfort now deepened by a touch of curiosity.

'I have tickets to attend,' replied Conti, 'and I was wondering if the *questore* would also be attending? The Contessa does have a splendid reputation for the high quality of her concerts and singers … and refreshment is provided during the interval.'

Bramanti glared at him for a few seconds, his earlier icy expression now positively glacial and charged with disbelief at the inanity of his junior's question.

'Pascoli! Where the hell is my milk?' he bellowed, angrily waving Conti away.

19

'*Buona sera, Signora* Litelli … and thank you, as always,' called Riccardo Fossi from the comfort of his padded leather armchair.

'Everything is in order and completed for the day,' replied a voice from the inner office. 'I will see the *Signore* in the morning, as usual.'

The nightly ritual of securing the office was all very formal and perfectly correct – exactly as things should be in such a highly respected organization.

'*Buona sera, Signore,*' she continued, her voice receding until it was finally silenced by the click of the lock on the front door to the office. She was always the last of his small number of staff to leave. It was as if the custodian of so many of the company's secrets felt obliged to stay after everyone else had left, in order to secure those same secrets for the night.

Alone in the calm silence of his little empire, Fossi smiled and allowed himself to sink even further into the luxury of his chair. He was very pleased. Things were going very well; the business was growing steadily (his father would be proud of him), he had his singing and a loyal following of supporters in Lucca, and he and Renata had all the excitement that sailing close to the wind engendered. What more could a man possibly want?

After a few minutes of contented silence he sat forward, unlocked the top drawer of his large wooden desk and opened it. He removed a large pile of innocuous papers and reached in to the furthest recess of the drawer, feeling for a slightly raised square in the underside of the desk top. As he pressed it, there was a deep click and the bottom of the desk drawer sprang up at the front. Fossi was humming softly to himself as he carefully extracted a flat, leather-bound book from its secret hiding place. He kept details of his 'special' clients in it – details which were also a kind of insurance policy against future detection or betrayal. One couldn't be too careful when dealing with a certain kind of client. He opened the book, picked up his pen and started to write up notes of his meeting with *Signor* di Leone, the new client who had been sent to him with the personal recommendation of Don Amico Forno. Such a recommen-dation was very valuable, as it could well be the vanguard of future contacts leading to yet more high-powered clients joining his 'special' list. It was a discreet, not to say, danger-ous business, this 'special' list, but as long as one main-tained the outward appearance of being a true pillar of towering respectability within the community... *Well, what people didn't know couldn't hurt them – or myself, come to that.* Riccardo Fossi smiled as he looked up from his writing, gazed across his darkening office and out of the large window at the skyline of Lucca beyond. He had worked hard to foster a carefully nurtured appearance of absolute respectability, which successfully masked the hidden network of his 'special' clients.

If any of these names ever became public knowledge... Well... he thought, but a complacent smile had already spread across his face. There was no chance of that. On the other hand, the reality of such an event actually happening – the names on his 'special' list falling into the unsympathetic hands of the law – would spell disaster for his highly respected reputation and public standing. To be either remotely connected with the name of the Sicilian Don Amico Forno, or even to be connected to the shady machinations of that specific geographic location, would place him well beyond the point of salvation. If truth be told, over the years, Fossi had thrived on the hidden danger of his darker, less-respectable side. He pondered the sudden thought that perhaps the ever-faithful *Signora* Litelli knew of the book; but, then again, if she did she would be implicated and that was enough to ensure her silence in the event of an emergency.

He suddenly added words to his humming: '*Dei mi bollente spiriti,*' from Verdi's *La Traviata*. At the very thought of the beautiful Violetta, Alfredo's passion bubbled through the music – much the same as his own passion would be aroused long before he met Renata at tomorrow's rehearsal for the COGOL concert.

But why wait for tomorrow? He decided on a course of action and sat forward to use the telephone. He didn't have to think about the number, which fell automatically under his fingertips. As a precaution he had decided not to program the number into the phone's memory. *Signora* Litelli might look like an old dragon, but she was far from stupid and had a habit of finding out about things. At least, without hard evidence, any suspicions she might develop would remain just that.

That's the way it's done, he inwardly chuckled as he heard the number dialling. Then, without warning, a cloud suddenly drifted across his handsome features. He froze, staring at the desk in front of him, and quickly replaced the handset. What was it that *Signor* di Leone had said, sitting at that dreadful *Café del Mostro* on the *Piazza Napoleone?* Engulfed in the smell of that establishment's awful coffee, the two men had sat talking, hinting in the broadest terms at what one of them wanted and what the other could possibly deliver. He could hear di Leone's voice again.

'Therefore, you have to conclude that it is a ludicrous situation. The more successful you become in business, the more you are legally robbed by the State ... if you understand my meaning. Do you not agree that there should be some provision to keep some small part of one's success for oneself? After all, do you not think that such a desire is only fair?' The clouds on Riccardo Fossi's face deepened as he heard the other man's voice fill his head. 'If we live in an egalitarian society, how can fairness be anything other than that?'

Fossi stared straight ahead into the emptiness of his office. He was not at all sure why he harboured the suspicions that had made him replace the telephone so suddenly; something had tripped the first stage of an alarm in the back of his mind, but he couldn't put his finger on it. There had been many, many questions from the olive grower during the course of their meeting, but no more than was usual in meetings of this nature. And di Leone had come with the personal recommendation of Don Amico Forno, so surely he was what he appeared to be? A frown suddenly added to the disquiet on Fossi's face. The Sicilian Don was known to a great many people – people on both sides of the law. On reflection, perhaps Fossi's present alarm was grounded on the simple fact that di Leone had not offered any kind of tangible proof of his contact with the forces further south. Then again, di Leone had given no obvious reason to even suspect that he was anyone other than whom he claimed to be.

Fossi shrugged and leaned forward on his desk, reliving the meeting in some detail. He had 'special' clients, as this man hoped to become, and years of experience had taught him to be extremely cautious in his dealings with them. Despite this, he could not remember having such feelings of apprehension with any of the others on his list. And yet he had no reason to believe that this man was anything other than the Sicilian olive oil magnate he professed to be. So why had the nagging doubt suddenly clouded his thoughts? He sat for some time in his nearly dark office, trying to rationalize his concerns. After the second cigarette he suddenly became aware that he had started to hum '*E lucevan le stelle*', as he had done earlier in the day on his way to that meeting at the *Café del Mostro*. He lit a third cigarette, but the tune continued to reverberate through the cloud of smoke he exhaled. Was he like the condemned painter Caravadossi in Puccini's masterpiece? As he had walked innocently enough through the picturesque streets of Lucca on his way to the *Piazza Napoleone*, humming Caravadossi's aria, was it a precursor to his own doom and his imminent appearance in front of the firing squad of the law, a victim of the overzealous and omnipresent forces of justice? Lately, he had read of several instances of less than honest people having been caught through entrapment by the undercover forces of the law. Was *that* what was alarming him? Was di Leone a plant? Or perhaps he was a double agent, playing both sides for what he could get out of it? Fossi felt decidedly uneasy about the situation and resolved to carry out some investigations himself. Once decided on that plan, he felt better and could now attend to his more basic needs; he reached for the telephone.

'*Buona sera, cara mio*,' he purred into the mouthpiece, no trace of his earlier concern over *Signor* di Leone even tinting his voice. 'I have my lips around your nipple and your ripe breast in my eager hands...'

He heard the surprised intake of Renata's breath and smiled. However, despite the velvet seductiveness of his words and the thought of the erotic fulfilment he hoped to achieve later in the evening, the melody of the condemned tenor's aria still played incessantly in his head.

The stars were brightly shining, he recalled as he continued whispering into the telephone. It occurred to him that this *Signor* di Leone could be an unknown force, which might just cause his own stars – which had been shining very brightly for many years – to dim somewhat and for a very long, lonely time. No – he was being ridiculous! There was no reason to suspect that this man was anything other than a greedy industrialist – like the rest of his 'special' clients. Besides, he had let di Leone do almost all of the talking and had said nothing remotely contentious or incriminating; he had far too much experience to be that stupid on a first meeting. So, why was he still even considering the ludicrous idea that di Leone was an undercover policeman?

'And now I am licking your navel and going lower and lower...' he continued, filling his mind with the image of Renata di Senno in all of her sexual glory.

At the other end of the line, she giggled softly. 'The Contessa wants to hold another rehearsal ... tonight?' she said, innocently. 'Well, my husband was called away to Florence this afternoon... Yes, a meeting with someone from the Foreign Ministry in Rome...'

'And now I've reached that part of you that only I can truly excite...' continued Fossi.

'...I could perhaps attend, but I'd have to make arrangements for my maid to have my husband's meal ready for when he returns home...'

The telephone extension was in the large farmhouse-style kitchen. Renata had her back to the large window, in front of which were twin sinks and *Signora* Tabita Agostini – the di Senno's maid of many years. She had learned to recognize the sound of her mistress's dalliances long before. She paused in her preparation of the vegetables for the evening meal and stood as if looking out of the window. In reality, she was carefully observing her employer's reflection in the glass, which appeared against the darkened sky like an image on a television screen.

'Yes, that should be possible, then. Please tell the Contessa I will come,' continued Renata.

'You will ... many times, I hope,' purred Riccardo Fossi.

'My apartment ... as soon as you can.'

'Very well ... and thank you,' said Renata, replacing the telephone and only just managing to suppress the snort of excitement Fossi's statement had just provoked.

'Tabita, I have to attend the Contessa's extra rehearsal. Can I leave you to see to my husband when he returns from Florence?'

Tabita Agostini didn't bother to turn around. She had seen Renata's reflection disappear from the window and knew that she was once again alone in the kitchen. She looked down into the bowl of vegetables she was peeling and was not in the least surprised to find that she was holding a rather large courgette. She smiled knowingly to herself as she proceeded to gently wash it.

20

With just a few days to go, the Contessa was still fussing around ensuring that everything was in place and would be ready for the concert. Even so, she was still able to find the time to complete another of her duties within the confines of Lucca. It would be a chance to get away from the worries of the organization of her concert and to seek a passage of time in some peaceful and tranquil surroundings talking to an old friend.

It was almost mid-morning before the Contessa, accompanied by Carlo Quinto, found herself in the top north-western part of Lucca on the well-worn steps of the convent of Saint Jerome Emiliani in *Via delle Conce*.

'Not long now,' she said, looking down at the dog, 'and then you can have some water.'

She manoeuvred the large 'Pisa Museums' bag and the dog's leash so that she could reach up and pull down on the antique bell-pull, which dangled from a rusty chain next to the heavy wooden double doors. Somewhere in the dark, secret recesses of the building a bell tinkled softly in response to her tugging. She had nearly tripped over Carlo before almost toppling off the top step herself, as she held the ornate bell-pull in her hand.

'Ooh! You really are a *bad* boy at times,' she said as she regained her balance. 'Why can't you just sit still and wait like other dogs?'

Never one to miss an opportunity to take the upper hand, Carlo Quinto smiled calmly up at her, fangs clearly visible, the picture of innocence. It was a peculiar sort of smile – a mixture of humour and something else almost bordering on affectionate aggression, as if to silently say, 'Don't worry; if you'd fallen I'd have caught you.' As ridiculous as this promise seemed, it nevertheless underpinned the deep bond of affection which existed between the two; theirs was a bizarre relationship, not unlike that which had existed between the Contessa and Elizabeth for over half a century. Carlo Quinto yapped twice and then dusted off the top step with several energetic wags of his tail.

'You really are a funny one,' muttered the Contessa. 'Sometimes I just don't under –'

She was stopped in mid-sentence by the sound of a bolt being drawn back on the other side of the doors. A small flap in the centre of the left-hand one suddenly flew open and a pair of bright-blue eyes peered out into the freedom and glare of the street.

'Yes?' came a soft voice from the deep shadows below the smiling eyes.

'Good morning, sister,' replied the Contessa. 'I've come to see the Reverend Mother.'

As quickly as it had opened, the flap suddenly closed again and the bolt was driven home. After a few seconds there was the sound of a much heavier bolt being withdrawn and then, slowly, one half of the heavy, carved doors swung majestically open on its huge, worn, iron hinges. It creaked loudly as it did so – like a hopelessly out of tune choir. As the gap slowly widened, the Contessa became aware of a figure clothed from head to foot in flowing black, the folds of which – stirred by the breeze from the street – billowed gracefully towards the darkened interior of the building. The blue eyes were encased in a not unpleasant, smiling face, which was only separated from the mountain of black fabric by the thin white outline of her wimple. So complete was the appearance of the pale face in the darkness that the Contessa found it difficult to distinguish where the cool, welcoming darkness of the entrance lobby ended and the bodily form of this nun began. The nun stood respectfully back and motioned to them to enter. Behind them, she closed the door on its complaining hinges, symbolically cutting them off from the world outside. Then she glided past them and, gesturing to them to follow, she walked off silently.

The little procession made its way through a maze of short, twisting corridors towards the centre of the ancient building. Everywhere was scrupulously clean and a faint smell of something bracingly antiseptic hung in the air. The Contessa couldn't place it at first, although it was not unfamiliar. Borax? Borax and something else – incense, perhaps? Or was it just mustiness, bordering on decay? As they continued, the only sounds were their measured footfalls and the regular, staccato clipping of Carlo's claws on the marble floor tiles. They passed rooms that had once echoed to the sound of children's voices raised in the recitation of the times tables, verb declensions or the Catechism. The sounds belonged to the ghosts of the past, as the rooms were now mostly empty and unused. The children had long since been removed from the orphanage.

'Oh, my goodness... How beautiful!' exclaimed the Contessa as they passed through a doorway and entered the shade of a colonnaded cloister. 'I don't think that I have ever seen your garden looking so enchanting,' said the Contessa pausing to take in the vibrancy of the colours. It was a dramatic contrast to the almost bleak austerity of the interior of the building. 'How magical...'

Realising that her footfalls were the only ones to be heard, the nun suddenly stopped and turned.

'*Si bella no? Questi fiori...*' said the Contessa, realising that the nun probably did not speak English. The nun smiled and bowed her head gently. She said nothing. In fact, in the many years that the Contessa had visited the convent – since the dark days of 1947, shortly after Enrico had been taken from them – she couldn't remember any of the sisters ever saying anything. Originally she had thought it odd, as they were not a silent order, but then she had put it down to the fact that their devotion to God occupied so much of their waking time that they simply didn't feel the need to talk to anyone else. That had been the case over the years and seemed to be so now. As they walked on, the Contessa mused silently on how strange this type of life was, especially when one considered how much the world had changed and how organized religion now seemed to play such a marginalized role in it – at least in the West. This nun, who couldn't have been much older than her mid-twenties and had probably grown up in the Church orphanage system, would probably never know much about the over-commercialized, self-centred materialism of the world, although her convent was surrounded by it. The Contessa smiled gently at the thought.

Peace of mind and body, I suppose. Perhaps it's one way of avoiding the reality of life, she contemplated as the nun smiled at her, gestured ahead of them and turned to continue their progress. Carlo growled and resumed his clipping on the worn stone floor.

They passed through the pleasant ambience of the cloister and re-entered the building on the far side. The Contessa had to pause for a moment to give her eyes the chance to adjust from the bright vibrancy of the cloister's quadrangle to the darker, more sombrely restrained interior of devotion and service.

No, she decided as she continued to follow her guide, *definitely not a world for me. Thank heavens for the Reformation!*

Ahead of them loomed the end of yet another passage-way. The Contessa found it hard to believe that such a modest-looking building on the outside could contain so many corridors on the inside. They reached a stout door and the nun knocked softly. In response to the answer, the nun opened the door and stood respectfully back, head bowed, as she ushered the Contessa and Carlo into the presence of the Mother Superior.

'My dear child,' said the elderly head of the convent. She spoke softly in English, which was as fluent as the Contessa's Italian, 'how very good to see you again.' She extended a gnarled hand in the Contessa's direction and smiled broadly, the lines on her wrinkled face forming a spaghetti-like mass around the partly open mouth.

'Mother Superior,' replied the Contessa, taking the hand and shaking it gently, 'I hope that you are well?'

'As well as God sees fit to make me,' was the reply. There was a look of unquestioning faith on her face.

'Insha'Allah' in another religion, remembered the Contessa, who had made a few Egyptian and Jordanian friends over the years through the International Cultural Exchange Programme. *How convenient it is to be able to blame everything, even the inevitability of old age, on the whim of an intangible, unaccountable entity.*

Carlo growled softly and sat on his haunches, fangs bared.

'Some water for our guest,' said the Mother Superior to the nun, who still stood filling the open door, waiting for either further instructions or dismissal. She bowed respectfully and closed the door softly behind her. 'We make all God's creatures welcome within our walls,' continued the Reverend Mother, smiling down at Carlo, 'even those with four legs and sharp-looking teeth. Please ... do take a seat,' she continued, indicating the empty chair across the desk from her own. 'How can I help you today?' she asked as she rustled gently back to her own chair and sat down.

It was the same ritual they had followed over the years; years which, the Contessa had noted with silent alarm on each successive visit, had not been all that kind to the Mother Superior. Although there could not have been more than a few years between their ages, the Mother Superior now looked old enough to be the Contessa's biological mother.

Is that part of the reward for a lifetime of service and devotion to God? Perhaps it is, wondered the Contessa as she settled herself onto the hard, un-giving seat of the chair. 'You have been kind to give me of your time, Reverend Mother, and that is all I ask,' she said.

The reality was that it was the Contessa who was, once again, about to do something for the Mother Superior.

The conversation was interrupted by a soft knocking on the door, which swung silently open. The young nun placed a bowl on the floor near, but not too close to, Carlo. Careful to keep eye contact with the little beast, the nun retreated from the bowl and left, closing the door behind her once again.

'You were saying, my child?' prompted the Mother Superior, despite the fact that, from past experience, she knew full well the course her annual meeting with the Contessa would take.

'Reverend Mother,' began the Contessa, 'it is once again time for me to enquire as to how you are progressing with all of your good works.'

'It is kind of you to remember us. We carry on as we have always done,' answered the Mother Superior, a hint of longing for what her life had once been clouding her grey eyes, 'even if our precious charges are no longer under our roof.'

Any orphans in the care of the convent had long ago been transferred to a much larger convent in Pisa. When he had broken the news to the Mother Superior, the bishop had delivered the bombshell as if he was ordering a pizza: 'A rationalization of operational capability,' he had said. In her turn, she had thought of it more as a dismantling of the spirit of the *comune* – the community – rather than any advancement in pastoral care. Many years of obedience had taught her not to question instructions. However, despite this blind compliance, underneath her wimple she had a mind that jealously guarded her right to think for herself – as long as her thoughts did not show. As a result of what, to her quite worldly wise rationale she saw as a money-saving exercise, the orphans and their teachers had all been duly removed to Pisa. The continued generosity shown by this grateful woman towards the place from where she had collected her son, now seemed to be but a painful reminder of busier, happier times for the Mother Superior. A gentle smile hid her sadness. The Contessa's generosity would be duly passed on to the office of the Archdiocese and it would eventually filter down through the system, until it benefited those of their charges in Pisa who needed it the most. That was what always mattered. The Reverend Mother's smile deepened and she folded her hands together on the desk blotter in front of her.

Despite the absence of orphans at this convent, the nuns did some work for the *comune* and the Mother Superior was pleased to tell her visitor of their success in harvesting honey from their bees and of the convent's tentative steps into herb growing; all ways that raised money for the poor and the orphaned. She was eager to find out about Luigi's career and was delighted to hear of the Contessa's pride in what he was achieving at the hospital. The two old friends chatted on, each respectful of the other's status, but nevertheless enjoying their exchange of news.

As they continued talking in this timeless setting, it was inevitable that they each would revisit the memories of their first meeting, over half a century ago. It was in this very office, almost to the day, that *Il Conte* and *La Contessa* di Capezzani-Batelli had collected a little crying bundle; the little bundle that had contained their Luigi. He had been another of the countless orphaned victims of the *Anni di piombe*, the 'Years of Lead': the merciless civil war that had engulfed Italy as the Nazis retreated and the Allies drove them ever northwards up the peninsula towards the Alps.

'Give him a good home, my children,' the Mother Superior had said, standing behind the self-same desk on which her hands now rested, 'but not as a replacement for Enrico; that would be unkindly wrong. Bring him up as a child in his own right and in the Light of God.'

And so, over the following years, it had proven to be.

'Luigi would very much like to be more involved in the hospice project we started some months ago, but his work at the hospital doesn't leave him much spare time.' The Contessa had made an expansive gesture with her hands as she spoke, which brought the Mother Superior's concentration back to the present. 'It is a pity, as he has such a good manner with the sick.'

For a second the Mother Superior stared at the Contessa blankly, as if she did not understand.

'What is "hospice"?' she asked.

'Oh … we have them in England, so I thought it about time we had one here in Lucca. People are sent there from the hospital … mostly.'

'Is that for treatment?' asked the Reverend Mother, who was still none the wiser.

'Well, not really … but I suppose yes, in a way… We offer them dignity and peace … and compassion,' continued the Contessa, who saw from the expression on the other woman's face that she had still not understood what the project was about. 'It's really a … how can I put it … *e un ospedale specializzato nell'assistenza ai malati terminali*,' she said, lapsing into Italian.

'A place for the terminally ill to die?' replied the Reverend Mother.

'Exactly so,' said the Contessa. 'We make no charge for what we can do to help. I play the piano there several times a week. It is of no medical help, but it seems to please the patients and Doctor Bardini is convinced that it is a form of mental therapy and that it does cheer the poor souls up.'

The hospice – the first in Lucca and quite possibly the only one in the whole of Tuscany, if not all of Italy – had been started in one of the family's disused buildings, in the far north-eastern corner of the city. The building had been thoroughly cleaned, the small garden tidied up and one or two suitable building alterations – mysteriously approved at near breakneck speed by the *comune's* planning office – carried out.

'That is, no doubt, a great blessing to those who need it most,' replied the Mother Superior, finding it hard to hide in her voice the genuine admiration she felt for this English woman. For one who possessed so much and, in consequence, had the privileged opportunity to do so little, the Contessa di Capezzani-Batelli was a powerhouse of good deeds, all fuelled by the fire of genuine, often anonymous altruism.

'Perhaps, there is something the convent could do for the hospice?'

Although the Contessa didn't see religion, of any faith, being an important part of the palliative care programme the hospice would offer, the presence of Catholic nuns in a country such as Italy may have a relevance to some of the patients. She knew that any additional offered help would have to be accepted by Doctor Bardini at the hospice and certainly, any suggestion of work by the convent in the *comune* would have to be verified by the bishop in Pisa. Nevertheless, it was a good idea; if nothing else it would get some of the sisters out of the rarefied atmosphere of the convent and would expose them to the outside world.

'Maybe it would be sufficient to just visit and perhaps read to the patients if required,' she suggested.

Now that the seed of interest in her new project had been sown, the Contessa decided to move on as time was flying by and she still had much to do before the day was finished. 'May I now enquire as to Christina's progress?' asked the Contessa, abruptly changing the subject. 'She should be in her final year.'

'Indeed, Christina will qualify as an architect at the end of this academic year. That is all thanks to your generosity ... not that she will ever know that,' added the Reverend Mother, 'exactly as per the conditions you requested. Those lucky ones whom God places in our care and who progress well through their education will never know it was not Holy Mother Church who paid for their university education,' she continued, nodding her head slightly towards the Contessa.

For years, the Contessa's grant had allowed for two adopted orphans – a boy and a girl – to benefit from the privilege of a university education and a springboard to a professional career. It was a rather complex selection process, in which the Contessa had no wish to become involved, but it seemed to work.

'And Guido?' asked the Contessa.

'He, too, will graduate at the end of this academic year. And I am reliably informed that he has shown such promise that he has been offered a junior position with a highly respected law practice in Siena and that again is all thanks to you, Contessa.'

The Contessa smiled dismissively and waved the leashed hand in the air. There was the sound of water slopping on the stone floor as the bowl scraped across it when Carlo was tugged unexpectedly forwards and collided with it.

'I rather think that Guido's good fortune is more a result of his own hard work,' she said.

The Reverend Mother smiled as a series of short grunts rose above the level of the far side of her desk. 'I have enjoyed our conversation and have detained you for quite long enough. Now I must get on. We have a concert on Friday and there is still much to prepare. Come along, Carlo,' she said as she got up from her uncomfortable chair. 'Oh, you are a messy little boy! Look what you've done!' she looked down at the landscape of puddles. 'He's flicked water all over the floor. I am so sorry.'

The Mother Superior rose from her own chair and peered down over the end of the desk. Carlo smiled smugly back at her.

'Do not concern yourself, my child,' replied the elderly nun. 'That is a problem which is easily remedied.'

Over the years there had been far worse mementos to clean up resulting from the various Carlos who had visited. Water would present no problem at all.

'How kind,' muttered the Contessa as she took up the slack on the leash and turned to go. 'Oh, I almost forgot,' she said, turning back and balancing the 'Pisa Museums' bag on the end of the desk. She rummaged around in it and took out two large white envelopes, each of which bore the lily logo of the *Banca Toscana* in the top left corner. 'I'll just leave these here,' she continued, putting the envelopes on the desk. 'I am very pleased to be able to say that we have had a good year.'

The Mother Superior's face seemed to suddenly fill with the light of admiration as she looked straight into the Contessa's eyes. She did not look down at the envelopes – she had no need to. Rather, she kept her gaze on the Contessa's face. The Contessa di Capezzani-Batelli's contributions to the good works of others, which were usually far from modest in their financial generosity, were well known and had she not said that it had been a good year...?

'God will bless you for your compassion, my child, as will

we all. Go in peace,' said the Reverend Mother as the door opened and the young nun appeared once more.

A few minutes later, the Contessa and the complaining Carlo were once again out in the morning sunshine, strolling away from the convent down the *Via Galli Tassi*. Suddenly, something made her stop and turn. The convent and former orphanage of Saint Jerome Emiliani stood on a corner, where it had done so for several hundred years. Next to it, set back a little, almost hidden behind protective barriers and festooned with surveillance cameras and *Keep Out* signs, stood the regional headquarters of the *Polizia di Financia*, the branch of Italian law and order charged with stamping out anything even remotely illegal in the world of finance.

How very odd, thought the Contessa as she and the dog resumed their progress down the ancient road. *One building only too keen to invite you in and the other one – the next door neighbour as it were – only too keen to keep you out and yet to know all about you. It is a sad mirror of modern society.* 'Come on, you naughty boy,' she concluded. 'It is time to be on our way.'

Carlo growled at a passing cyclist.

21

As usual, *Via Fillungo* was crowded with an army of tourists. Some walked purposefully, first studying their guidebooks and then following the instructions that they had just read, pausing to study both the ancient architecture and the more recent Art Nouveau shop fronts that lined the street. Others ambled along aimlessly, uninterested in the riches of the abundant heritage that seeped out of almost every surrounding stone. They were concerned only with how much farther their guides would drag them before they had the opportunity to eat or drink something.

At Number 102 *Via Fillungo*, the *Casa dei Gioielli* glittered like a beacon of good taste, displaying its treasure trove of exquisite antiques in the most alluring way possible – not that the average tourist paid the contents of the shop window much attention. The lure of the echoes of blood sports in the nearby Roman amphitheatre – long since restored to expensive and much sought-after apartments – proved far stronger than any attraction the finest craftsmanship of previous centuries had to offer. Inside his shop, Gregorio Marinetti was late finishing off his mid-morning snack of a mozzarella and tomato *panino*. He stood in front of the counter at the rear of the shop, his back to the window. For a change, he was feeling contented. It had turned out to be a reasonable morning, following the unexpected appearance of a long-standing client from Pistoia, who had made a rather expensive purchase.

'Is it not funny how the smallest and most delicate items

often carry the largest price tag?' the customer had quipped.

Marinetti had smiled knowingly and shrugged in that peculiar Italian manner. If it had been an attempt to obtain a small discount, it had been unsuccessful. Marinetti needed every euro he could get his hands on.

He screwed up the greaseproof paper that had encased his *panino* and tossed it over the counter and into the bin that stood in the corner, discreetly hidden from view. It narrowly missed Nicola Dolci, his assistant of many years, who was standing on the other side of the counter facing him. In front of her, she was wrapping the item for Pistoia in bubble wrap and cardboard, ready for the client's collection later that same day. Being a Wednesday, it was also Marinetti's afternoon off. This was a time he found to be full of conflicting, contradictory emotions; half of him deeply resented leaving all of his beautiful objects in the care of someone else – even if it was the faithful and totally reliable Nicola; the other half couldn't wait to get back to his modest villa up in the cool of the foothills behind Lucca. After a restorative swim in his pool, he would run through his exercise routine, before donning his pure silk dressing gown and giving himself over to the other great obsession of his life – his singing. The rest of the afternoon and early evening would be spent at the piano, practising his arias and ensembles for Friday's concert.

'Before I go, I must tell you about that chair over there,' he said, flicking a few crumbs off the lapel of his tailored jacket. 'That is the one the Contessa wishes to use for our concert on Friday.'

He was always immaculately groomed and presented. Some secretly accused him of dangerous vanity, but had he been party to any of those comments, he would most certainly have ignored them, treating them with disdain. He waved a finger in the chair's general direction. It was an ornately gilded, seventeenth-century throne-like chair from the Bologna region and it was quite valuable, at least in terms of the potential profit to be made from an excessive mark-up. It had been moved from position to position in the shop over the past month and it had still not sold. In fact, over the last three months, very little *had* sold, which had largely given rise to Marinetti's current financial predicament. He took consolation from the fact that it was a difficult situation, which was shared by a great many in these hard times, including his arch opposition, Alonzo Adriani. The rumour was that this rival antiques dealer was about to go under. Marinetti considered himself more fortunate than the rest, especially the over-opinionated Adriani, because his situation was about to be remedied. The solution now resided safely hidden away in his lock-up, up in the hills close to his villa and well out of the way of prying eyes.

'You have told Francesco?' he asked, raising his eyebrows at Nicola. 'He does know to collect the chair from the lock-up on Friday? If he collects it at about four o'clock and then delivers it to the *istituto*, it will be in good time for the concert; none of his last-minute appearances please.'

Nicola looked at him tolerantly as she put the roll of bubble wrap back in its position under the counter. She could often be as sweet as her surname, but that softness hid a hard side to her character, something she had learned to develop over the years.

'Of course,' she said flatly as she stood up again. She was used to Marinetti's worrying. He had the habit of carrying on like a mother hen at times and she had learnt that it was far easier just to agree with him. There were also times when she had to hide her amusement at the prima donna attitude of her employer, an attitude that was emphasized by an excessive use of expensive cologne.

'And tell him to be careful with it. I would do the job

myself, but I shall be resting prior to the concert.' Marinetti had decided that he would take the gilt chair, which was to be used in the concert, to the lock-up that afternoon on his way home. Also, it was an opportunity to double-check on the screen to ensure it was ready for collection tomorrow when his client's agent would come to take it away. *Then my worries are over*, he thought gleefully. 'You haven't forgotten that I will not be available on Friday, have you?'

'No, I haven't forgotten that you will not be available on Friday, because you will be resting before the concert,' repeated Nicola, smiling at him as she drummed her fingers on the counter top. She had been to several of the Contessa's concerts over the years, but more out of a sense of job-preservation than any interest in opera or singing generally. To her untrained ears, the singing always sounded good and she quite often recognized the tunes. However, she had tickets for this Friday's concert and had purchased a new frock in which she would sparkle.

Not that Nicola would have known, but Marinetti would also be doing something else on Friday afternoon as part of his pre-concert relaxation – something he preferred no one ever found out about. In a discreet gay club he knew of in the back streets of Pisa, he had found a leaflet advertising 'A way of relaxation and stress reduction'. It promised a weekly programme of one-to-one sessions with Tezziano, a bronzed, bearded Adonis who resembled both a Greek god and, in certain other respects to judge from the leaflet, a virile stallion. In the misguided hope that it might lead to something, Gregorio had promptly signed up. He had struggled to pay the fee, but he had consoled himself with the thought that *something* might happen and that his recent anxieties would soon be released – one way or the other. He had indulged in the fantasy that his over-stressed body would be soothed by the laying-on of the Adonis' hands. Words had failed to describe his total disappointment when he had appeared for his first session, the previous week, only to discover that he got exactly what was advertised – no more, no less. Tezziano ran a nude yoga studio. Whilst he displayed his highly desirable attributes in a mind-boggling variation of positions, Gregorio Marinetti valiantly attempted to emulate the master, but, in reality he suffered, lusted and dreamed.

Perhaps this week will be different? If nothing else, I shall be really relaxed before the concert, he anticipated. 'I'll take the chair with me now and drop it off at the lock-up. Tell Francesco to collect the spare key from you on Friday. I have left it in the top drawer of my desk in the office as I must not be disturbed.'

'Yes, I'll tell him,' she said, *and don't forget to touch up the grey roots before the concert*, she observed.

Francesco was Nicola's drop-out brother and Marinetti's general odd-job man and, like Nicola, was totally trustworthy.

'Good, then I'll load up,' said Marinetti as he picked up the chair. 'Oooff!! It's heavier than it looks,' he said, straining to lift it before almost staggering across the shop to the door, which Nicola obligingly held open for him. 'I'll be back in a minute,' he puffed, pausing in the doorway, 'so, in the meantime, can you please turn your imaginative attention to how best to fill that empty corner with those new items in the stockroom.'

'Of course,' she replied, amused at the rather grand name for what she secretly called the closet. She thought this label more appropriate to describe the facility's true dimensions.

The door swung closed and with some difficulty, Marinetti battled his way through the tourists before turning sharp right and entering the relative tranquillity of the dead-end side street that ran adjacent to his shop. As usual, he had parked his little van in the recess at the rear of the shop. As he struggled towards it he asked himself silently – and not for the first time – why no one had thought of putting a door in the back of his building when it had been built centuries before. Now, the *comune* planning office – guardians of Lucca's architectural heritage – steadfastly refused to even consider an application for such a cosmetic triviality. Planning permission was totally out of the question.

'I'll get away in a minute,' he puffed as he re-entered the shop, his appearance as dapper as ever, despite the beads of perspiration that ringed his forehead like the illuminated lights sometimes found around the head of the Madonna. 'I need to make a notice, so that Francesco knows which chair to take on Friday. The partial set of dining chairs is also in the lock-up. The Contessa would not be pleased if she was presented with a straight-back dining chair, even if it was once sat on by Ambrogio de Medici!' He sniggered slightly, a gesture which ended in a little snort.

'Do you have any news on the delivery of the two missing chairs?' asked Nicola.

'Any day now, I should think,' he replied, 'and sooner rather than later, I hope. I need to move some of the items into the shop. There is a crisis of available space at the lock-up at the moment.'

That's because we haven't sold much lately, so there's little that needs replacing, mused Nicola, but she thought it unwise to say so. 'Um hum,' she mumbled as she busied herself with displaying the items she had removed from the closet.

'That should do it,' said Marinetti as he clipped the cap back onto a thick, black felt pen. He looked down at his handiwork on the counter in front of him. 'Take this to the Institute' it read in large, well-formed letters. 'I'll be off then, Nicola,' he said, picking up the notice. 'Enjoy your siesta and fingers crossed for a sale or two when you

reopen. Give me a ring if anything exciting happens …
otherwise not and I'll see you tomorrow.'

'There is just one thing before you go,' said Nicola.

'Yes, my dear and what would that be?' he asked, his free
hand balanced on his hip, one foot slightly in front of the
other. It was his usual stance.

'Those,' she replied, stabbing her well-manicured finger
with its shimmering red nail polish towards Marinetti's
chest. 'They are quite fetching, but I think not really an
improvement on the original pattern.'

He looked down at his white silk brocade waistcoat and
saw to his horror, that across the top right-hand side, just
clear of the lapel of his jacket, a jagged line of tomato pips
descended.

'Oh, my God,' he muttered, his voice rising several
pitches as he desperately tried to flick the offending objects
off his waistcoat without damaging the surface fibres.
'And you let me go out into the street like this?' he asked,
incredulously.

'Don't worry about that; I've only just noticed them, so
nobody else would have, not in that crowd,' she replied,
turning her attention back to her display. 'It's nothing a
good dry clean won't fix. Just make sure you ask for the "P"
cycle.'

That is 'P' for precious, she added silently as the door swung
shut behind him.

Some forty minutes later, Gregorio Marinetti reached the
concealed security of the foothills. As he bumped his
way along the dirt track, drawing ever nearer to his secure
treasure trove, his mind – quite involuntarily – had turned
to the highly valuable and potentially extremely dangerous
von Hohenwald screen, which resided in incongruous
splendour against the wall of the crowded garage. It was
large and rather heavy – as was his present secret burden of

debt – and he regarded it as the object of his salvation or damnation, depending on the mood of the fates. Of late it had always been the same – Marinetti felt the bile rise and his unease grow with each passing kilometre, as the distance between his van and the garage lessened. He was hopelessly inadequate at being dishonest – at least, in everything except his true self.

He looked yet again in his rear mirror, just to make sure that he wasn't being followed, before instantly feeling a little stupid. Who on earth was going to attempt to follow him? Then he remembered only too well the tension-ridden interview with that inspector and promptly changed his mind. Perhaps he had good reason to be over-cautious at present. He cast another glance up to the mirror. There was nothing behind him, just dust rising from the dirt road. Then he noticed the tell-tale sign of his untouched-up roots.

How thoughtful of Nicola not to mention it.

He cast his eyes down to his waistcoat, the top of which, if he sat upright to his full extent, he could just see in the mirror. The tomato pips had left a dry residue of pale red, which, as Nicola had predicted, would only be vanquished by a good dry clean.

He covered the last few kilometres to his lock-up, bounced to a halt and switched off the engine. He got out of his van and stood in front of the door of the lock-up. It was a small, free-standing building on the smallholding of one of his neighbours. They were an elderly couple. As a result of macular degeneration, the husband had gone almost blind and the wife had never learned to drive, so they had been obliged to sell their ancient Fiat. As a result, their garage became a painful reminder of happier, more mobile days now long past. Never one to miss an oppor-tunity, Marinetti had commiserated over their unexpected mis-fortune and had then quickly moved to obtain an agreement with them to use the now defunct garage, with its convenient up-and-over door, as his lock-up. It was watertight, easily accessible on his way to and from the villa, secure in its anonymity and – above all – inexpensive to rent, at least by Marinetti's standards.

As the door swung upwards and the sunlight streamed in through the opening to illuminate his Aladdin's cave of wonders, Marinetti's attention was drawn immediately to the screen, hidden under a large, heavy cloth. As he looked, he felt the butterflies flutter into life in his stomach. *Too late to go back now,* he reasoned as he took a step forward and carefully removed the cloth. He felt uneasy as the Lion of Saint Mark, from beneath its layers of centuries-darkened varnish, glared at him accusingly from the central panel. He had been obliged to open the screen out in order to accommodate it in the only available space against the wall. Space in his lock-up was at a premium; it had, after all, been built to house a modest little Fiat. As he stared at the object of his disquiet, Marinetti felt himself working up to one of his 'nervous episodes' – something with which Nicola was only too familiar. The sweat was starting to trickle down the small of his back, but that was not due to the pleasant warmth of the afternoon. 'No you don't!' he said, half to himself, half out loud. 'Oh no you don't!'

He flung the heavy cloth back over the screen, as if to blot out the accusing glare. His conscience felt no better, although he fancied that some of the butterflies could possibly have landed. *Just stay safe until tomorrow,* he reassured himself as he patted the cover around the edge of the screen.

He turned his attention back to the large table and the incomplete set of Medici chairs. *Blasted middle-men! How long does it take someone to package two chairs and send them on to me?* He was looking at the space occupied by the ornate table and the matching chairs. Only ten of them at the moment, but when the other two arrived, the set would then be saleable and he could free up space by moving the items to the shop. He had tracked down the two missing chairs on a recent antique-hunting expedition, following a tip-off from a fellow dealer, but he always preferred to fool himself that the subsequent discovery came as an unexpected surprise. He got more of a buzz out of it that way. For the moment, the table and the existing chairs would have to remain where they were, as big a nuisance as that was. He carefully threaded his way further into the garage, drawn in by the invisible allure of his treasures. As he squeezed past the table, his thigh caught the protecting cover and pulled it with him as he shuffled past. He looked down at the table top, polished by so many hands over the centuries, and being a true antique dealer, he could fully appreciate the patina and character the surface displayed.

'Ah … how beautiful,' he purred as he ran his fingers a few millimetres above the surface not wanting to touch it for fear of leaving greasy finger marks. He twisted round with some difficulty and managed to pull the cover back into place, but his passion had been awakened. He turned into the garage once again and his attention fell on a tall, glass-fronted seventeenth-century Neapolitan display cabinet, with its bevelled glass panels and highly ornate gilded carvings. 'Ah … exquisite,' he muttered as he reached out towards it. Then he noticed the large mirror, which had started its existence nearly two centuries earlier in one of the royal palaces in Piedmont. The mercury reflective backing was still in excellent condition and the exuberantly decorated heavy wooden frame, a festival of cavorting *putti* and fruit, was capped by a shield bearing the Cross of Savoy and surmounted by a crown. It was in need of a little restoration here and there, but Marinetti could easily do that once he had the space to use the skills that his father had had the foresight to apprentice him to all those years ago. To tell the truth, Gregorio Marinetti was a little older than he liked to think people believed him to be. Still, that issue did not occupy his mind at present. The mirror would fetch a good price once he could get it into town and display it in pride of place in the window of the *Casa dei Gioielli*. Then he turned once again and his gaze fell upon another of his treasures, but before he could squeeze his way over to it, his common sense finally took control and reason prevailed.

'Not today, my beautiful things. Today is only for music. We have a concert on Friday and I must prepare. I am sorry.'

A few minutes later he had extracted himself from the garage and had removed the heavy chair from his van. He manhandled it carefully into position in the front of the garage – not that he could have put it anywhere else, considering the chronic lack of space. Then he carefully checked to ensure that the chair would clear the line of the closed garage door. As he did so, his foot caught the edge of the heavy piece of cloth, which he had flung back over the screen with such force. He nearly stumbled and was only saved by clutching hold of the arms of the throne-like chair he had just placed in front of everything else. The squadron of butterflies took flight once again – exactly as they had often done since the screen first crossed the threshold of his shop. His palms were wet with sweat. He took a step backwards, as if the screen was repelling him and he knew that the lion was still glaring at him from behind the heavy cloth. The frenzied beating of the wings in his stomach had created a feeling of nausea. Anxiously, he looked around to see if anyone was watching, which was highly unlikely considering that the garage was in the middle of nowhere and surrounded on all sides by now largely unkempt fields.

'Get a grip on yourself, for God's sake!' he muttered as he turned back to the garage and reached up to close the door. It was halfway down when he remembered the sign he had made. Without it, Francesco – who was not the brightest bulb in the chandelier at the best of times – wouldn't have a clue which chair he was supposed to take to the *istituto* for the concert. He pushed the door up and walked back to the van. He returned, clutching the sign, but with his attention fixed once again, involuntarily, on the covered screen.

'Why does life have to be so complicated?' he asked himself as he put the sign on the chair, his eyes still half on the ominous bulk beneath the heavy cloth. It seemed to be exercising equal shares of fascination and dread upon him and it was all becoming just a little too much. He hastily reached up, closed the door gently, secured the two bolts and locked his treasures away behind the security of the two heavy Chubb padlocks. He then got into his van and in almost a total muck-sweat, retreated back down the dirt track in a cloud of swirling dust.

What he could not have known was that, in his haste to escape the accusing glare of the lion, he had flung the protecting cloth back over the screen with such defensive force that the top corner of it had ridden up too high and had draped itself over part of the lifting mechanism that supported the door's weight when opened. As he had closed the door, despite the care with which he had done so, the action of the movement had started to dislodge the cloth. Almost imperceptibly at first, the fabric started to slip, egged on by the encouraging embrace of gravity. What had started out merely as a suggestion of momentum now assumed increasing velocity as the cloth slid gracefully towards the concrete floor, uncovering most of the screen as it did so. On its way down to earth in the darkness of the garage, the cloth flicked across the seat of the throne-like chair and caught the edge of the sign, dislodging it. Not that Marinetti had even noticed, being obsessed as he was

171

by the presence of the screen, but he had put the sign on the chair upside down. This oversight was now corrected, as the sign slid gracefully under the arm of the chair – like an ocean liner being launched – bounced once on a little pile of the accumulated fabric on the floor and toppled over to the left, righting itself in the process. Leaning neatly and purposefully against the screen, it came to rest in the folds of the fabric. The Lion of Saint Mark seemed to be smiling broadly in the gloom.

'Take this to the Institute', said the sign at its feet, written in Marinetti's own neat and distinctive writing.

22

Riccardo Fossi had come to Florence to get some information about Daniele di Leone. Having made the decision that he should find out more about this Sicilian before committing himself to any business arrangements, he had made a phone call to a long-standing friend and suggested they meet up for a drink. Accordingly, he was now sitting at one of the attractive tables outside *Il David*, his favourite café in the *Piazza della Signoria*, the large public space in the heart of the city. He felt relaxed and was his usual confident self, hidden behind the dark anonymity of his Gucci sunglasses. The bright Tuscan sun beat down on the city and it was hot – even under the shade of the café's umbrellas. Fossi took a mouthful of his cold beer and replaced the frosted glass on its little paper doily on the table in front of him. He licked his mouth, just to make certain that none of the thick froth from the head of the beer had remained in the stubble of his upper lip. Although it was only mid-afternoon, his five o'clock shadow had already made its appearance. Out in the *piazza*, the usual flood of humanity choked the place: groups being herded around by knowledgeable city guides; smaller groups wandering about on their own; couples who knew what they wanted to see and others who seemed to be in shock, overwhelmed by the crowds and by the realization that they had finally arrived in the beauty of Florence. Fossi lit a cigarette and relaxed more into his chair.

'*Ciao*, Riccardo,' said a voice from behind him. 'Apologies

173

for being a little late; we had a case that came up. You know what police headquarters can be like...'

Fossi had no idea what police headquarters could be like, apart from what he had seen in TV dramas. '*Ciao* Doriano, *come stai?*' he asked, smiling and standing up to embrace his friend, who was doing him a favour by finding the time to meet him during working hours.

'I am well, thanks. And you?' replied Doriano.

Fossi smiled broadly and shrugged. 'Okay,' he said as they both sat down.

'I see you're having a beer. Good idea on a day like today. Thank you, I'll join you.'

Fossi turned around and caught the eye of a waiter, indicating the need for another couple of beers.

'So, my friend, what is it that tears you from your columns of figures and brings you to Florence on such a warm day?' continued Doriano as he took out a cigarette and lit it. He put his mobile phone on the table in front of him. 'It is turned off... Officially I am investigating and am uncontactable. Unless, of course, *she* wants to get hold of me,' he added with a wink.

The two men, who had been friends for many years, grinned at each other from behind their sunglasses.

'*She?* Is this the same one you were talking about the last time we met?' asked Fossi.

'You bet it is! I can't remember one like this before... Well, perhaps Giesla, but she was German. My *mamma* always hoped I'd find a nice *Italian* girl, and you know what *mammas* are like,' replied Doriano, laughing. 'And you, Casanova?'

'Still handsome, physically attractive and available,' replied Fossi.

'Are you telling me that you haven't got anybody special at the moment?' Doriano asked, his voice heavily laden with mock disbelief. 'That I find truly hard to believe.'

'Believe it or not, as you wish,' said Fossi, 'but it is sometimes best to allow a refreshing break between liaisons to recharge the batteries.' He was not about to admit to his steamy affair with Renata di Senno. If it were ever to become public knowledge that he was sleeping with the respected wife of the assistant regional state prosecutor, Fossi faced the prospect of being ruined by a vengeful husband. Such revelations could become even more serious and detrimental to any subsequent recovery of his career if they were to spread beyond Lucca. *Signor* di Senno frequently came to Florence to consult the forces of law and order and Doriano Peri was a senior member of the flying squad, with information at his fingertips on a vast range of subjects covering just about everything – including the latest 'palace gossip' and social scandals. Fossi preferred not to think of the consequences of such a revelation. Better to be safe than sorry.

'There will be someone soon, I have no doubt,' he lied, smiling.

'Ah,' agreed Doriano, 'so, moving on to more mundane things. 'What is it that brings you to see me in the middle of the week? Business a little slow?'

'Not at all, thank you. Business is very brisk at the moment and everything is firmly under control.' In his mind's eye he saw the aged *Signora* Litelli running the office in his absence with her usual accomplished professionalism.

'I wanted to have a little informal chat with you, Doriano – off the record.'

Peri looked at his friend. He narrowed his eyes slightly behind his sunglasses, which, unlike Fossi's, were definitely not by Gucci.

'I have recently been approached by a prospective new client and I was wondering if you might…' He broke off as the waiter appeared with the two bottles of beer and a complimentary bowl of potato crisps and put everything on the table. 'I was wondering if you might know of a certain person?' continued Fossi.

'*Salute!*' said Doriano, holding out his glass.

'*Salute!*' replied Fossi as the two glasses clinked.

They each took a long draught.

'We know a lot of *persons*,' said Doriano, emphasizing the other's choice of word. 'I presume that you have a definite *person* in mind for your enquiry – off the record, naturally.'

'Naturally. I am interested to know if you are acquainted with a certain *Signor* di Leone – Daniele di Leone.'

'That is a southern name, is it not?' asked Peri, sitting back in his chair. 'We know of many persons from the south. Do you have a reason for wanting to know about this particular one?'

'I might well have,' replied Fossi, 'because I would rather make sure that this person is who he says he is before I decide to take him on as a client.'

'What makes you think that he might *not* be who he says he is?' asked Peri. Although his eyes were hidden behind his sunglasses, Fossi knew that this man's brain was running in top gear. There were no outward signs of any inquisitiveness, but the questions were coming in an organized, logical way. That was, after all, what this man did for a living; he asked questions, pieced together the answers and solved crimes.

'I don't know. I have met this person once for an introductory interview ... following the same professional procedure I always adopt with a new client.'

'And?'

'And ... well, I'm not sure why I have to ask you if you know of him. Everything seemed absolutely above board, but I have a twinge of uneasy feeling about things,' continued Fossi. He firmly believed that nobody knew anything about the darker, more murky side of his business dealings and he was absolutely certain that he would never tell

Doriano anything about them, for obvious reasons – friend or not. Fossi decided to play the innocent card. He did not see that he had any real option.

'A twinge?' repeated Peri, sitting forward in his chair. 'What sort of twinge?' Fossi's friend of many years had suddenly become the professional policeman. A natural curiosity, developed over years of investigations, had automatically switched itself on. Fossi sensed that his question, which to him had seemed perfectly innocuous, could be laced with a hidden danger. From behind the smokescreen of his sunglasses, Fossi suddenly felt uneasy about the situation he had created. He had started asking questions, but had had to do so by framing them in a context that would hide his own involvement in something that he already knew was decidedly illegal and rather dangerous. He would have to hide that dangerous fact if he was to maintain his squeaky clean appearance with those bent on removing the influence of organized crime from the tainted legal system. He was also only too well aware from stories he had heard that those from within the ranks of organized crime had little forgiveness and were often bent upon revenge. Discovery and betrayal were two things neither side tolerated and Riccardo Fossi suddenly fancied that he had managed to place himself firmly in the crossfire from both.

'You must know of the recent reports of professional people taking on new clients, those clients then turning out to be involved in illegal activities, which then involve those professionals.'

Doriano looked on, but said nothing.

'Of course, if they had had any idea that these activities were illegal, I'm sure the professionals would not have taken on the clients in the first place, although there were reports of a couple of them being trapped by police posing as the very people who were trying to commission their services.'

'Riccardo, my friend, are you trying to tell me that you have taken on a new client who is not clean?'

Fossi wished he could just ask Peri outright if he could check to see if this di Leone character was genuine, or if he was a police entrapment operative cruising the upper echelons of the professional market, bent on trapping the greedy or careless. Naturally, he realized immediately that he could not.

'Me? Good God no! What on earth makes you think that? I just ask before I find myself possibly put in the position I have described … in the future. Better to be safe than sorry,' he concluded with a smile, the falseness of which was largely masked by the sunglasses and the beer glass, which he held to his mouth.

'Hmm…' said Doriano, who was obviously chewing things over in his mind. 'I have to say that, if such a professional person found himself in a predicament of this nature, immediate contact with the authorities might be taken as a redeeming factor in mitigation … should such a circumstance arise. Having friends in high places sometimes works, but it cannot be guaranteed to do so every time.'

'Believe me, my dear friend, as I have said, I am not one of those professionals,' replied Fossi, careful to keep his voice evenly modulated. 'I simply ask *before* I might find myself unwittingly becoming one.'

'Then you are wise to do so, my friend. Daniele di Leone, you said the name was? What does he do, that he sought out Lucca's finest accountant … whose services certainly do not come cheap?' He drained his glass almost to the bottom. The afternoon was marching on and he would shortly have to get back to the *Questura*.

'Olive oil and crystallized fruit, amongst other things. He said that his family is from Sicily: the north-western tip of the island, as I recall,' said Fossi.

'If his business is *that* extensive, then why hire an accountant on the mainland? Why not use the company accountant?' asked Doriano softly.

Fossi began to feel a little trickle of panic fight its way up
through the beer bubbles in his stomach. It was a strange
feeling – one that he was most certainly not used to. 'I have
absolutely no idea. I, too, thought it a little strange, which is
why I asked for your advice – off the record, of course,' he
said.

'Advice?' repeated Peri, a grin crossing his mouth.
'Surely, my dear Riccardo, you mean *information?*'

'Well…' replied Fossi, shrugging. 'Yes … I suppose that
could be how your policeman's mind might see things.'

An hour later, Riccardo Fossi sat in the air-conditioned
comfort of a first-class railway carriage as the train pulled
out of Santa Maria Novella Station in Florence on its way to
Genoa. There would be several stops before he would have
to change at Viareggio to catch the local train to Lucca, but
that was an inconvenience worth tolerating as it meant he
was able to leave Florence at an earlier time. As the train
picked up speed he settled back and tried to process the
conversation he had just had in Florence. Doriano Peri had
indicated what would happen to those who were foolish
enough to involve themselves in illegal dealings. He had
said that the CID had no knowledge of any undercover
operations in the Florence-Pisa-Lucca area, although he did
let slip that there had been something similar recently,
further north in Bologna, even if it was a local issue. Parts of
the conversation kept bouncing around in Fossi's head, but
he had been assured that Doriano knew of no undercover
operation going on in his area.

Fossi was not certain if his expedition to Florence had
accomplished anything. At best, he had hoped for possible
confirmation of a police entrapment operation in the area.

He had come away with nothing, except the assurance that his life-long friend would run a check on di Leone's name through the police records – strictly off the record, naturally – to see if they had anything in the database on him.

23

'I'm after tellin' yourself what 'twas himself said – no more, no less,' said Elizabeth in her off-hand yet totally devoted way.

'And exactly what was it he said?' asked the Contessa as she propped her bicycle against the wall of the entrance vestibule of her apartment in the *Piazza Anfiteatro.* Carlo remained perched in the wicker basket over the front tyre, looking like a white, curly-haired marble figurehead. He looked at the Contessa in full expectation of being picked up and gently returned to *terra firma.*

'Come on,' she said as she lifted him out of the basket, 'time for tea, I think.'

The Contessa had been busy with her extensive rounds, which had included a piano-playing break at the hospice, and now she was thirsty and tired.

'Tea? Nonsense! Himself said nothing about tea!' snorted Elizabeth from her position at the head of the short flight of stairs that led up to a pair of imposing double doors. This was the formal entrance to the spacious apartment and Elizabeth McGraunch, in anticipation of her employer's return, stood filling the open left-hand door as if she owned the place. In a hypothetical manner of speaking, she probably did.

'Is he coming for tea, then?' asked the Contessa as she started to climb the steps. Carlo's leash had been unclipped and the dog was up the steps and through Elizabeth's bow legs in a flash. This was an action which happened on an almost daily basis, but which always managed to destabilize the aged domestic. She grabbed hold of the closed half of the door to steady herself.

You hound from hell! she thought, swaying back into as vertical a posture as her curved spine would allow her to adopt, but she said nothing, having learned several Carlos ago that such comments were very unwise, even allowing for the Contessa's extremely tolerant nature. 'If yourself'll just be listening for a change, yourself'll know that himself phoned and tells Elzeebit something about a *cream* that doesn't smell. Himself has found it at the hospital and will have it delivered to the *Insingtote* for your hooley.'

Elizabeth always referred to Luigi as 'himself', even to his face.

'What cream?' asked the Contessa as Elizabeth swayed backwards to allow her through the door, before closing it resolutely behind her. In the confines of the entrance vestibule the loud bang sounded like a howitzer being fired.

'How should I be knowing? And it doesn't smell, so it doesn't,' mumbled Elizabeth as she dutifully followed the Contessa across the marbled entrance hall. The two women progressed further up the stairs to the first-floor rooms. 'I'm just a'tellin' yourself the message … not *interpring* … *intersper* … I'm not after explaining what 'tis himself meant.'

They climbed the stairs in silence for a few seconds.

'Yourself's not having something she shouldn't be havin'?' asked Elizabeth, her eyes fixed firmly on the back of the Contessa's head in her own peculiarly concerned way.

'Screen!' said the Contessa triumphantly, suddenly stopping as she did so. 'Luigi's found me a screen for the concert. Oh, the dear boy!'

Elizabeth was taken completely by surprise by the sudden halt in their progress and nearly careered into her employer. She was obliged to steady herself against the balustrade. 'That's what himself said,' she muttered. The

182

sudden, unexpected stop had caused her curved spine to extend to its fullest extent, but her mouth was still only just level with the Contessa's shoulder. 'And it doesn't smell,' she repeated. 'So, is yourself ill?'

Elizabeth was nothing if not forthright at the best of times. She also had a habit of locking herself into a verbal loop, which the Contessa had discovered over the years was best treated by simply changing the subject.

'Tea, I think, please,' her mistress said, resuming her upwards progress.

'Would that be before or after I finish me ironin'?' mumbled Elizabeth as they reached the top of the stairs.

'There 'tis, yourself's tea,' said the maid as she put the tray on the folded cloth, which covered the piano lid, 'and now Elzeebit will be back to the ironin', which won't do itself, so 'twon't,' she added closing the door loudly behind her.

From the comfort of his cushion, Carlo growled softly. Seated at the keyboard, the Contessa did not look up from the piles of operatic scores that surrounded her.

'Thank you, Elizabeth,' she said, ignoring the comment about the ironing. Long years of interaction had taught her that her resident Irish terrier's bark was far worse than her bite and that her pronouncements were merely un-barbed, muttered statements of fact. Across from the keyboard and piles of scores, where the tray of tea had been placed, a strong column of steam could be seen escaping from the spout of the teapot. It was bisected by an early evening sunbeam, reflected off a window across the arena and it highlighted the cloud of dust motes the tray had disturbed from the fringed throw covering the bottom half of the grand piano. They swirled about happily in the glow of the sunbeam, like a densely packed corps of graceful ballerinas. The Contessa sighed. Perhaps the opportunity for even the simplest dusting and polishing had now passed; she had long ago begun to think that the time for reminding Elizabeth to do so certainly had. As she shuffled the scores, she wondered why the singers in COGOL – her silver-voiced angels – had not been affected by the dust, which obviously lingered in plentiful supply.

I think I'll let that cool a little, she decided as she sorted her pile of scores, many of which would be needed for the concert. Luigi had offered to find her a suitably discrete bookcase in which to store them in some sort of order, but his kindness was always met with a postponing reply. The Contessa felt securely happy surrounded by the tools of her trade and had no desire to change things. She stopped at a rather battered score of Puccini's *La Bohème*, the cover of which had a long tear down it. The once-white, thick paper exposed by the tear had turned a deep sand colour over the years. Now, it almost matched the shade of the brown paper tape that had been used on the inside of the cover to repair it.

Poor Elizabeth; she's a bit like this book ... rather torn and quite faded, thought the Contessa as she gently fingered the tear. *Still ... we have to carry on.*

It never occurred to her that she was also in a state of ever-noticeable decline as the years progressed, but it had never been in her nature to notice or even admit to such a thing. She had always been an active person. When she was younger, there were those who remarked that she was hyperactive, and she saw no reason why things should change now, simply because of the intervention of the passing of time.

'Let's see now... Musetta's Waltz Song,' she muttered as she paged through the well-worn score, which had originally been Giacomo's and was now hers. She put the score on the piano's music stand and turned the pages slowly towards Act Two, enjoying the memories she encountered along the way and humming the melody of the Waltz

Song softly as she did so. In her mind's eye she saw herself sitting in front of a different keyboard, the score still balanced on the music stand, but now held in place by the well-tanned, olive-skinned hands of a man.

A melodious, deeply placed voice drifted into her ears. It was tinged with the faintest hint of its foreign origin.

'...and this is one of the most beautiful parts of the opera,' he said softly, his voice full of affection for the dots printed on the staves of the page. 'Please ... play...'

As she played, she noticed out of the corner of her eye that he had closed his eyes and was following the curve of the music in the air with his hands. When she reached the end of the Waltz Song, she stopped, letting the last sounds from the piano linger in the large room.

'That is really beautiful,' she said, turning on the piano stool to look at him.

For a moment he did not reply, but continued to sit on his chair with his eyes closed, his hands in the air in front of him, as if inviting an invisible cast of singers and orchestra to pause in their music-making and savour the genius of Puccini's melodic creativity. Then he opened his eyes and smiled at her. It was the familiar, warm, gentle smile she had always found so exhilarating – so alluring – right from the first time she had seen it.

'It also sounds just a little sad, as if someone has lost something that means a great deal to them, perhaps? I don't know.' She had no idea what the words meant and there was no English translation included in the Ricordi edition score in front of her. 'What is Musetta singing about? *Is* it sad?'

'They are all poor. Musetta is pretty and coquettish and moves from man to man in search of a better life – you know the sort of situation which poverty drives people in to.'

Penelope Strachan was not at all sure that she did understand what he meant, but smiled and nodded anyway.

'She used to be with another of the Bohemians, Marcello, but she abandoned him in favour of the much richer and older Alcindoro. So yes, in a way it is about loss, but not Musetta's loss; it is rather Marcello who has lost something, for which he still desperately yearns.'

'And yet the music is so beautiful,' she said, turning back to look at the pages of the score in front of her.

'And that is the true genius of *Maestro* Puccini; he paints bare human emotion in the subtlest of musical colours. This whole scene is a complicated dialogue between the principal characters. Each is voicing their own opinion of Musetta, of Marcello and the rest. Even Mimi and Rodolfo comment on the situation. And it is all held together by the music.'

'Oh ... how clever,' Penelope replied feebly. She was finding it increasingly more and more difficult to follow the complex situation, and the seemingly endless flow of Italian names wasn't helping. She wondered how anyone ever remembered them all.

'This scene has a happy ending ... for the moment,' continued Professor Capezzani-Batelli, looking at the score as if he were standing on the stage in the middle of the scene. 'Musetta sends her elderly lover away to buy her a new pair of shoes and then throws herself back into Marcello's eagerly waiting arms. Sadly, the happiness they then feel will not be shared by the two central characters.'

'Oh ... dear, so it is a little sad, then.'

'We Italians all have the embers of sadness smouldering deep within us,' he continued. That was something which Penelope Strachan, with her limited experience of the jagged web of life, did not fully appreciate. 'We have so much, but always desire something more. Sometimes we find it and manage to keep it; sometimes we find it and then lose it ... have it taken away from us.'

He fell silent for a few seconds, a distant look clouding the handsome, chiselled features of his face. She was suddenly curious as to what it was he might have had taken away from him, but couldn't find a polite way in which to ask such an indiscreet question. The resulting silence engulfed the room.

'That is what happens in the reality of life and that is what will happen to Mimi and Rodolfo. *Maestro* Puccini was better able than most to express these complex emotions through his music. Perhaps that was because his own life was often something akin to a plot from one of his own operas,' he said, his mood suddenly lightening and the smile once again creasing his face. 'You have a very accurate saying in English, which says everything that needs to be said about the *maestro*. He was very much a "Jack the Lad" and had a reputation for enjoying life to the full ... in all of its many aspects.'

She had heard the expression before, when her parents had been discussing her father's cousin, Richard. She had walked into the sitting room one Saturday evening for the usual pre-dinner sherry and had been in time to hear her father's muttered opinion of his cousin.

'Richard is a disgrace to the good name of the family. His Jack the Lad attitude to everything is going to end in tears. One girl too many and the resulting pregnancy will –'

When her presence had been suddenly noted, the subject had been abruptly dropped, but it was plainly obvious that her father was rather angry.

Now, in the comfort of Professor Capezzani-Batelli's studio, she cleared her throat and turned back a few pages to where the music staves were headed 'Mimi' and 'Rodolfo'.

'Who are Mimi and Rodolfo?' she asked softly, turning to look at him once again.

He turned and for the first time that day, looked her straight in the face. 'They are the two lovers. They love each other for who they are, not for any material benefit that one might possibly obtain by loving the other. They find everything they ever wanted in each other and are then forced by fate to give it all up again.'

The look of distant loss once again flicked across his face. For a split second, she thought that she saw the light of something go out in his eyes, as if he was involuntarily remembering the pain of having something of inestimable value taken away from him.

'Listen to this,' he said, getting up from his chair and sitting next to her on the double piano stool. He turned to the last few pages of the opera then reached across her and started to play. 'This music is so powerful ... it rends the human spirit in two with its pathos and loss.' He played a few more bars. 'And here, finally, what they have found together is taken from them.' He continued playing to the end of the opera. 'At the end the *maestro* suggests some of the musical material from the first act of the opera, when the lovers meet for the first time. So, as in life, the opera goes in a full circle – we find and then we lose.'

'Oh dear, did Mimi go away, then?' asked Penelope, unable to read the Italian, but noticing that the musical stave marked 'Mimi' had stopped before the final pages of the score.

'Yes, in a manner of speaking she does go away...' he replied, the emotion in his voice threatening to overwhelm him. 'She dies.'

The silence returned once again to engulf the room. She turned from the score to look at the professor.

'Mimi is ill from the very beginning ... even when the lovers first meet. It is as if fate is playing a cruel game with their emotions.'

'Oh ... I see,' she said, taken a little aback by the revelation.

'I hope I have not upset you,' he said, reacting immediately to the colour of her tone, 'but that is life. This kind of opera plot is called *verismo*, which means "realistic". There are no gods and goddesses to the rescue at the eleventh hour ... no cavalry to rescue you from the Indians, as happens in those American western films. There is just the bleak, ugly reality of the hand of fate that life sometimes deals out to us.'

She turned her head back to the score, but said nothing. He had become very emotional during his description. Perhaps he really was affected by the tragedy of the plot. She had heard people say that the Italians were far more passionate about things that the English took for granted. And yet it occurred to her that there must be something really deep-seated in this man, which provoked such feelings of deep emotion – feelings of loss. Her curiosity now came into play and she once again toyed with the idea of asking him, but was foiled by her inability to phrase so delicate a question in such a manner as to make the asking of it not sound blatantly impertinent. After all, this man – as handsome and charming as he was – was almost old enough to be her father. Her fingers caressed the keys once again as she started the Waltz Song from the beginning. She had a photographic memory and an excellent ear, both attributes affording her the extraordinary gift of being able to look at a piece of music once and then forever have it cemented in her memory.

'Is all of Puccini's music like this?' she asked, turning her head to look at him again. 'I should very much like the opportunity of getting to know it better.'

'And so you shall, Miss Strachan. Please do not think me presumptuous in any way, but would you care to accompany me to the opera? Covent Garden has a production of *La Bohème*, this very opera, opening at the end of next month. My position here at the Royal Academy affords me easier access to the performances than most. I would be honoured if you would accept.'

For an instant, Penelope Strachan's pulse raced all over her body and she felt as if her head was about to spin right off her shoulders. She wanted to shout out, *Yes, of course I will*, but her upbringing restrained her from such a common course of action.

'Er ... well, yes. That would be very pleasant, but I really think that I ... that is to say...' She suddenly felt very stupid and childish, as the words refused to come out the way she wanted them to. She felt herself going quite red – not so much from embarrassment as from anger with herself for her lack of control.

'Please do not concern yourself with any thoughts of impropriety. I ask you as one musician to another.' He paused, smiling that smile at her once again. 'And there *is* no Mrs Professor, if that is what concerns you.' His smile deepened as he raised his eyebrows in anticipation of her reply. How handsome he looked, with his white teeth and blue-grey eyes.

'That would be lovely,' she said, reaching up to the piano's music stand, misjudging the distance completely and sending the score tumbling down onto the keys with a loud discord. 'Oh ... how very clumsy of me!' she blurted out, wishing that she could disappear straight down into the academy's basement. 'I am so sorry... I'll pick it... Oh, no, I've torn the cover... I really am most...'

'My dear Miss Strachan, it is only a book. A little piece of brown tape and some water and it will be as good as new again. Please do not concern yourself over it.'

In the confusion of her retrieving the score from her lap, where it had finally landed, he had reached out to help her. They both had hold of the score by its long sides, their fingers touching, and she felt the sparks of attraction fly between them.

'Thank you, Professor, I would love to accompany you to the opera, but please understand that I must ask my parents' permission first.'

'But naturally you must,' he beamed. 'That is only right and proper.'

She smiled at him and then started to play the Waltz Song again. He sat next to her, playing the same music an octave lower. The room filled with the sonorous melody and harmonies, which engulfed them.

As she played, she became increasingly aware that the richness of the doubled parts gradually decreased, until she was once again seated in front of her own piano, her fingers, released from their arthritis by the music, moving with consummate ease over the keys as they caressed the composer's genius.

'Himself is here,' snapped a gruff voice, 'so shall I be after puttin' her in the kitchen on alert to make more for dinner?'

The Contessa turned towards the source of the question, without stopping her playing. 'Luigi's come to visit?' she asked. 'Where is he?'

'Gone to do what only himself can do,' replied Elizabeth as she stomped past the piano and started to close the shutters on the two large windows. 'Himself will join yourself when himself's finished ... and washed his hands,' she added, admonishingly. She still thought of Luigi di Capezzani-Batelli as the little boy she had helped to rear all those years ago, back in the time when Mister Giaco (that was what she had insisted on calling the Count, for she had never managed to get her tongue around any more of his name than that) had still been with them.

'He's probably come to tell me about his screen,' said the Contessa as she swung effortlessly into a passage from Cimarosa's comic masterpiece, *Il Matrimonio Segreto*. That extract, together with the Humperdinck and the Mozart, were the items on the programme that called for a screen.

Having closed the shutters, Elizabeth was crossing back to the door when the full meaning of the Contessa's last remark – at least, as the maid interpreted it – sank in. She stopped in her tracks and fixed her beady eyes full on the Contessa. She had still not been told what it was that was wrong with her mistress, what it was that had created the need for this cream – which did not smell – in the first place. The music swelled, so she thought better of bringing up the subject again. *When herself is that involved in her playing, 'tis a waste of time asking her anything at all.*

As she reached the door, she caught sight of Luigi crossing the lobby towards her.

'Himself's here,' she called over her shoulder as she marched past him.

24

Round about the same time that Elizabeth was pouring boiling water into the teapot and onto the worktop around it, an old, but well-maintained Fiat slowed to a halt at the order of a red traffic light at the top end of *Via Matteo Civitali* – the road which led to Lido di Camaiore. The two occupants never went as far as the beachfront delights of the Lido; that was a dream their finances would ensure remained just that – a dream.

'The girls have made plans for us on Friday evening, so you'll have to look after the kids,' said the woman in the passenger seat. She spoke in a clipped, aggressive way, as if issuing orders to an underling. She sat twisted in her seat, facing out of the car window, and she had addressed her remarks to the driver without even looking at him.

'But you know that I have my concert with the Contessa on Friday night,' replied Tito Viale as he fought desperately to avoid being drawn into the spiral of hopelessness, which was all too painfully familiar to him. The light still glared at him, as red as his frustrated, impotent anger – as red as a bloodstain.

'So what do you expect me to do about that? I'm going out with the girls, so you'll have to sort the kids out. That sounds quite straightforward to me. Besides, all the time you spend with your singing hasn't done you any good; you're still tied to your office desk with no hope of a singing career, so why bother?' She spoke spitefully, looking down at her expensively manicured hands, admiring the new shade of nail varnish as she did so. 'I don't know how you keep your self-respect, expecting me to exist on the pittance you bring home each month. And you call yourself a man?' She raised her glance and studied a large hoarding advertising cheap Ryanair flights around the world. Her eyes narrowed as she changed the angle of her attack. 'And I haven't been able to afford a holiday in years,' she added with a heavy sigh.

'But that is unfair; you know I give you everything,' replied Tito in a feeble attempt to stand up for himself. 'There is nothing else to give.'

'And I'm supposed to be comforted by that, am I?' she snapped, turning her head and glaring at him with a look that barely disguised the loathing she felt for him. To her, *he* was the reason she never had enough money; *he* was the reason keeping up with the rest of the girls was always such an embarrassing problem; *he* was the reason she was cemented into the level of society from which she so covetously desired to graduate. She hated *him* for all of that.

'But ... I made an excuse to get off work early so I could come and collect you ... just as you asked,' he answered feebly, looking at the back of her head. She was gazing longingly at the hoarding once again. 'And I do more than my fair share with the children and around the house...' He faltered, wondering if he had already said too much. 'And my singing is only once ev –'

'And that is once too much!' she snorted, without even turning to look at him.

Tito Viale, who was kind-hearted and gentle by nature, was no match for the corrosive vitriol which bubbled up from his wife in an unstoppable flow. Rather than being drawn into an argument, which is what Letizia would have liked, he gripped the steering wheel firmly and, gathering some inner strength from his newly acquired sense of purpose, stated quietly and firmly, 'I shall be singing with

COGOL on Friday night. It is a long-standing arrangement. If you feel you have to go out as well, then we will have to organize a baby-sitter for our children. I will ask our neighbour.' Inwardly, Tito was shaking and he knew if he continued his voice would break and he would retreat back into his shell. Before any reaction could erupt from his wife, he became aware of the chorus of blaring car horns behind him: the traffic light had changed to green and the expectation was that he should move forward. Despite his continuing insecurities, something deep down – something that he was not yet ready to fully accept – had started to formulate. As he released the handbrake to start driving away, it occurred to him that *maybe the road ahead is starting to clear.* He also wondered if Letizia had actually heard him!

25

Riccardo Fossi lay on his bed in the darkness, thinking back over the previous few hours of the evening. His muscular, tanned form was covered only by the lightness of a fine silk sheet. At the beginning of the evening he had hoped to see Renata, but his plans, which had caused him to be aroused on more than one occasion that afternoon, had disintegrated into disappointment when she had phoned and told him that slipping away from home that evening would be impossible.

'*Amore*, I cannot, not this evening,' she had whispered into her mobile.

She had gone for a stroll around the olive trees outside the *Villa Legge*, the better to make the call without the chance of being overheard. The fact that it might seem a little odd that she had gone for a stroll in the near blackness of the early evening and a question or two might arise as a result had never entered her head.

'...yes, and I need to feel you, too, but not tonight. Benito is having some of his colleagues over for dinner... He says it is the pleasurable side of business.'

Riccardo had made some lurid reply involving a detailed description of his interpretation of the word 'pleasure', which made her stop walking and shiver with suppressed anticipation.

'Stop it!' she had whispered into the mobile. 'You are cruel to entice me so, when I cannot get away.'

She had returned to the house looking a little flushed and entered through the large kitchen. Tabita Agostini looked up from the food she was busy preparing. She paid little attention to the flushed cheeks and the slightly desperate look of disappointment that hung about her mistress's face. She had seen it often enough over the years.

'Ah, there you are, my dear,' Benito di Senno had said as she entered the formal sitting room. 'I was wondering where you had got to. You look lovely, as always. Our guests will be with us in about an hour. Does Tabita have everything under control, as usual?'

Renata had nodded and mumbled some incomprehensible reply as she took a seat.

'Are you quite well, my dear?' asked her husband, noticing the flush in her cheeks, which had not quite faded back to normal.

'Of course,' she had replied, smiling. 'Absolutely fine.'

Despite his legal training, Benito di Senno was not as astute a judge of human nature as was his cook-house-keeper.

That telephone conversation had scuppered the plans for the early part of Fossi's evening. Suddenly finding himself at a frustrated loose end, he had decided to go out to *La Cucina d'Oro* for supper. The food at the Golden Kitchen had, as usual, been delicious, as had the bottle of Barolo, but it had done very little to lift his mood of frustration. He had left the restaurant quite early by his usual standard and had walked back to his home. With only the first part of the evening gone, and unable to settle down to anything even remotely resembling either work or relaxation, he had turned in. With his head full of the vision of an aroused Renata and of the erotica he had planned for that evening, he found sleep impossible. Now, shortly before midnight, he flung off the single sheet under which he had tossed and turned, and slowly started caressing his chest and nipples. His other hand slowly traced its way down the hairy path of his chest, towards the object of his pleasure, which had risen up to welcome it. In the coolness of his air-conditioned bedroom, he slowly and rhythmically began to satisfy his frustrated desires. As he did so, for some reason which he was beyond the point of being able to either fathom or control, Renata's face had slowly changed. It had become thinner, younger and the features had become finer – much finer, like a fine china tea cup, like an English Rose, ripe for the plucking. By the time he reached fulfilment, the face of his object of desire – Renata di Senno – had been replaced with that of the new COGOL member, the English teacher who lived in Pisa – Yvonne Buckingham.

26

On the top floor of her apartment block, Maria Santini felt herself sliding into one of her pools of neurotic helplessness. A trail of silver *Carezze* wrappers led from the bedroom to the dining table and then onwards towards the balcony. Also scattered intermittently along this route of increasing despair were assorted pieces of paper torn from the 'New Releases' section of the current *Gramophone* magazine. Maria's bright-red, manicured talons had made short work of shredding these harbingers of unwelcome and painful memories – especially the page containing the announcement of the new recording of *Carmen*.

'Bastards!' she muttered through tightened jaws. 'Why should you be the ones? What about me?'

She sat on a chair, half in the spacious sitting room and half out on the balcony. This action in itself was revealing, inasmuch as it demonstrated her inability to make a decision. She sat facing outwards, half in shade and half in the morning sunshine; it was a metaphor for her own existence, of the career she still desired, but had abandoned when her nerve had gone. It was a desire usually held in check by COGOL and chocolate, but it was also a desire which became depressingly all-consuming when she saw the names of those – her former friends – who had gone on to 'make it'. She rocked backwards and forwards gently, staring not at the already lively scene of the *Piazza del Giglio*, the Square of the Lilly, which spread itself in front of her apartment block, but at her two feet, which were firmly planted on the marble floor tiles. She had created a crisis in her own mind and slowly felt herself being drowned by it. As she moved rhythmically she muttered and occasionally burst into a sustained fit of humming. It wasn't loud humming – her jaws were too tightly compressed to allow for that – but it was persistent: arias from the operas or snatches of them. The very thing which caused her all of her trauma was the one thing in which she took refuge.

'You think you are good?' she muttered, turning to look at the mangled remains of the bulk of the magazine on the floor. 'Well, I also have *my* audience to please ... tomorrow at the *Istituto Musicale!*' She sounded like a little child who thought that her helping of ice cream was smaller than anyone else's. She returned her gaze to her feet and continued to rock gently.

'*Stride la vampa...*' she hummed.

The two faded herons on her kimono-like gown seemed to flap graciously as she rocked back and forth. They floated in the faded confines of the woven material with each rise and fall of her chest. The truth was that they had been reluctant participants in this sort of scene on many, many previous occasions – ever since that unfortunate night of the oranges in the opera house in Barga. They had long ago decided that the best thing for them was to simply float and watch. They had seen it all before.

27

As her neurosis closed in around her and she became imprisoned in her own void of bitterness, Maria Santini paid little attention to the day-to-day life as played out in the *piazza* below her balcony. Whilst she hummed and rocked, the spacious *Piazza del Giglio*, which spread itself like the archetypal picture postcard of Tuscany, continued to fill with people going about their business. The first customers of the day had settled themselves at the tables of *del Mostro's* and the early guided tourist groups had emerged from the *Via del Duomo*, stopping to admire the statue of Garibaldi in suitable heroic pose, which stood in the middle of the large public space. Then they continued across the expanse of the *piazza* to admire the faded glory of the *Teatro del Giglio* with its classical architecture. The guides never failed to point out the large lily – the symbol of Pisa and Tuscany – which adorned the sculptured oval in the centre of the pediment.

On the ground floor, four storeys underneath Maria's gently swaying form, lilies and flowers of all sorts played an important part in the small, successful business run by Gilda Ignazio. *Belli Fiori* aptly described her enterprise. She owned a florist shop. In fact, it was *the* florist shop in Lucca.

'…yes, we can do all of that for you,' Gilda said, speaking softly into the telephone. She had a practised telephone manner and her husky voice was as seductive as the scent from the flowers that filled her shop. '…but of course, any number you require,' she continued after a short pause.

'Please hold on. I will make a note of that… We will have to order in extra, but it should not be a problem.'

As she reached across her desk, she suddenly became aware of a shape standing in the corner of her shop, admiring the generous displays of roses, chrysanthemums and – naturally – lilies. Gilda knew instinctively who it was. Even from the back, there was no mistaking the familiar outline of the Contessa. The caller continued speaking and Gilda returned her attention to her order book.

'…yes, everything will be ready by six next Thursday. Will you be collecting your order…? Yes, we can deliver.' She wrote quickly and in a firm, decisive hand, the way her father had taught her. She thanked the caller for the order and replaced the handset in its cradle.

'Good morning, Contessa,' she called out, looking up at the figure in front of the floral displays. 'I hope that you are well.'

The elderly woman nodded her head, but did not turn around. 'Very well, thank you, my dear,' she replied, 'and how are you? I hope that you are in blooming health,' she continued, smiling at her own pun.

'The Contessa is too kind to ask,' replied Gilda, 'and yes, thank you, I am in good health.'

'You are lucky to be surrounded by such beauty,' continued the Contessa, indicating the flowers; 'much better than working in an office.' She looked up through the large bunches of massed flowers and out towards the *piazza*. In front of the shop, basins and buckets on tables and trellises held further forests of multi-coloured blooms. 'You have done very well for yourself, but I think that you are going to have to find a bigger shop…' The elderly woman suddenly seemed distracted; something had caught her attention.

'The Contessa is too kind to say so,' said Gilda softly.

There was a short silence. Gilda waited for the Contessa to speak. Her visitor was watching a child in one of the tourist groups running amuck around the lower step of the plinth on which Garibaldi's statue stood. The child tripped and cascaded inelegantly to the paved floor of the *piazza*. Howls suddenly filled the air, shattering the morning peace. None of the adults in the group seemed to pay the child any attention, except for the mother, who seemed more embarrassed by her offspring's actions than anything else. As the two women watched the spectacle outside in the bright sunlight, the telephone suddenly burst into life.

'If the Contessa permits?' asked Gilda, half turning to point at the desk.

'Of course, my dear. Off you go,' replied the Contessa expelling the breath that she had been holding. 'I'm in no hurry this morning.'

The tour group had moved on and the howls of self-pity had receded with it, but the Contessa remained looking out through the stacked baskets and buckets of flowers at the now empty steps.

In her mind she was looking at a different plinth, one on which Garibaldi had been replaced by an ancient Roman statue of Ceres, goddess of the crop and of fertile nature. Leading from the statue, forming a kind of ceremonial way, stretched a long flight of broad marble steps leading down to well-manicured lawns and terraced borders. Beyond the ornately decorated balustrades flowed the extensive vineyards and fields of the *Villa Batelli*. In the cool hills to the north-east of Lucca, the villa was one of the numerous residences owned by the newly returned *Conte* di Capezzani-Batelli. It had once again become a family home – the Count, his young English wife and his four-year-old sickly son and heir. The scene recalled in the recesses of her memory was every bit as beautiful and fragrant as that created by the contents of Gilda's small shop. Despite this, it was a frightening scene and the Contessa tried valiantly not to look down the flight of stairs. Over half a century later, she still saw everything as vividly as the day it had happened. She knew that she would look down – she always did – and she knew that she would see the crumpled form of little Enrico lying there, spread-eagled on the unforgiving marble expanse of the last step, his head twisted in grotesque confirmation that his little neck was broken.

What they found at the foot of the impressive stairs beneath Ceres's statue was the unfortunate conclusion of what had started almost from the moment their only child had inhaled the air of wartime London.

The awful truth manifested itself as soon as he had started to crawl. He would suddenly buck – like a frightened horse – and would scream the place down as he shuffled away into the nearest corner in what seemed like abject terror. Giacomo had watched this condition develop with even more alarm than had his young wife.

'Please God, not *il malocchio*,' he muttered after a particularly frightening manifestation of Enrico's seemingly worsening condition.

Penelope had looked at him quizzically. 'What was that you said?' she asked, her voice betraying the strain of the previous few hours.

'*Il malocchio*,' he repeated, taking her hand in his. 'In English you call it the "Evil Eye". I hope to God that he is not the victim of it.'

'The Evil Eye,' she repeated, turning to look at him. 'What on earth is that?'

There was a lengthy silence as she looked at her husband and he looked at his wife. He seemed to be fighting an inner battle of the Titans. If she did not know about the Evil Eye, did he have any right to tell her about it? It was, after all, only peasant superstition, but it was implicitly believed by many. They had enough of a burden to shoulder with their sickly firstborn, without adding to the burden by bringing in the intangible elements of the supernatural.

'It is nothing,' he said softly, moving nearer to her to kiss her gently. She nestled her head against his chest. He turned his head to look in the direction of the room in which their son had finally fallen into a fitful sleep. Outside, war-torn London slumbered, vigilant against a repeat of the air raids and of the Blitz of 1940. Inside the airy space of 26 Prince Consort Mansions, a recently married couple seemed to be just as vigilant over their infant son.

Penelope suddenly sat up straight and looked at her husband with iron determination, which far outweighed her youthful years. 'Was it something about a *malady* … about Enrico?'

Giacomo sensed that his wife would not give up until she had an explanation. He took a deep breath and held her even closer to him. 'The Evil Eye – *il malocchio* – is a curse. Someone puts it on you and you … well you' – he seemed to be struggling for words – 'you have a very bad time of it afterwards … that is what happens.'

'A curse?' she repeated, looking at him in a disbelieving seriousness. 'A curse … on whom? Surely nobody would put a curse on us?'

Giacomo shrugged. He knew his wife would probably not believe him. And why should she? After all, she had not had the exposure to such things he had had. He knew that the English were a superstitious people, but he was not sure if the Evil Eye was a superstition they subscribed to. It was quite a different matter in Italy. He did not respond to his wife's question.

'Who on earth would put a curse on us? Why?' repeated Penelope, turning a grave face towards her husband.

'I have absolutely no idea at all, *cara*,' he replied, sighing. 'The war is over for Italy and there are many grudges to be settled. Such a thing is possible, I suppose, if there are those who feel wronged by my family … for whatever reason.'

'I don't believe that for a moment. What wrong could your family have done to anyone?' she asked with child-like simplicity. She looked at him with wide eyes, not inviting a response as much as underlining her reply to his outlandish claim. In truth, she knew almost nothing about her husband's family. She knew he came from Lucca in Tuscany – not that she had had any idea where that might be when he had told her. She also knew that he had an elder brother and that they owned land. And that was just about the sum total of her knowledge of his roots. Giacomo knew far more about her family, whom he had obviously met prior to the wedding. Comfortably settled in their Hampshire house with its extensive gardens, spaniels and horses – not to mention the young Irish maid who had 'found' Penelope on Waterloo Station – the Strachans presented a picture of domestic happiness that he had not been fortunate enough to share in his own past.

'It is late, *cara*, and we are both tired. Such thoughts are only too eager to creep into a tired brain. Do not concern yourself with *il malocchio*. It is, as you English say, only an old wives' tale.' There had been hardly any conviction behind the statement.

Only upon their arrival in Italy, had Penelope Strachan discovered that her husband came from an old aristocratic family and was now *Il Conte* di Capezzani-Batelli and that she was now *La Contessa*. The significance of her new title and surroundings did not truly permeate her consciousness; her mind was too full of concern for the wellbeing of her son. They had entertained hopes that the freshness and warmth of Tuscany would help and up to a point, it had. There had been days when Enrico's breathing had seemed like any normal little boy's – days when he had played with his toys on the carpets of the villa, watched over by his anxious parents and his devoted nanny. Elizabeth also helped where she could, but lacked the medical training thought necessary to become his full-time nursemaid. And then, when it seemed as if the improvement might just be permanent, the other thing had reared its head again – the other thing, for which they had absolutely no explanation. Enrico would suddenly cringe away from something – an unseen, frightening something – which seemed to terrify him.

On such a day, Penelope entered the spacious grandeur of the *Villa Batelli's* main reception room. Despite her youth, she looked drawn and tired and she was wringing her hands in a manner not unlike Lady Macbeth.

'The doctor says Enrico's chest infection is a little better and that he has given him an injection. He thought him a little distressed and uncommunicative for a four year old' – there was a pause – 'so he says he will call in again to-morrow...' Her voice trailed off, leaving the final cadence of the sentence unfinished. Giacomo was standing at one of the high French windows, his hands folded across his chest, a lit cigarette, un-smoked, smouldering in his left hand. Most of it had been transformed into a compacted column of ash and seemed in imminent danger of tumbling to the floor. At the sound of his wife's voice, he turned and put the cigarette into an ashtray, oblivious to the fact that the action had caused the ash to fall down the front of his immaculate waistcoat.

'*Cara*,' he said, embracing her warmly. He felt the anxiety and worry in her body as he did so. He had anxieties too, but felt it his duty to maintain the strength they both needed. That was the husband's role in Italian life. 'I am sure that the good doctor is doing the very best he can for Enrico. Let us hope that the injection will help his chest.' They had spoken in English, as Penelope's Italian was nowhere near good enough to hold a conversation. 'Perhaps it would be best for the boy if we *were* to move him to Florence ... or even Rome: wherever we can find care that is the most modern and up to date.'

She turned wearily towards a pair of brocade-covered couches, took his hand and led him across to one. They sat down next to each other, hands held lovingly.

'You mean psychiatric care... in an institution,' she said softly, so that her voice was lost in the sounds of birdsong, which filled the sun-drenched gardens outside. Despite the opulence of the surroundings, the mood inside seemed to be one of darkness and gloom.

'If that is what is required, perhaps that is what we should seek out,' he replied, his face creased with the worry of his son's condition. Apart from a weak chest, the doctors had found nothing else wrong with him – at least nothing physical. However, his attempted escapes from his invisible demons had continued – sometimes frequently and sometimes less so, when the demons seemed to have left him alone. But any respite was tempered by their return, each time with a little more intensity than the time before. That had led them to question an illness of the mind. Harley Street specialists had said that it could well be a passing phase and that he might well outgrow his demons; it often happened that young children had imaginary friends, whom they left behind as they walked through adolescence. It was very difficult to tell with one so young – one so uncommunicative in all respects – one who seemed to be devoid of even the most basic of responses to stimuli of any sort. Nothing further had been done, but the demons persisted. Enrico was gaining greater and greater mobility every day – a physical development which seemed to be at odds with the lack of any mental advancement. He had a full-time nanny, but even that was not going to be enough to constantly monitor him every hour of his waking day. Now that he was almost four, perhaps here in war-ravaged Italy, something could be done. Something would *have* to be done.

They had sat on the sofa, each smoking a cigarette, the silence acting as confirmation that their son's condition could well lead down the path Giacomo had already suggested.

'Do you know of any doctors?' Penelope had asked, eventually, as she stubbed out her cigarette. A few weeks later, however, the need to know of any leading psychiatrists was brutally and quickly dispensed with, as Enrico di Capezzani-Batelli – in a terrified world of his own – sought to escape his demons by running out of the villa as fast as his still unsteady little legs would carry him. With saliva dribbling out of his silent, open mouth and arms flailing the air against the pursuing demons, he tottered across the narrow corridor of well-maintained lawn. He reached the statue of Ceres with her arm raised in an imperious blessing of fertility to the vineyards which spread before her, turned on the top stair to fend off his invisible pursuers, caught his foot on the ridge at the end of the lawn and flew headlong out and down to the lower terrace.

There were those in the district who mourned along with the family; those who admired Giacomo's stand against Mussolini. There were also those who muttered that it had been an appropriate sacrifice to the goddess. After all, had not *Il Conte's* elder brother been a diehard Fascist with blood on his hands? There were many still living in the surrounding area that were as vehemently anti-Fascist as Giacomo's brother had been pro-Fascist. They felt nothing; they had also lost family members recently to both the Fascists and the SS; the Germans had been no friends of Italy. To some of Giacomo's fellow countrymen, one Capezzani-Batelli was much like another.

When the grapes were harvested a few months later it was a bumper crop and the resulting vintage was one of the best anyone could remember. Matteo Ignazio, Gilda's father and also the hard-working overseer of the villa's vineyards and extensive gardens had just reason to be proud. Ceres, the smiling marble goddess, had, indeed, been bountiful.

'Everything is as the Contessa always requires: blooms which are magnificent in themselves, but without any fragrance ... to protect the singers' voices.'

Gilda Ignazio's voice echoed hollowly in the Contessa's head. She forced her mind's eye to dim the unwelcome scene at the foot of the goddess's marble stairs as she returned her attention to what Gilda was saying.

'What was that, my dear? I'm afraid that I didn't quite catch what you said. I was thinking of something else. I do beg your pardon'

Gilda smiled patiently. She had come to realize that elderly people sometimes did tend to drift off during a conversation. 'Your bouquets will be ready for delivery tomorrow afternoon, as usual,' she repeated. 'Everything is as the Contessa always requires: blooms which are magnificent in themselves, but without any fragrance ... to protect the singers' voices.'

'Ah yes, the angels,' corrected the Contessa. 'They have the voices of angels, every one.'

Gilda smiled good-naturedly.

'It promises to be a very fine concert. They have all worked very hard towards it. We have a final rehearsal tonight and then...' The Contessa smiled happily, closed her eyes and raised both hands, as if playing the music she had started to hear in her head.

'And where is Carlo today?' asked Gilda pleasantly, noticing, with relief, that neither of the Contessa's wrists were tethered to a leash. Every time the little beast came into her shop a trail of devastation, of chewed or mangled foliage, bore grisly testament to his movements. And speaking of movements, there had been that time when... But

Gilda Ignazio was spared any further dwelling on *that* topic by the Contessa's reply.

'He's at home having a bath with Elizabeth. She seems to be far better at it than I am these days. My back, you know...'

This simple statement of fact produced two quite different responses in the two women. For her part, the Contessa had a mental picture of the irascible maid hell-bent on getting the better of a snarling and snapping Carlo. He would be standing in the bath, resembling a chipolata sausage – a largish one at that – on four thin toothpick-like legs. Once his luxurious curls got wet, the true proportions of his grumbling form made themselves clear. Elizabeth would be covered in more suds than there were in the bathtub or, for that matter, on Carlo. That expensive dog shampoo purchased from the vet didn't go far at all. There would be water everywhere, but, with a little luck, it would soon dry and Elizabeth would neither slip on anything nor trip over a bedraggled pedigree bent on canine revenge. Gilda Ignazio, on the other hand and despite her pleasant smile, had only the image of the little beast meeting its grizzly and waterlogged end. She had been scared of dogs – especially bad-tempered ones like Carlo – ever since she had been badly bitten on the arm by Carlo Terzo (the third of the Contessa's Maltese poodles) when she was a girl of just five – not much older than Enrico had been.

Carlo Quinto could hardly be held responsible for the actions of one of his predecessors, but as far as Gilda was concerned, one Maltese was the same as another. Because of this firmly held belief, she wished the Contessa's current Carlo nothing but the very worst. She had absolutely nothing against his mistress. In fact, Gilda Ignazio had an enormous amount of respect for *La Contessa*, and that was not just because the Contessa had recently given her the huge green awning that stretched over the front of the shop and in the shade of which a considerable portion of her stock was now comfortably displayed. Gilda also remembered the emotional support she had received when her father had died and the financial assistance she had been given to set up her florist's shop. The Contessa regarded her as one of the family and 'families should always stick together', she had said on the day the shop had opened nearly ten years before. Gilda loved the elder woman for that and admired her simply for being a good member of the human race.

Somewhere in Lucca a clock chimed the half hour. 'I had best get on,' said the Contessa. 'I know I can leave the flowers in your capable hands, my dear,' she said, 'and you know we're performing at the *istituto* as usual.'

Gilda nodded and smiled. 'All will be delivered and ready for your performance.'

'Thank you, my dear,' said the Contessa, 'and now I really must be getting along. Things to do, you know.'

She almost made to tug at the leash to get Carlo into a walking position, but remembered in the nick of time that he was at home, hopefully washed and dried by now. She made a theatrical gesture to her cheek to hide the unnecessary movement.

'Such beautiful flowers,' she said as she turned to go. She seemed to be trying to find a way out of the shop, through the large phalanxes of greenery and perfumed colour. 'I must say that you've done really well for yourself, my dear,' she continued as she carefully picked her way through the buckets and display stands, 'but I think that you are going to have to find a bigger shop, you know.'

Four stories above them, Maria Santini was still rocking gently backwards and forwards. She continued humming softly to herself. It had not escaped the notice of the two herons that the intricate, yet faded, beauty of the cherry blossom that entwined them was now flecked with several random blotches of melted chocolate. Even more silver *Carezze* wrappers lay on the floor. Though Maria's considerable bulk prohibited direct communication, the herons knew that they would be in for a rough flight before the day was out.

28

Amilcare Luchetti had a girth of ample proportions, which was well-matched to the glorious velvet of his deep bass voice. He was COGOL's totally reliable vocal foundation. He loped, perspiring, into the main hall of the *Ufficio Postale* on the *Piazzetta della Posta*. The day was edging towards its hottest part and tempers in the large expanse of the crowded post office were rising in sympathy. Luchetti took a ticket from one of the machines serving the postal side of the hall. Other machines dispensed tickets to those wishing to use the banking and business side of the same hall.

Clutching his ticket in his free hand, he made his stately way across to a seat and sat down to await the appearance of his number over one of the service counters. In his other hand he held a small packet, the size of which was diminished by the podgy fingers of his hand. He rolled in his seat, removed a large white handkerchief from his pocket and mopped his face. His weight seemed to be out of control these days. He had always been well-built, but that solid construction seemed to be leaning a little too much towards simple bulk these days.

And what is one supposed to do? Luchetti deliberated. *There is no competition between a bowl of salad with no dressing and either a steaming dish of fresh cannelloni in a cream sauce or generous ravioli in a rich tomato passata with extra olive oil!'*

The image of these delectable delights – despite the high calorific content promised particularly by the cream sauces – caused his mouth to start watering. He switched the cotton handkerchief from his face to the flow of saliva that had suddenly started to well up on his lips. Suddenly, he felt a little stupid as he held the handkerchief over his mouth and looked over the top of the crumpled folds of the fabric at the other people in the hall. The action of clamping the cloth to his mouth had pushed his ample cheeks, which were not quite jowls, but were well on their way to becoming such, up into his face. This produced the undesirable effect of a pig-like appearance. His eyes, reduced in size by the restructuring of his cheeks, peered out over the rolls of flesh in a somewhat startled manner. He suddenly felt that the entire hall was staring at him, which of course was not the case at all. The saliva suddenly dried up. He coughed and replaced the handkerchief in his pocket without even folding it back into its neatly creased squares. He rolled back onto the iron mesh of the seat, so that with protesting equality, both ample buttocks once again supported his bulk, which towered above them. Others of less substantial build often complained about the discomfort of these utility seats at the post office, but Amilcare had to confess to never having felt the same discomfort himself.

A number flashed above one of the counters. 89. His ticket was 95, so it should not be too long now. At least, he hoped it would not be as it was getting close to lunchtime and... He closed his eyes tightly and tried, in a half-hearted sort of way, to banish the highly appealing pictures of food that had suddenly appeared in his imagination. He fought to regain control of himself as the saliva started to fill his mouth once again. He opened his eyes – 90 flashed above another desk – and he sighed.

He suddenly became aware of a heated discussion at the counter nearest to where he was sitting. Without turning his head he moved his eyes towards the noise, which was of sufficient intensity to be heard above the general din of the hall.

'Aaww ... come on, mate!' said a young man in accented English. 'Ya gotta be joking! How's a fella supposed to know which is which? Where's the English on it, then?'

The counter clerk glared back in barely hidden contempt.

'*Siamo in Italia...*' he said, a smirk appearing on his face, '*...quindi la forma è in italiano.*'

'What's that?' said the young woman who was standing next to the young man with the accented English. '*Non comprendo,*' she said, using the universal expression for 'I haven't a clue what you're talking about'.

'*Ah! Lei parla italiano?*' continued the clerk, his smile deepening. He knew perfectly well that she did not.

'Geeze, mate, all we want to do is send one miserable little packet back home.'

'Eh?' replied the clerk, whose expression indicated that he understood far more than he was about to let on. This was sometimes the case; those Italians who were working with the public would often have a good comprehension of English and would be able to respond where necessary. But in his opinion, these two, who were obviously backpackers and foreign, had been quite rude and he wished to satiate his position of power behind the safety of the post office counter. At least the man had been rude, he thought; the young woman, however, was very attractive in an adventurous sort of way with her firm young breasts filling her T-shirt with its message, 'Enjoy the Delights of Siena'. The nipples were erect, so that the taut fabric seemed to place undue emphasis on the 'Enjoy the Delights' part of the message. The clerk's mind was dwelling on that very thought as he surreptitiously eyed her up from behind the restrictive barrier of his counter. Her attitude had been no worse than the average local customer.

'Excuse me, please,' boomed a deep, molasses-like voice in English. 'Perhaps I can be of assistance? I use the post office regularly and I know this gentleman,' he continued, moving his head slightly in the clerk's direction.

Just in time to catch the movement, the two backpackers turned to face Amilcare Luchetti, who had padded across the short distance of marble floor to join them at the counter. Further on down the row, 91 flashed above another service point.

'I am 95,' he said, smiling and waving his ticket in the air with his free hand.

'Oh ... right y're mate,' replied the man, a look of relief crossing his face. 'We just want to post this packet back home and they're making such a performance out of it.'

Luchetti smiled and shuffled nearer the counter.

'*Ciao*, Salvatore,' he said in Italian. 'What is the problem?'

'They have filled in this form, which is only for internal posting. They want the packet to go to Australia and so they have used the wrong form,' he replied rapidly, 'and he thinks he is so smart and yet he cannot read the instructions on the form and complains that they are in Italian. We are in Italy and he cannot read Italian. And suddenly that is everyone's fault, but not his own! At least she is not so arrogant – quite attractive, actually, wouldn't you say?'

'What was all of that?' asked the young man, a look of non-comprehending expectancy on his well-tanned features.

Luchetti flushed slightly. Wanting to placate the situation, he realized that the moment could be a little tricky, given Salvatore's observation of the stretched message on the Siena T-shirt.

'It is simple,' he said, switching back to English. 'It is just a case of using the wrong form.' Amilcare turned back to the clerk. 'She is like a ripe peach ready for the picking,' he said, 'but a little of the wild beast about the quarry often heightens the excitement of the chase and eventual capture, would you not agree?'

Salvatore burst out in a peal of lecherous laughter, breaking the tension of the previous few minutes. Luchetti continued, smiling.

'We must keep our grip on reality, must we not? Some fruit in wild orchards is simply not attainable, no matter how desirous.' He smiled and shrugged, his ample cheeks vibrating as he did so. 'So, my dear Salvatore, can you remedy their ignorance and fill out the correct form ... for Australia.'

Number 93 appeared, a fact which, despite the jocularity and relaxed laughter between himself and Salvatore, Luchetti did not fail to notice. He was not about to lose his place in the queue.

'What was all that about?' asked the young man.

'He will fill out the correct form for you ... to Australia.'

'That's great,' said the young woman, smiling and leaning forward towards the counter. 'Enjoy the Delights' wobbled as she did so. Salvatore kept one eye on the message and the other on the form he was filling in.

'Yeah, that's great,' echoed the young man. 'Thanks, mate.'

Salvatore looked at him with an expression of intolerance. '*Prego*,' he muttered.

'He says that you are welcome,' translated Luchetti. Further up the row, 94 suddenly flashed. 'Excuse me, please, I must prepare for my number, which is next. I wish you a pleasant stay in Lucca. Goodbye.' He did not tell them that the implied tone of Salvatore's voice really meant 'idiot'.

The Contessa emerged from the subdued interior of the *Cattedrale San Martino* – the *duomo* – into the warmth of the early afternoon. Speaking to those two Australians the previous week, about the choir stalls now displayed in the Museum Guinigi, had reminded her that it had been many years since she had been into the *duomo*. It had been built after the erection of a *campanile* or bell tower, and so – a little like the Contessa's mind at times – was a little disorganized in its layout. The usual symmetry of cathedral architecture was largely lacking and the building was of a quixotic, cramped and unbalanced design. Still, it held many interesting features, not least of which included a painting by Tintoretto and the *Volto Santo*, the so-called Holy Face of Lucca, a much venerated wooden crucifix. Indeed, such was the fame of this object that Dante even mentioned it in his *Inferno*. The Contessa had tried to read Dante, but it had been many years before she had managed to master some, if not all, of the colloquialisms and other turns of phrase the great author had used. She had not been particularly religious since Enrico had been taken from her. Although she found some comfort in the silent tranquillity of the buildings themselves, she now debated if there had ever been a God in any of them. Such was her loss of faith.

She turned left and continued eastwards down the *Via del Duomo*. She was humming quietly to herself as she strolled into the *Piazzetta della Posta* and did not see the two backpackers as they bounded down the steps and out of the post office. She collided with the man.

'Geeze, I'm sorry about that,' he said, grabbing hold of the elderly woman before she could fall over. 'Are you okay?'

'Er … yes … quite well, thank you, if only a little winded. No damage done, I assure you.' As she replaced her glasses on her nose, it seemed to the Contessa that increased dangers on the roads from tourists on hired bicycles and on the footpaths from tourists reading guidebooks instead of looking where they were going, was a small enough price to pay for the continuing prosperity their presence brought to the city.

'Oh! Hello again,' said the young man's female companion in a friendly voice. 'Fancy meeting ya here, as they say.'

For a moment the Contessa looked blankly into the face of the young woman.

'It's Victoria,' continued the young woman, realising that some sort of prompt was necessary to assist identification. 'You remember; you helped us with that ticket business on the station platform last week.'

'Oh yes, of course … I remember now… You are the nice young couple from Australia. I had just been thinking of you both. What a pleasant surprise. How are you?'

'We're just fine, thanks,' continued Victoria, 'and we've had a really great trip.'

'Have you been in Lucca for the whole week?' asked the Contessa, all the time recalling more and more about these two youngsters and the circumstances of their last meeting.

'No. We've been around quite a bit,' said Jez. 'That tip ya gave us about Roberta in the Tourist Information Office … what a find! She gave us a map and pointed out all sorts of things we should go and see.'

'She even helped us plan a little trip further afield,' continued Victoria. 'She wrote it all down for us, so travelling was dead easy, 'cos all we had to do was show the paper and point to where we wanted to go.'

'Oh … how very exciting,' replied the Contessa. 'So where did you go?'

'In a big circle on the train,' replied Jez. 'Down to Arezzo, then to Siena, back to Florence and then Pisa and now back here for our last couple of days. We go home on Sunday. We want to go and look at the architecture of the *Café Margherita* in Viareggio and then go and look at a town called Petersinta, where there are a lot of artworks and artists and so on … sculptors, too.'

The Contessa was sure that he had meant to say

Pietrasanta, where she knew the retired actress Gina Lollobrigida had established a reputation as a sculptress, but she kept that to herself.

'And guess what?' asked Victoria, without waiting for a response. 'We've decided to spend our last night in Lucca at a Puccini concert.'

'Yep ... we did the Puccini stuff, like ya said, and thought that if the guy was that important to this tow... city, we'd better check out what he's all about. So we had just enough for two tickets.'

'How interesting...' replied the Contessa, who found it a little difficult to keep up with both the accent and the speed at which Jez spoke. 'I'm sure that you'll enjoy yourselves. The music is ravishingly beautiful at times ... very romantic.' She smiled at the mention of 'romantic'. Her dear Giacomo had been right when he had told her about the magic of the *maestro's* music. 'I'm having a concert of my own on Friday night – the Chamber Opera Group of Lucca. We call ourselves COGOL for short. I'll give you some tickets... Do come along and listen to us. We raise money for all sorts of charities, so don't tell anyone I gave you the tickets. You are both to come as my guests.'

She wore a sling bag over her shoulder, like a Sam Browne belt. She pulled it around in front of her and rummaged through the contents.

'Will there be any Puccini on the programme?' asked Jez.

'But of course... We are in Lucca... What would a concert be without Puccini?' replied the Contessa, a sparkle in her eyes. 'Here we are ... two tickets for tomorrow. They're the last two, so we should have a full house.'

Jez took the tickets and they both thanked the Contessa.

'It starts at seven-thirty sharp and we perform in the *Istituto Musicale Luigi Boccherini*. We also have a glass of wine and a little something to eat at the interval. It's all included in the ticket.'

221

Victoria was visibly gladdened that, if the music was no good, at least there would be food on offer.

'Where's did ya say the concert is?' asked Jez meekly.

'The Music Institute... It is named after the famous composer Luigi Boccherini ... just off the top end of the *Piazza Bernardini*. The venue is on the ticket and there are signs to show you the way to the *piazza*.' The Contessa had finally recalled everything she could about these two and was feeling quite relaxed and at home in their company. The young man, though of a much slimmer build, reminded her of her Luigi when he was in his early twenties.

'Do you sing?' asked Victoria, politely trying to hide the incredulity in her voice.

'Me? Good gracious no!' snorted the Contessa as she slung the bag back to its usual position and straightened her glasses. 'Me ... sing?' she chuckled. 'No, my dear, but I do play the piano.'

29

A few minutes later the Contessa reached *Café Alma Arte.* It seemed to her that the throng of tourists filling the *Via Fillungo* was as big a crush as ever. She was glad that Carlo had been left to Elizabeth's tender ministrations for the day as she found herself thinking it best not to imagine the fun he would have had with his leash and the many legs of those in the street. She had entered the aromatic oasis, exchanged the usual pleasantries with Gianni, enquired as to the health of Fiorenza and the expected arrival of the baby and been assured that all was well. Then, as was the established custom, she had been ushered to her reserved table in the far corner of the café.

'You only have to let me know if there is anything you and Fiorenza need, Gianni. You do know that,' she said as she sat down at the table, to the suspiciously watchful glares of many of the other café patrons, many of whom were squeezed somewhat uncomfortably around their own small tables.

'The Contessa is too kind,' Gianni had smiled warmly back at her offer. 'It is a comfort to us. Let us hope that the Blessed Virgin will smile on us this time. Will it be your usual tea and something for the palate?' he continued. He knew perfectly well what her answer would be – it was always in the affirmative – but asking the question was somehow part of the tradition of a Thursday afternoon.

It was some time later when the Contessa, whose mind was filled with the music for the forthcoming concert, suddenly became aware of a middle-aged couple approaching close to her table. The man walked with a heavy limp and his female partner seemed to be in the early stages of exhaustion. As they continued to walk towards the rear of the café, the man suddenly stumbled and nearly fell over. It was only the action of his partner that stopped him from doing so.

'Goodness me, are you all right?' asked the Contessa, a little alarmed. 'Please do join me and take a seat.'

'You speak English?' asked the man, who seemed to be embarrassed by his near fall in such a crowded place. 'That's very kind of you. We could do with a bit of a rest; we thought a cup of something and a sit down would be just the thing.'

For what seemed an age, three pairs of eyes looked at each other expectantly. The Contessa's invitation had been well-meant and gratefully received, but she, herself, occupied the only chair at the table.

'Oh! How silly of me!' she said suddenly, realising this with a chuckle. 'There are no other chairs, are there? Let me catch Gianni's attention and he'll soon fix that.'

Within a minute two chairs had been produced and the couple had been seated to the continued accompaniment of quizzical glances from the other customers.

'This is very kind of you,' said the man after Gianni had departed with their order. 'I'm Ewan Morgan and this is my wife, Margaret. We're here on holiday ... but I suppose that's quite obvious,' he laughed.

His wife took his hand in hers and laughed, too.

'How do you do? I'm Penelope Strachan and I've lived here in Lucca for' – there was a pause as her expression tallied up the years – 'well, for quite a long time,' she said simply, smiling. 'Have you seen the sights and visited the Puccini Museum? He is one of our more illustrious sons you know, but we have others as well.'

They chatted on amicably for a few minutes, until Gianni reappeared with the couple's order, which he placed expertly on the table in front of them.

'Two *cappuccini* and some unforgettable *dolci* to excite the mouth,' he said, grinning broadly. 'Does the Contessa require any more tea?'

'No, thank you, Gianni ... the pot is still half full.'

'*Buon appetito*,' said Gianni and left them alone once more.

'He speaks very good English, doesn't he?' asked Ewan Morgan, turning to watch Gianni's receding back.

'Please excuse me, I don't wish to appear rude, but did I hear the waiter call you *Contessa*?' asked Margaret, a look of curious respect on her face.

'Hmm?' replied the Contessa, but in such a way that she didn't answer the question directly.

'The waiter ... did he call you Contessa?' she repeated.

'So comforting to see that the younger generation still have respect, don't you agree? Of course, we don't make a song and dance about such things in Italy these days ... not since the king went. But we still have the old family titles.'

Mrs Morgan almost rose from her chair and was about to embark on her next question when her husband cut across her and to save any possible embarrassment, changed the subject.

'I must compliment you on your English,' he said, adding some sugar to his cup.

'How kind,' smiled the Contessa, as she selected two *dolci* and put them on her plate. 'I was born in Hampshire, actually,' she added. 'I do hope that your leg will soon be back to normal,' she continued, avoiding Mrs Morgan's questioning gaze.

'Sadly, not,' replied Ewan Morgan. 'It is an artificial one.'

'Oh ... I am sorry,' replied the Contessa. 'I ... er...'

'It was during the war in Yugoslavia,' said Margaret, 'at a

field hospital helping the local people... They were attacked and...'

'How awful ... the hospital was attacked?' repeated the Contessa, indignation showing in her voice.

'Ewan was hurt, along with many others,' continued Margaret, her voice trailing off.

'Were you in the army out there?' asked the Contessa.

'No, I was a surgeon with Global Medical Outreach,' replied Ewan softly, the suggestion of what could have been a smile creasing his face, 'but no longer, I'm afraid. The old hand can't be relied on to behave itself all the time,' he said with no trace of anger in his voice. 'These things are sent to try us, I suppose.'

The Contessa noticed that his hand, which Margaret still held in hers, twitched from time to time. 'I really am very sorry for that,' she said with genuine concern.

'But I wasn't killed; that was lucky,' he continued. 'Perhaps you've heard of Global Medical Outreach?' he asked, stirring his *cappuccino*. 'GMO: it's a charity working in trouble spots and disaster areas around the globe.'

The Contessa had not, but she smiled demurely and nodded sagely as if she had.

'How admirable that people should put themselves in such danger to help others,' she said.

'Anyway, such is life,' continued Ewan. 'After such a narrow scrape, we decided that life was too short to just think about things, so we decided to get out and about and see the world, to celebrate my lucky escape, as it were. And here we are in Lucca,' he beamed, his lust for life all too evident.

The conversation drifted between what to see and do in Lucca and the declining state of the Old Country on the other side of the Channel. The Contessa suddenly found herself musing on the unpredictability of life: on the cheerfulness of this man, who had been dealt a cruel slice of it;

on Gianni and Fiorenza with the on-going difficulties of their first child; of her own tragedy all those years ago at the foot of the goddess Ceres's statue; of the uncertain future facing the Mother Superior and sisters of the Convent of Saint Jerome Emiliani; of her own dear Giacomo, who had been taken from her unexpectedly, when he was barely out of his forties. Life could be kind and life could be cruel.

'...so that's what we plan to do with the rest of today,' said Margaret, 'so perhaps we had best get a move on.'

As the Contessa watched the couple leave, she felt her usual enthusiasm return, dispelling the more sombre thoughts of life she had felt earlier. Mr and Mrs Morgan had not let adversity pin them down any more than she, herself, had; to her, life was for the living. She felt the teapot; it was still warm and like herself, still contained the glow of life. There were a couple of things to do before her angels arrived at the apartment for the final rehearsal before tomorrow's concert and time was marching unstoppably on.

30

As the end of the day approached, two crises – one real and one largely imagined – had arisen in the otherwise placid city of Lucca.

At Number 102 *Via Fillungo – Casa dei Gioelli –* the owner, Gregorio Marinetti, was becoming progressively more and more irritated as the day wore on. Nicola Dolci, his long-suffering assistant, had already fallen foul of his tongue and was busily dusting to keep out of his way. She was quite used to his erratic behaviour on the eve of one of his COGOL concerts, which she had long ago put down to his over-excitable artiste's temperament. In fact, she looked forward to the actual day of the concert, when her employer would absent himself from the shop for the whole day in order to prepare himself for the rigours of his fleeting moment of stardom at that evening's concert. At least her day would be quiet and reasonably stress free – which, she surmised, was more than could be said of his. She flicked her duster at the lined and pock-marked face of a minor Roman Emperor for the umpteenth time. The marble bust, which had been accustomed to being shown far more respect in a time long past, glared belligerently back at her. Nicola was not to know that the reason for Gregorio Marinetti's excessive display of pre-concert unpleasantness had nothing to do with the build-up to that august musical event. Rather, it had to do with a stolen art treasure, bought illegally to be sold on – again illegally – at a considerable profit. More accurately, it had to do with the collection of the piece – or the non-collection, as it seemed to be. She turned her head and caught a glimpse of her employer seated at his desk in the other closet he fondly referred to as his office. He was sitting dejectedly, his head resting on his left arm, his hand clamped over his mouth. He was staring at the telephone, which had been silent since they had reopened following the afternoon siesta. Something else Nicola Dolci was not to know was that it would remain open until well past closing time that evening.

The palpable mood of despondency, which Nicola Dolci had felt blowing off the dejected bulk of her employer, was mirrored in the apartment of Maria Santini. Steam rose from the narrow stream of boiling water as the Contessa poured it into the cup, stirring the camomile teabags around with a teaspoon as she did so. She had arrived at the apartment with a packet of the tea in her sling bag. It was an indispensable part of her therapy equipment and was most effective in a very strong dose. She picked up the saucer and the cup, with its soothing contents and walked through to the spacious sitting room with its trail of discarded silver *Carezze* wrappers pointing the way to the balcony.

'Here you are, my dear,' she said kindly as she put the steaming brew on the table in front of Maria. 'Sip this and you'll feel a lot better. Be careful; it's hot,' she added as an afterthought, looking at her principal mezzo-soprano, who looked all the worse for wear.

'Thank you. The Contessa is too kind,' mumbled Maria, keeping her gaze firmly on the cup and its strongly coloured contents. 'I do n...' There was a long pause, during which nothing was said. The Contessa had been through these sessions before and knew the best way to proceed, which was at a pace dictated by Maria.

'You have a truly beautiful voice, my dear, and do you not

wish to share that special gift with everyone?' she asked, quietly, after several minutes.

The pair of herons said nothing as they danced behind the steam rising from the cup.

'Naturally, I... I want to sing... That is what...'

The silence descended once again as Maria took another tentative sip of the hot liquid. The Contessa sat quietly opposite her, her hands resting in her lap. It had been some time since the last Maria *pazzia* – Maria madness – as the other members of COGOL referred to such bouts of self-doubt and withdrawal.

'What is it you want to do?' asked the Contessa encouragingly. She was patient and supportive, although she had more than enough to do herself, what with the looming rehearsal and a host of other things to prepare.

Earlier, the Contessa had reached her apartment in the amphitheatre, quite exhausted from the many activities of her day. Her anticipation of a light snack, yet another cup of restorative tea and half an hour with her feet in a soothing basin of hot water laced with lavender oil had been dashed when Elizabeth had met her at the front door.

'Herself sounded in a right fix, so she did!' she said as she opened the door for her mistress.

'Which "herself" would we be talking about then?' asked the Contessa, who, after all these years and a long day of organizing a concert and chatting to visitors to her beloved city, still found herself slightly irked by her maid's wonderful ability to be so vague.

''Twould be the large one with the low voice. Muttering like an angry swan, so she was. Something about not being able to *reverse* tonight. So I told her yourself will be ringing her.'

'You mean Maria not being able to attend tonight's

rehearsal?' replied the Contessa, automatically correcting the maid's malapropism.

Elizabeth grunted confirmation.

'Oh dear…' replied the Contessa, 'not again,' she said, *and as usual with appalling timing*, she thought. 'Thank you, Elizabeth.'

The Contessa continued walking into the vestibule as the door was loudly banged shut behind her.

'Will you be after *trellifoaming* her now then, before I bring the tea?'.

'No, I think the tea will have to wait. I fear that I will have to go to Maria and speak to her in person. I had better go straight away.'

'Of course, I want to sing…' said Maria Santini softly, as she fidgeted nervously with the teaspoon in the saucer, 'but I have such anger it causes me to not want to sing … at times,' she muttered.

'Then you *must* sing and beautifully, too,' replied the Contessa softly, 'as you always do, my dear. That will defeat the anger.'

'I find it difficult … to' – Maria seemed to be searching for the right words – 'to … understand…'

'To understand what?' asked the Contessa, realising that Maria had slowly started to open herself up to the conversation. She knew exactly what was coming next, as an encounter with Maria and her insecurities was nothing new. The therapy of getting Maria back into her comfort zone and out onto the concert platform always took the same route.

Yet another silence engulfed the room and its occupants.

'…to understand why I did not have the career everyone told me I would have. It is unfair that I should not have had one, when the others I knew did. I saw them again … in that…' She waved a hand vaguely in the direction of the torn remains of *Gramophone*, which lay on the floor in a tangled heap.

'Which opera is it this time?' asked the Contessa, who suddenly feared that the tone of her question leant itself more towards the bored enquiry of a regular occurrence, rather than towards an enquiry of legitimate concern.

'Carmen ... *that* one ... again,' muttered Maria, her eyes still on the cup that was now half empty, but which still emitted tiny wisps of steam.

She had taken the question at face value. The Contessa felt relieved as she did not want to make a difficult situation more so.

'Maria, my dear, what happened in Barga was an unfortunate accident... It was nothing against you personally... It could have happened to anyone.'

'But then why did it happen to *me*? I don't understand.'

'And perhaps you should not try to understand,' replied the Contessa calmly. 'Sometimes things happen for a reason which is not yet apparent, or which might never become apparent. It does us no good to look for the answer. If we are truly meant to know the reason why, it will be shown to us without our having to look for it.'

'But *they* are not looking for the reason why *they* have their careers.'

'My dear, are you taking this all far too much to heart? You *do* have a career ... here in Lucca, with COGOL,' said the Contessa, pausing. 'The *Istituto Musicale* might not be La Scala or Teatro San Carlo,' she continued, being careful not to include the name of La Fenice, with its painful memories of a blossoming career that never was, 'but our audiences appreciate our efforts – *your* efforts and *your* talent – with the same appreciation and enjoyment. Would you not agree with me, my dear?'

Maria Santini shrugged slightly and slowly nodded her head, but she still stared down at the now empty cup. The two herons moved gently as she heaved an enormous sigh. It was the usual sign that the Contessa was winning the argument.

'The important thing to remember is that you must live for the moment. You have only the one chance to perform at your best, then the opportunity is gone until the next time. That takes courage, determination and perseverance.' The Contessa leaned nearer to Maria and continued. 'The people you remember from an earlier time … the people in the recordings in that magazine … they can sing a piece as many times as it takes before they get a near-perfect performance. You do the same thing, my dear, but you create that near-perfect performance with just a single opportunity and that is the sign of a true artiste. I would suggest that those same loyal supporters of ours, who appreciate our musical talents, will be very disappointed if COGOL's favourite mezzo-soprano is unable to perform for them tomorrow night.'

'Do you really think so?' asked Maria, looking up at the Contessa for the first time since her arrival at the apartment.

'Of course I do, my dear, and I think you do as well. You do not have to sing in a major opera house to have your performance appreciated by the audience. Besides which, what would your friends in COGOL do tomorrow night if you do not sing? We all rely on each other and we are all just as important as each other. Perhaps *they* are your true friends … not the people you remember from a previous time.'

The Contessa smiled across the table at Maria, who seemed to be somewhat calmer.

'Well, if that is what the Contessa truly thinks, perhaps it *is* important for me to sing tomorrow…' As she spoke, she reached out and caressed the corner of a box of *Carezze*, which lay on the table at her elbow. The Contessa had quietly replaced the lid on the remains of its contents when she had sat down to face her troubled mezzo-soprano. Now, as she sat and quietly watched, she knew that, if Maria Santini decided to remove the lid then the case would not yet have been won and further persuasive talking would be necessary.

'Perhaps I should perform,' continued Maria, still running her fingers over the corner of the box, 'if that is what the Contessa thinks is best.'

'The important thing is what Maria thinks,' replied the Contessa, 'and I think that she already knows what the Contessa thinks.'

The room was once again filled with the insecurity of silence.

'Very well, then,' said Maria eventually. 'I will sing for the sake of the concert,' she said as she pushed the *Carezze* box just far enough away from her to make it almost unreachable.

The Contessa suppressed any outward signs of her relief. Trying to find a substitute mezzo-soprano who had the necessary repertoire at her fingertips in twenty-four hours would have been a next-to-impossible task.

'I think you know it will be more for the sake of Maria Santini,' smiled the Contessa as she stood up and took the cup and saucer to return it to the kitchen. 'Although, of course, your friends will be very pleased that you can join them in the concert. And, of course, so will I.'

Maria Santini smiled up at the Contessa. The two herons suddenly seemed to be a lot more relaxed in the folds of her gown.

'So … now I suggest that we prepare ourselves for tonight's rehearsal,' said the Contessa over her shoulder, as she made her way through to the kitchen. She felt a sense of achievement at having averted a possible crisis, but she also felt a sense of trepidation. Maria was prone to these bouts of depression, although the Contessa wasn't quite sure what the exact medical term was for them. What was obviously apparent was that they were occurring with more frequency than before. She had broached the topic with Luigi at one of their weekly suppers – not mentioning anyone specifically of course, but speaking in general terms. He had said that such a condition was usually the result of a mental attitude, rather than the result of anything purely medical. He had confirmed that there was a range of treatments available, depending on the severity of the individual case. It all depended on the mental state of the patient and, in some instances, whether the individual concerned had the ability or the will to realize that something was wrong and had the desire to be guided towards putting that condition right.

The Contessa stood in front of the sink, looking out of the window and down across the *Piazza Napoleone.* She wondered how long it might be before Maria Santini finally surrendered to her insecurities; either deliberately to get cured, or unintentionally and have the decision made for her.

31

Penelope, *La Contessa* di Capezzani-Batelli, sat propped up in bed against a pile of pillows, her glasses perched on the end of her nose, with Carlo Quinto snoring gently at the foot of the bed. The rehearsal had gone well enough, including one or two minor slips, thereby confirming the old theatrical maxim of a bad final dress rehearsal leading to a first-class opening night's performance. The Contessa had thought that Gregorio Marinetti had been on edge – again. Not when he was singing – that had been as pleasurable to listen to as it always was – but when in conversation. He had been like that for the last couple of weeks. She had allowed herself a moment of improper contemplation and wondered if he was having trouble fulfilling the more base side of his nature again. She had heard of the yoga teacher and the course for which Gregorio had signed up, as well as of the disappointment of his thwarted desire; there wasn't much that did not eventually filter back to the Contessa's ears. At the rehearsal she had felt a momentary twinge of sympathy for him, although he did look a little better for the exercise.

Why can't you just be yourself and be who you are? Whilst she could think this, the Contessa would never have dreamt of asking him about it. It was not the situation Maria Santini found herself in, where she exhibited the signs of actually *wanting* to be helped and those around her who cared could respond. No, Gregorio's problem was a delicate matter and his sexual preference would have to remain personal and out of bounds. She suddenly thought of Maria's and Gregorio's situations in contrast to Renata di Senno and Riccardo Fossi. *Subtlety is definitely not their strong point*, she mused as she plugged the earpieces into her ears and switched on her Walkman. The strains of the slow movement of Shostakovich's Second Piano Concerto floated softly into her brain. At bedtime, she preferred something a little more soothing than opera. It helped her to relax after the hectic activity of the day.

She reached out to her bedside table and picked up the book she was reading. As she did so the gold locket that she wore on a chain around her neck swung out from underneath her nightgown.

'Dear Giacomo,' she whispered softly over the strains of the music. She caressed the locket lovingly. 'You would have been pleased with the angels this evening. I think that the concert will be one of our best ever. But, of course, you'll be there with me and can hear that for yourself.' She smiled, raised the locket to her lips, kissed it gently and then tucked it back into her nightgown. She then sighed as she thought of their life together – Giacomo's and hers – how they had had so much to look forward to and had made so many plans together, before it was decreed that she would have to meet the achievement of their aspirations and dreams on her own – for both of them.

'Good night, my darling one,' she whispered, before propping the book against her knees and adjusting her glasses.

'Oh, Elizabeth! You gave me quite a surprise!' said the Contessa loudly as she suddenly caught sight of the hovering shape of her faithful maid out of the corner of her eye. 'Did you knock?'

'As if the very staff of Saint Peter himself was in me hand,' came the acerbic reply.

'What was that?' replied the Contessa, who hadn't heard

clearly over the sound of the music. She removed the right-hand ear-piece. 'What about Saint Peter and his staff? Did Saint Peter have a staff?'

'I was after saying that... Away with ye. 'Tis of no matter. Where will you be wantin' this, then?' she asked, holding out a cup and saucer of steaming liquid towards the Contessa. She shook if she had to carry something for a protracted period; that explained the cocoa in the saucer.

'Oh, how kind. I'd forgotten all about the cocoa. I think on the bedside table will be quite in order, thank you. It smells appetising.'

'And I found this in the music room,' she said, holding up a gold lipstick case in her other hand.

'What's that?' asked the Contessa.

''Tis a lipstick. "Whore's Red" from the look of it. If y'ask me 'tis from the one who sings high – her with all the rings.'

'You mean Renata?' replied the Contessa.

Elizabeth made no reply, but stood shaking the cup and saucer in one hand and clutching the offending lipstick between two fingers of the other, as if she didn't actually want to touch it at all. She had a knowing look in her eyes.

'I wonder why she forgot to take it with her?' asked the Contessa.

''Tis because she and that smarmy one is havin' *cardinal* relations and they couldn't wait to get out of here and on with it, so they are,' replied the maid with a deadpan face. ''Tis blindingly obvious to those that can see.'

The Contessa was about to reproach her retainer for even suggesting such a thing when she was cut short.

'On the bedside table, says yourself. Will you be after takin' care of this thing, or will I be puttin' it in with the cleaning things in the cupboard?'

The aged retainer shuffled around to the far side of the bed and deposited the cup and saucer with an alarming rattle of the fine bone china. As she did so, Carlo observed her suspiciously through one half-opened eye. The servant certainly did not enjoy the same level of trust and affection as did the mistress.

''Tis hot,' said Elizabeth, stating the obvious in her own inimitable fashion, 'so drink it now,' she ordered as she shuffled back around the bed towards the door. 'I'm now away to me bed,' she continued, eyeing the Contessa with one raised eyebrow, 'but not before I'm telling you, herself in the kitchen is going to need a seeing to.'

'Why?' asked the Contessa.

'I'll not be going into that now; 'tis late and I'm tired. I'm just after telling you for yourself's information that herself will need a seeing to ... and that's the end of it.'

Elizabeth stood halfway between the door and the bed, a look of triumphant achievement on her face. The Contessa did not have the faintest idea what had seemingly upset her. Besides, it was late and the Contessa was also tired.

'Very well, Elizabeth, we'll discuss your concerns in the morning,' she said, reasonably confident that by that time Elizabeth would have forgotten all about it.

'I'm away off, then,' replied the maid as she wheeled, unsteadily, on her heels and shuffled off towards the door.

'Good night,' called the Contessa, and plugged herself back into the right-hand ear-piece of her Walkman. The Shostakovich had moved on into the final movement, with its uneven seven-in-a-bar beat pattern, which was far too vigorous for so late an hour. The Contessa fumbled with the controls and rewound the tape. Then she picked up her book once again and opened it.

'Oh!' she suddenly exclaimed as she was presented with a crumpled envelope held in a gnarled hand. For the second time in as many minutes, the book fell shut again and the ear-piece was removed. 'Yes?' she asked, her voice tinged with the edge of uncharacteristic annoyance. 'What is it this time?'

'*Afore* I'm off to me bed, I'll be giving you this. It came with the post this morning. Yourself was out and about at the time, so I put it in me apron pocket and forgot to give it to ye. Now I'm giving it to ye; then I'm away to me bed. Good night.' The whole speech was delivered in a single breath.

'Thank you,' replied the Contessa who, thanks to Elizabeth's performance, was now more awake than asleep, 'and a goo...' She stopped in mid-sentence as a rather unpleasant aroma caught her nostrils, cancelling out the appealing attraction of the hot cocoa. She glanced down the bed at Carlo, who was snoring softly with both eyes firmly closed, now that the threat of contact with the aged maid had, for the time being, receded.

'How odd,' thought the Contessa, sniffing the air gingerly. 'It certainly wasn't me .... and if it wasn't Carlo ... Elizabeth?'

A loud click signalled the latter's departure as the tongue of the heavy lock on the bedroom door shot home.

'Oh,' muttered the Contessa for the third time, 'and she's gone off with Renata's lipstick.'

She replaced the ear-piece, moved the book further down the bed, reached across to take the saucer in her hand and took a long draught of the still-hot liquid. It was strong, good-quality cocoa and it was sweet, not because the Contessa liked it that way, but because Elizabeth was becoming more and more forgetful when it came to simple matters such as remembering the number of teaspoons of sugar she had stirred into a drink.

'Oh ... well,' muttered the Contessa for the fourth time, and replaced the cup on the table. She then turned her attention to the crumpled envelope, which had enjoyed most of the day in the confines of Elizabeth's copious apron pocket. Tearing it open, she removed the contents. Then she flattened out the single sheet of paper, discovered a pair of tickets and started to read.

My Dear Contessa,

    I do hope that you will forgive the directness of my approach, but I have always believed this to be the best policy. Please allow me to introduce myself. My name is Arthur Crowe and I am the founder and musical director of La Banda Inghiltalia. *We are a group of keen amateur musicians based in the Pescia area and are about 50% Italian and 50% expatriates, mainly English. That explains our name, which is a contraction of* Inghilterra *and* Italia. *Some of our players are former military bandsmen or orchestral players, so our standard of performance is very high.*

    The purpose of my letter is to enquire as to the possibility of our working together on a joint concert. I have attended one of yours and was very impressed by what I heard. I feel that our combined efforts will produce a musical event not to be forgotten in Lucca. I prepare much of our music and would be willing to arrange the orchestrations for whatever pieces your singers might wish to perform.

    I enclose two tickets for our forthcoming Starlight Concert and hope that you will be able to join us as my guest for the evening.

    I hope to receive your favourable reply in the near future.

    Yours faithfully

    Arthur W. Crowe

'Oh!' said the Contessa for the fifth time.

32

'When did he call?' asked Gregorio Marinetti, clutching his DECT phone as he stood in the shade of the umbrella, his naked body still glistening with the refreshing sparkle of water from his swimming pool.

'Immediately before I phoned you,' Nicola Dolci replied tersely. 'You know I don't like phoning you on the day of one of your concerts, but the gentleman who telephoned was quite insistent that he speak to you. He said that you did not answer your mobile, as arranged, so he phoned the shop.'

'My mobile hasn't rung at all – not yesterday afternoon, not today, not...' He broke off as he bent towards the wooden recliner to retrieve the offending object from the pocket of his cotton beach wrap. Nicola wondered what the significance was of the mobile not having rung the afternoon before, but she thought better of saying anything. Her boss seemed twitchy enough as it was.

'Look, I have no messages or...' There was a pause accompanied by a considerable amount of mumbling. 'Shit! Fucking thing's flat – no fucking power!'

'Pardon?' asked Nicola, who had heard perfectly well; Gregorio had shouted it loudly enough for half of Lucca to have heard.

'What!' barked Marinetti as he flung the dead wonder of the technological age angrily onto the recliner on which his robe was piled in a mangled heap.

Nicola thought it best to simply continue the conversation. 'The gentleman asked when you would be available and he also seemed quite a bit put out. I did not want to give him your home number. You've told me not to.'

That was true. In the past, he had been unlucky enough to have made the odd liaison, which had subsequently gone wrong, and thought it best to remain 'non-contactable' until the emotional threat of these depressing occasions had passed. But this caller had not been one of his recent disastrous affairs. He knew that this caller had wanted to talk to him about an important collection – one which should have taken place the previous day and one which had caused him to be preoccupied during the final COGOL rehearsal. As a result, he had made two silly musical mistakes. Eventually, he had had to force himself to switch his attention away from the source of his suppressed panic and onto his music. He not only had a stolen object to dispose of, in return for a substantial sum of money, he also had his considerable musical reputation to live up to. Everything had caused him to have a virtually sleepless Thursday night. Now, at what for him was an early hour of the day, his mind was giving a highly convincing impersonation of a tumble dryer in full revolution.

'Did you take a telephone number?' he asked, already knowing the answer. Agents who represented clients such as this one were not in the habit of giving out their contact telephone numbers. Any contact in matters of this nature was definitely a one-sided affair.

'I did ask, but he said that he would call back later, at approximately four o'clock. I did not want to say that you were not in today. He was well-spoken and I thought that he might be interested in something with a high price ticket. He didn't say what it was he wanted. As you know, we could do with the business...' Nicola let the unfinished sentence hang in the warm morning air. Lately, with business being as quiet as it had been, she had often wondered how long it would be before she was told that her services were no longer needed at the shop.

'Four o'clock. Alright, Nicola, I'll be in at about a quarter to four. Oh shit … there is something I will have to collect first. If I can't manage it on my own I'll phone for Francesco to help me. Can you tell him that I might need his services a little earlier than planned.'

Snap your fingers and your lapdog comes running, thought Nicola. The way Marinetti treated her brother – even if he was a little different in the head from most other people – really annoyed her at times, but the money was reasonable and Francesco had little hope of finding anything else that would pay as well.

'I will tell him,' she said. 'See you later.' And then she replaced the receiver.

'Blast it!' snapped Gregorio as he spread his towel on the paved surround of his pool and tried to settle down to his yoga routine. Despite the fact that his principal, misguided reason for enrolling in Tezziano's yoga course had come to nothing, he had kept up the exercises and felt much better for it. He was finding it difficult to remain calm and would have preferred to have kept his mind clear of everything except the evening's concert. The reality was that he was becoming more and more worked up about everything with each passing moment. He would have to go to his lock-up, collect the screen – hopefully without having to summon Francesco's reliable but painfully slow muscle power – then drive into Lucca and close the deal. After all of that, he then had a concert to sing. It just was not fair on him!

'Fucking people!' he shouted out in uncharacteristic fashion. He was not prone to the use of socially unacceptable language, but he was making up for his avoidance of it now. 'They say one thing, do another and then change their minds again! Bastards!' he yelled. In his jangled state, it never occurred to him that he had not charged his mobile for well over a week and that possibly the present situation was largely of his own making. Acknowledgement of his appallingly bad decision to try gambling his way out of his financial woes also never entered his head.

A flock of birds, alarmed by the sudden shriek, took flight from the safety of the row of tall trees, which lined the southern boundary of his property.

'Take steady breaths … in … out … in … out,' he gasped as he tried to create the pre-concert ambiance, which was so vital to his preparations for a good performance.

After five minutes of pointless effort he was no nearer a state of inner calm than he had been before Nicola's telephone call.

'It's no use,' he muttered angrily, finally admitting defeat; 'there's too much going on to let me relax.'

He got up and was about to dive into the pool once more when he remembered that his mobile needed charging.

'Fucking thing!' he snarled as he picked it up and glared at the dead screen. 'I now have to abandon my concert preparations and plug you in to charge!'

He had not had a good week and, so far, he was not having a good day either – and it was not even noon.

33

Inspector Michele Conti looked questioningly at Sergeant Pascoli, who stood in the doorway of his office with an 'it's to be expected' look on his face.

'Well, Sergeant?' asked Conti, who had been distracted from reading a discreetly folded copy of that morning's *La Nazione* newspaper.

'Not really, sir... Seems he's quite ill, actually. At least, that was the message *Signora* Bramanti left.'

Questore Bramanti's health had been a topic of debate for some time amongst the staff of the *Questura*.

'Is he in?' asked Conti, leaning back in his chair.

'No. So I suppose that makes you senior officer until he gets back,' replied the unsmiling sergeant, who was well known for being an expert on finding things via the Internet, but not for possessing a detectable sense of humour, 'or until Florence decides to send someone else up here,' he continued.

For a moment, Michele Conti sat and thought what this situation implied. Then, being a policeman who usually followed thought with action, he sat upright in his chair. 'Right then,' he said in a very matter of fact manner, 'let us get on with the business of the day. What do we have?'

Whilst Pascoli had filled the doorway, Conti had been reading yet another speculative article about the Lucca murders. Lack of any progress in the cases – including the latest one in Montecatini – had pushed the reportage to page five, but it was still there and the public were still unhappy with the lack of results.

'Anything new on the murders?' he asked, thinking that it was as good a place as any to start.

'Well, yes and no,' replied the sergeant, who still stood in the doorway.

'What do you mean, yes and no?' asked Conti.

'No, nothing new of any significance has turned up since yesterday … and yes, something new has turned up this morning.' He took a couple of steps into the office and stood next to the inspector's desk.

'So…?' prompted the inspector, who found Pascoli's occasional attempts at theatrical revelation, which were anything but convincing, rather annoying. 'What's new?'

'This…' replied the sergeant, putting a sheet of paper on the desk in front of Conti with a flourish. 'It's hot off the fax machine.'

The inspector stood up, clutching the fax in his right hand. It had been sent from Florence, copied to Assistant State Prosecutor di Senno and it was, indeed, 'hot'. He finished reading to the end and then turned to look at his subordinate. It was his first, totally unexpected day in charge of the forces of law and order in Lucca and this had to be the first thing to cross his desk.

'The Foreign Ministry in Rome has been contacted by the German Government in Berlin and has requested the *Carabinieri* to "assist" us with the investigation into the murder in Montecatini, due to its international dimension,' he said, reading from the sheet. Sergeant Pascoli had adopted an 'I know' expression, because he had already read it on the way to Conti's office. 'That means they'll be all over us with their arrogance and innuendo at our perceived incompetence. Blast it!' He put the fax back down on the desk, thought for a few moments and then crossed to the door. 'If anyone wants me, I will be in the lavatory. I could be gone quite a time.'

34

'I have a call for you,' rasped the elderly voice of *Signora* Litelli. 'It is *Signor* Doriano Peri from Florence.'

'Thank you, *Signora*,' replied Riccardo Fossi as he settled into his comfortably upholstered leather armchair. He mused that the ever hyper-efficient *Signora* Litelli, given another ten seconds with the caller, would probably have deduced his eye colour, the colour of his hair and when he had last had sex. She had a knack of finding out all sorts of things. 'Doriano, *come stai?*' he asked warmly, using the less formal form of address, usually reserved for family members or very close friends.

'Good. And you?'

'Fine ... fine,' replied Fossi, turning slightly to look across the expanse of his office and out of the large window. He was in a good mood. There was Renata, the evening concert and the as-yet-unconquered Miss Yvonne Buckingham. He was in a very good mood.

'Just a quick call,' continued Peri, 'to let you know that the matter we discussed earlier in the week – well, I have no information whatsoever on that topic ... nothing locally, anyway.'

He was careful not to give any details away. Even calls made from the Florence Flying Squad Headquarters ran the risk of the occasional eavesdropper and it was always advisable to err on the side of caution.

'That's good news and a big relief,' replied Fossi, turning his attention back to his large desk and fiddling with a pen, which lay on the desk blotter. 'Thanks... I owe you one, my friend,' he continued.

'Funnily enough, Riccardo, I had thought of that,' replied Peri, chuckling. Then his voice suddenly took on a sharper edge. 'Just because I haven't found anything doesn't mean to say that the topic of discussion does not exist. It could be that we just don't know about it. You know the sort of thing – left hand doesn't know about the right hand.'

Fossi stopped fiddling with the pen. 'How do you mean?' he asked.

'I was thinking that perhaps you could help us, you know. If you proceed with the topic and then find out something we don't know, about the topic, you *would* let us know ... wouldn't you?' There was a prolonged pause as Riccardo Fossi's pleasurable good mood suddenly developed a slightly sour tinge. 'It's nothing more than we would expect from an upstanding pillar of the community such as you. It would be your duty,' continued Doriano.

'Of course.' Fossi's voice caught in the back of his throat. He coughed and it returned to its normal placing. 'Of course,' he repeated, the melodious sonority of his voice restored, but the doubts he had harboured about *Signor* Daniele di Leone and his olive oil were as alive as ever.

35

Julietta Camore sat at her piano doing a leisurely warm-up routine of vocal exercises and scales. It was still early in the day and she would mark her arias until the evening, when she would give full voice to them in the performance. She had wanted to sing the showpiece aria '*O don fatale*' from Verdi's *Don Carlo*, but had had her nose put out, somewhat unkindly, when she had mentioned it to Renata during a casual encounter in Lucca, only to be told that the Contessa had already approved Renata's choice of the same aria. Julietta had suspected that Renata had walked on past the next bend in the street and then phoned the Contessa to lay her claim to the piece before Julietta could. There had been little love lost between the two sopranos for some time now. As a result of Renata's perceived dishonesty, Julietta had been obliged to select something else. She had settled on Abigail's aria from the second act of *Nabucco*. The Contessa's fingers would make short work of the rousing introduction to the recitative, filling in the missing chorus and playing the accompaniment to the aria like a full orchestra. Besides, given the way she felt about *Signora* di Senno, the sentiments expressed by the daughter of King Nebuchadnezzar, the *Nabucco* of the title, seemed quite apt: '*O villains all! Upon all you will see my fury fall!*' Fair enough, Julietta had not just discovered a document proving that she was not actually her father's daughter, but the displeasure she felt towards Renata amounted to much the same thing in its building intensity.

Julietta spent some time polishing her interpretation of Abigail's great outburst. Then she reached up to the pile of scores on the piano to retrieve *Lucia di Lammermoor*. Last evening's rehearsal had gone quite well, but there was a section of the sextet which had been rather insecure, caused, it had seemed, by a sudden lack of concentration on the part of Gregorio Marinetti. The Contessa had covered it up from the keyboard, but Julietta wanted to run through it, just to be on the safe side. As she reached up and took the score she knocked her diary off the top of the pile. It cascaded over the piano's music stand and landed with a discord on the keyboard. It had landed open, face down, at the page on which she had written the name of Ruggiero Mondini. She had still not told the Contessa about this young man with the outstanding voice, this un- believable find who had been personally recommended by her sister, Mirella. Julietta had never met this young Mondini, who was shortly to commence his studies at the university in Pisa. Unfortunately for him, his association with Mirella had tainted any hope of a pleasant relationship with Julietta. She slammed the diary closed and placed it on the piano stool beside her with a thump. She had already resolved to tell the Contessa about him and his marvellous voice only if this 'singing angel', to quote her sister, actually telephoned her. Mirella had given Julietta's phone number to others in the past, much to the latter's annoyance, but in her own inflated opinion, it was Mirella's firmly held convic- tion that *all* of her friends were socially improving contacts. Despite this, nothing had ever come of Mirella's assurance that by doing so, her sister would benefit from any possible contact.

36

'Can you put my mother on the line please, Elizabeth?' asked Luigi di Capezzani-Batelli. He had been busy with an intriguing case of suspected murder, which, of itself, was nothing new to him. That was, after all, what constituted a large part of his job; not the actual act of murder, naturally, but the often complex unravelling of the method used to send the unfortunate victim on their way.

'I'll have to be after doing the stairs. Herself is on the *balconie* upstairs, resting herself for the *conceit* tonight. Can you be doing with a message? 'Twould be easier than anything else.'

Elizabeth was always very down to earth in her assessment of a situation, particularly if she could avoid undue physical exertion.

'That's kind of you to offer,' replied Luigi, who had long ago learnt to hoist the maid with her own petard, 'but I really do have to talk to her myself ... if it's not too much trouble. I know how busy you are.'

'Oh, 'tis never too much trouble for Elzeebit to do this and to do that,' replied the housekeeper with more than a generous dose of sarcasm in her voice. 'Hold on to this thing,' she snapped before a deafening crash in the earpiece confirmed that she had unceremoniously deposited the handset on the hall table on which the telephone stood.

With the hindsight of many years of experience, Luigi had anticipated her action and had conducted the last few lines of the conversation with his handset held well away from his ear. He knew he would have to wait some considerable time, as the mumbling retainer went from floor to floor before summoning his mother to the telephone. As he sat waiting, he ran his eyes over the images of the scans the radiographer had taken of the victim, but they revealed nothing out of the ordinary. Then he turned his attention to the medical records, which accompanied the corpse. The elderly male had had a pacemaker fitted several years before, in order to stabilize the rhythm of his heart. Since then, he had been in good health until his sudden and unexpected demise. According to the *polizia* report, his son had found him dead in bed one morning and, in a state of extreme hysteria and distress, had reported it. The general assumption was that the victim's heart had finally given out, possibly due to the failure of the pacemaker. It was recorded that the victim's son had said that he couldn't remember when the battery in the pacemaker had been changed, if at all. The interesting thing revealed by Luigi's physical investigation was that the pacemaker was working perfectly and still continued to send impulses to the long-dead heart. His next step would be to investigate for signs of smothering. He was in the middle of making a note on the subject when Elizabeth, wheezy and a little out of breath, came back on the line.

'I'll be giving you over to herself,' she said and her voice was abruptly replaced by that of the Contessa.

Although Luigi conceded that Elizabeth was getting on a bit and quite possibly was almost at the point of being past many things, he never ceased to be amazed at where she found her reserves of energy. It had taken her some little while to negotiate the stairs, but she had managed to deliver the message and return to the telephone in advance of his mother.

'Hello, dear, what a nice surprise to hear your voice,' said the Contessa. In the background could be heard the muffled sound of several growls and a heated exchange of words.

'Hello, *cara*. This is just a quick call about the screen for tonight,' he said.

'Oh, dear,' replied the Contessa. 'They've all done very well in rehearsal making believe the screen was there, but we do need the real thing for our audience. I do hope that you are not going to tell me that we can't have it.'

'Good heavens, no,' replied her son, chuckling; 'quite the opposite, actually. I'm phoning to tell you that the screen is a brand new one from the central storeroom – unused.'

'Oh, I say, that *is* good news. How kind you are to me,' she continued affectionately. 'All of COGOL appreciates your help.'

She was not only pleased that COGOL would have the screen it needed for the Humperdinck and Mozart excerpts, but was equally as pleased that the item in question would be free from the possibility of the clinging antiseptic aroma of its origins. That had been of concern to her before.

'I have arranged for it to be delivered to the *istituto* last thing this afternoon. Perhaps you could just make sure that somebody there knows to expect it?'

'That is not a problem. I will phone *Signor* Orsini at the *istituto* myself. He is already expecting a chair and the little table from the drawing room. Gregorio is going to organize the collection and will take care of the delivery of both items for me. Are you busy with your work today?' she continued.

'An interesting case at the moment, but I cannot say much about it at present – *polizia* business, you know.'

The Contessa made a sound of understanding acknowledgement.

'Anyway, *cara*, I thought I would just confirm arrangements about the screen. The other thing for you to mention to *Signor* Orsini is that the cases of wine and glasses from the villa will also be delivered during the afternoon. I must go now, so I'll see you at the concert this evening. *Toi Toi Toi.*' He wished his mother good luck for the concert and hung up.

The Contessa smiled broadly as she replaced the handset. She let her hand linger on it for a few moments, as if reluctant to break the connection with her son. She had found herself growing closer and closer to him, the older she became. As she stared idly down at the telephone she thought that, if things had been decreed otherwise, Enrico would be Luigi's elder brother by five years and Giacomo – well, Giacomo would have been nearly a hundred. She sighed. She might be an idealist by nature, but she was far too much of a realist to dwell on that which was unattainable. Her momentary reverie was abruptly interrupted.

'Will herself be after havin' her tea down here in the sitting room ... or up the stairs on the *balconie*?' wheezed Elizabeth from the doorway leading to the kitchen.

37

Gregorio Marinetti was an unhappy man. His situation was not helped by the early afternoon heat. He was a sensitive artiste whose God-given talent of a beautiful voice obliged him to perform for the pleasure of his audience. It was his duty to prepare himself thoroughly, both mentally and physically, so that his audience might share in the beauty of his talent. He had tried very hard to separate the thought of the screen from his need to prepare for the concert – not that Nicola's news earlier that morning had helped – and had found that the more he tried to do so, the more unsuccessful he became. At last, in a mixture of anger and frustration, he had decided to sort out the screen first. At least he had spent the morning relaxing as best he could: he had had to wait for the mobile phone to charge up anyway, as he would have need of it during the day. So shortly after midday he set off to collect the screen before Francesco went to the lock-up to collect the chair at four o'clock. Instead of a restful build-up to the performance hour, he now found himself at the head of a cloud of dust as he drove along the dirt track that led to his lock-up: he faced the prospect of lifting the heavy screen into the van. The screen would now have to be stored in the van until such time as it was exchanged for the money from his client. As he bumped along the final stretch of the track, his elderly neighbour's wife, who was busy in the adjacent field, stood up from her work on the vegetables and waved at him. Marinetti, who was muttering loudly to himself, ignored her completely. He was in no mood for social niceties.

He screeched to a halt outside the lock-up and slammed the gears into reverse, executing a three-point turn before reversing up to the front of the garage, leaving just enough space for the door to swing up and open.

'This is all just so unfair,' he mumbled to himself with extremely bad grace as he fumbled around trying to unlock the padlocks. 'Stupid mobile!' he snorted, oblivious to the fact that the consequences of having let its battery run flat were entirely of his own making.

As the door swung majestically upwards, Gregorio Marinetti swayed backwards on his heels, like a stalk of ripe wheat caught in a breeze, until he almost hit his shoulders on the back of the van. As he regained the vertical, his mouth hung open in disbelief at what was or – more to the point – was *not* in front of him.

'Whaat ... the ... fuck!' he exclaimed, his mouth hanging limply open and his eyes bulging from their sockets. He was prone to the occasional over-reaction – indeed there were those who agreed amongst themselves that at times he could be a typical drama queen. This time, however, it was different and Marinetti had more than enough reason to exhibit this tendency. 'Whaa...?' he repeated, but he got no further than he had on his first attempt. In a state of semi-comatose shock, he ambled into the garage, banged into the Contessa's chair and stopped facing the empty space against the wall, which had formerly been occupied by the fabric-draped screen. In its place, lying on the floor with a large footprint upon it lay his hand-written note: 'Take this to the Institute'.

With his mind in turmoil, Marinetti retreated to the chair and sat down, heavily. He stared straight ahead of him – out of the garage door and across the expanse of fields. 'That bloody idiot, Francesco!' he suddenly shouted as he reached into his trouser pocket and withdrew his mobile. 'I tell him to do one simple task and the moron can't even get it right!' He stabbed his finger angrily down on the buttons until Francesco's name and number appeared on the screen and hit the dial button. 'When I get my ha… Hello!' he cut across himself as Francesco answered. 'What the hell have you done?' he shouted.

'*Scusi, Signore?*' answered Francesco as he bore the brunt of Marinetti's unexpected outburst. He had been expecting a call from Maurizio, one of his team mates on the local football team.

'Where is the screen … you … you idiot! Why did you go to the lock-up so fucking early: I said fucking four o'clock? Why did you take the screen and not the fucking chair? My instructions were clear enough, you … you … fool!' Marinetti was well and truly submerged in one of his 'diva' moments.

'What? I collected the items from the Contessa's apartment and then I went to the lock-up early as I didn't want to make the delivery too close to the starting time of the concert. I took what your note said I had to take,' replied Francesco, unsure as to what his boss was talking about. 'I read it carefully. It said "Take thi–"'

'I know bloody well what it said!' thundered Marinetti. 'I wrote the sodding thing.'

'Oh,' muttered Francesco from the safety of the other end of the connection, 'but it said to take the thing to the *istituto,*' continued Francesco, chipping in quickly between Marinetti's ranting. He was not *that* slow-witted. 'So that is what I did and it was very, very heavy,' he continued, seemingly unperturbed by the explosion out at the lock-up, which showed very little sign of abating. 'The sign was on the floor in front of that big folding thing – with the picture of the lion on it – like they have in Venice…'

'That *is* the Li…' Marinetti had been about to confirm

the provenance of the screen and then thought better of it. The old saying of 'pearls before swine' flashed into his mind. 'So are you telling me that you've taken the screen to the *istituto* and not the chair?' snapped Marinetti, who realized that, in part, it was a stupid question to ask, as he was sitting on the item in question.

'That's what the note said,' replied Francesco. 'It said, "Take this to" –'

Gregorio stabbed the 'disconnect' button on his phone and the call ended.

'I'm going to have to talk to Nicola about that idiot!' he muttered as he stood up and returned the mobile to his trouser pocket.

He knew that there would be several small deliveries to the *istituto* during the course of the day – there always were on the day of one of the Contessa's concerts. He hoped that the idiot Francesco had not damaged the screen through his manhandling and that it had been safely deposited at the *istituto*, preferably without anyone noticing what it actually was. He had started to feel nauseous. He hadn't eaten much since Nicola's phone call earlier that morning; he never did on the day of a concert, not until after the performance. But today was different. Perhaps, he thought, the unnecessary worry and rushing around had burnt up his reserves of stored energy. That was, however, highly unlikely, given his substantial proportions.

'Shit! Now I'll have to go straight into town to see if the screen is safe and deliver the bloody chair myself,' he muttered as he picked up the heavy, throne-like chair and manhandled it out to the waiting vehicle. He had suddenly become even more belligerent than before as the realization that even more of his preparation time before the concert had suddenly evaporated. There was definitely no time to go to his yoga session with the lithe Tezziano.

*

Gregorio Marinetti was even more of an unhappy man than he had been before. His usual pre-concert plans for a leisurely build-up to the evening's performance lay in ruins and he was now as tight as an over-wound main spring. The traffic had conspired against him and he had taken fifty minutes – almost twice as long as usual – to reach the *istituto*. By the time he had carried the chair into the auditorium and placed it on the stage he was breathing heavily with exertion. He almost started hyperventilating with relief when he spotted the errant screen, standing at the back of the performing area with a length of heavy blue brocade thrown over most of it in a generous swag.

'*Bravo*, Gregorio,' said a voice from the wings. 'You've brought the chair. I can always rely on you – you and all of my angels'. The voice had come out of nowhere and had taken Marinetti completely by surprise, so fixed had he been on the presence of the screen.

The Contessa had arrived shortly before lunch. She always spent most of the day of a concert at the *istituto*, setting up the properties, checking the sight lines, making sure that she had brought the correct scores with her and trying out the piano, the action of which she found a little heavy and, if the night was warm and the auditorium full, a little unresponsive to her touch. He spun around to stare into the Contessa's smiling face.

'And look,' she continued, 'we have your chair, the little card table and Luigi has even found me the screen we so badly needed.' Marinetti spun his head around in the direction of the Contessa's raised arm. 'It is a bit dark, so I chose the lighter of the two sides to face the audience. I think that the brocade just lifts it a little, don't you?' she asked.

'But … that is a very valuable…' blurted out the over-vexed antiques dealer. 'It should…'

'That's the strange thing, you know,' she continued,

patting Marinetti on his arm, much as a pleased parent would do to their prize-winning offspring on a school speech night. 'Luigi said that it came from a storeroom and hadn't been used, but I would say that it has seen a great deal of wear, wouldn't you? It's also a little grand for a hospital, don't you think?'

'A wha...?' said Marinetti, who was still having the utmost problem navigating his way through the rest of the word.

'Perhaps he changed his mind and found it in one of the offices. Some of them can be quite grand, you know...'

'We cannot use th –' but Gregorio Marinetti got no further with his protest.

'*Scusi!*' called a voice from the floor at the foot of the stage, 'but there is a telephone call for La Contessa ... from a lady who is hard to understand and who is talking over a barking dog,' announced *Signor* Orsini, director of the *istituto.*

'Oh dear, that sounds like Elizabeth,' mumbled the Contessa. 'Would you excuse me please, Gregorio. I had better go and see what she wants.'

For a few moments, Marinetti stood in the centre of the stage with his mouth still half open and his finger half raised in the direction of the screen. In addition to everything else he was feeling, he now also found himself confused. The Contessa had been speaking in English when *Signor* Orsini had brought his message. Marinetti was not sure he understood how the English could 'see' what somebody wanted by *talking* to them over the telephone. No sooner had the Contessa disappeared with *Signor* Orsini than Marinetti's confusion was interrupted by the sound of footsteps echoing on the polished wooden floor of the auditorium.

'Where do you want this?' asked a stocky man who seemed to be carrying a screen under his arm. It was a lightweight tubular affair, the panels of which had lengths of brightly coloured fabric stretched between top and bottom suspending wires. It was a hospital screen and Marinetti thought the pattern of the fabric was one of the most hideous things he had ever seen.

'Er ... over there,' he mumbled, gesturing towards the Venetian screen. 'No ... wait ...over there is better,' he added, pointing off into the wings.

'Right you are,' said the stocky man as he climbed the steps to stage level and deposited the screen in the safety of the wings.

As he did so, it occurred to Gregorio that he might be able to swap the two screens, if the Contessa's telephone call kept her out of the auditorium for sufficient time. He was just about to ask if the stocky man could help him when caution got the better of him. The Venetian screen was, after all, stolen property and the fewer people who saw it, even with the protecting veil of the brocade, the better.

'There you are,' said the stocky man, removing a pencil from behind his ear and smoothing out a folded sheet of paper. 'Can you sign the delivery note, please?' he said. 'I'll just fill in the date and the time.' He looked at his watch, 'three thirty-three. Better get that right – you know how they want you to account for every second of the working day.'

The announcement of the time had sent a thunderbolt through Marinetti's already over-tired brain. 'Shit! Three thirty-three! I have to go!'

'Has he called yet?' he asked as he ran into the refined coolness of *Casa dei Gioielli*. 'It's almost a quarter to –'

'*Buona sera,*' replied Nicola Dolci from behind the counter, where she was busy dusting a set of seventeenth century Roman plaster medallions in their protective wooden display case. She looked up from the baize-lined box and had to consciously fight to prevent herself from saying how dishevelled and unkempt her boss looked. 'A busy day?' she enquired softly, the irony of the question going straight over Marinetti's head. 'It's been very quiet here … again. Coffee?' she asked, closing the lid of the case and covering it with her duster.

Marinetti crossed to his inner sanctum and picked up the phone. The comforting dial tone did nothing to calm him. He wanted it to ring. No, he didn't want it to ring – not this close to the concert. Yes, he did want it to ring – he had to get rid of the screen, but it was in the wrong place and it was enmeshed in the Contessa's voluminous brocade. He replaced the handset and buried his face in his hands.

'One lump or two?' asked Nicola as she appeared next to his desk with a cup of steaming *caffe Americano* and a bowl of sugar cubes.

'What? Er … two,' replied her boss. He was sweating and his shirt was streaked with sweat and dust. She wondered what on earth he had been up to, but thought it best not to try and find out. Instead, she replaced the sugar bowl on the shelf behind the counter, where a small DeLonghi coffee machine stood, then returned to the medallions. Gregorio was busily stirring the bottom out of the cup when, almost to the second of 4.00 p.m., the telephone burst into life. Despite the fact that he was expecting the call, Marinetti got such a fright that he flipped the teaspoon upwards and splashed coffee in several projectile paths across the surface of the desk.

'Yes… Hello,' he said, trying to keep his voice calm.

'*Signor* Marinetti?' asked the calm voice at the other end.

'Yes, this is he,' replied Gregorio, trying to stem the spreading puddle of coffee as he spoke, before it reached the end of the desk and dribbled into his lap.

'I am, unfortunately, delayed by a short time. I now anticipate reaching Lucca at approximately eight thirty this evening. I will collect the item shortly after that time, as discussed.'

There was no indication that this was a negotiable arrangement. It was simply a statement of what was going to happen.

'Yes... Er, no... I mean to say that there will not be ti –'

'*Signor* Marinetti, I do hope that everything is as arranged. You seem to be a little undecided. I need hardly remind you that my superior is a very busy person and that I have much to conclude before the day is finished.'

Marinetti's mind was spinning faster than the slot machines in Las Vegas. 'Of course ... all is prepared,' he said, 'but the item is not at the shop... It is at the *Istituto Musicale Luigi Boccherini* just off the *Piazza Bernardini*. I will have it ready for you at the time you specify.' Given the circumstances, he did not feel confident enough to remind this man to bring the cash. There was a silence on the line, which seemed to bore straight through his ears. 'Hello?' he said, almost timidly.

'Why?' asked the caller, his voice ominously flat as if he suspected something was not as it ought to be.

'Why what?' asked Marinetti, without thinking, before he realized it was probably not the best answer to have given.

'Why have you changed our arrangements?' The voice maintained its previous quality of ominous calm.

'It is simply a matter of logistics, nothing more. I am performing in a concert there tonight and if I were not to do so, it would arouse far too much suspicion. I have a very well-established reputation amongst the musical *cognoscenti* here in Lucca. They expect me to sing.' Marinetti found that he had regained a little of his usual self; singing his own praises always did him the world of good. 'Everything is arranged and delivery will take place as planned at the time you have stated ... at the *istituto*. I assure you that the arrangements have been made with the utmost discretion.'

Marinetti crossed himself as he said this. There *were* no arrangements and he had absolutely no idea how he was going to affect the exchange. All he could picture was that bloody screen swathed in the Contessa's piece of second-hand cloth. The upside of this mess was that there was now nothing Gregorio could do until later that evening, hopefully at the time of the interval. Until then, he could at least try to concentrate on preparing himself mentally and physically for the concert.

'Very well... If your new arrangements are to my satisfaction – and only if – then the transaction will proceed as planned,' replied the caller. 'I will expect to see you there shortly after eight thirty this evening.'

'At the rear entrance,' added Marinetti quickly, 'down *Via Sant'Anastasia* ... to the right of the building.'

There was another pause. Marinetti, who was sitting with his eyes screwed tightly shut, hoped the man was writing down the new address details, but he also realized that he could just as easily be considering aborting the entire transaction. The nausea swept over him once again. If that happened, he was well and truly sunk!

'Until this evening, then,' said the caller, eventually.

'I look forward to it wi...' said Marinetti, before he realized that the caller had gone. People such as he did not waste time on polite small talk.

It was shortly before 4.10 p.m. Although he had recovered a good deal of his composure, he had not relaxed at all. He was still as tense as an over-wound mainspring and he had done almost no preparation for the concert. To compound matters, he would have to spend the next hour and a quarter driving through Lucca's crowded streets to return to his villa to shower, change, pack his music and then return to the *istituto* in good time, hopefully, to exchange the screens before the audience started to fill the auditorium. Tito Viale would be there adjusting his lights and setting the spots. He would also be able to help with the screen exchange. Tito never asked any questions. Besides, all this cloak and dagger stuff surrounding the screen had started to wear very thin on Marinetti's nerves, as he found himself slowly reaching the point of not caring about the consequences of his recent illegal action any more.

He was suddenly aware of someone standing next to his desk.

'More coffee?' asked Nicola Dolci, looking at the splashes on the desk.

38

The stage area at the *istituto* was a hive of activity, in the centre of which stood the Contessa. As always on such occasions, she was calm and unflappable, yet as firmly in command of her troops as had been any of the famous generals in history.

'That looks lovely, Tito... The way you have set those lights really gives the impression of sunlight streaming through a big window and into a room.'

Tito Viale smiled. He was happy doing something he loved and had not spared a single second's thought about the fallout he would encounter once he returned home.

'Actually, I have been helped today by my friend Piero. We work together at the municipal electricity offices and he volunteered to set up the lights for the concert, before he takes his seat in the audience.'

'That was very generous of him to give up his time for our little concert. Perhaps I can meet him after the performance? How useful it is to have friends like that: friends that offer support and assistance when it is most needed... you and COGOL are very fortunate.' Changing the subject abruptly, the Contessa continued, 'By the way, *Signor* Orsini mentioned that the *istituto* has installed some new equipment since our last concert.' The Contessa was now making interested, polite conversation. She had no head for the technicalities of electricity, nor of how Tito managed to achieve his magical lighting effects.

'They have one or two new spotlights up there,' he

replied, pointing up towards the fly bars, from which dangled a selection of theatrical lights, 'but they usually present only a soloist or possibly two musicians at *their* concerts. They do not have enough lights for a production such as ours. That is why we have to use one or two extra units.'

The Contessa nodded sagely, but very wisely did not attempt to add to Tito's comments.

'They also have a new lighting board over there. It is very modern and will link all the lighting changes through to a computer, which will control everything. I have been talking to their electrician and he tells me that they should have everything installed and running by our next concert.'

'Oh … how … modern,' replied the Contessa. 'Don't make yourself late. You still have to change. If you'll excuse me, I had better just go and quickly check on how they are progressing with the refreshments.' She walked through the empty, darkened auditorium and out through the central door. She crossed the foyer, her sensible heels clicking on the marble, and entered a large salon, which led off to the right. 'Don't those look absolutely beautiful?' she said, almost cooing with delight at the sight of several large arrangements of flowers and greenery, which were dotted around the room. 'Gilda has excelled herself … again,' she said, straightening a small printed sign, which read, 'Gilda Ignazio, Lucca's Florist'.

'*Buona Sera,*' called Gianni as he entered from a side door, carrying several large flat cardboard boxes, each of which contained a mouth-watering assortment of the best that *Café Alma Arte* could produce. He was followed by Anna, who was similarly laden. Verriano brought up the rear. Like the Contessa, they were all formally dressed: Gianni and Verriano in black slacks and bow ties and Anna in a simple, yet curvaceous, smart black evening dress. The Contessa noticed that Verriano was wearing trainers instead of black shoes. It would not matter, as he would be stationed behind one of the tables during the interval. She smiled at the thought that he had conformed to the expected norm, whilst at the same time managing to state his independence of youth. *Perhaps he will yet embrace his position in the family business.*

'Put those on the other table,' said Anna as Verriano staggered in carrying the largest pile. '*Buona Sera,*' she added, nodding her head at the Contessa once she had deposited her load on the table. 'Gianni has something to show you.'

'Oh...?' replied the Contessa. Gianni had moved behind the cloth-covered table and carefully put his load of boxes down. She turned to face him. 'That sounds intriguing.'

'I have had an idea,' said Gianni, carefully removing the top box and placing it on the table where the Contessa could better see its contents. 'The Contessa always asks us for that English *crostata,* which always looks so messy when we cut it into pieces...'

The Contessa smiled encouragingly; quiche had been an indispensable part of any cold buffet in her younger days, but that did not seem to be the case in Italy.

'I have solved the problem by making very small ones, which do not need to be cut up,' announced Gianni, removing the layer of aluminium foil with a flourish.

'Goodness me, don't those look delicious ... and look at everything else,' beamed the Contessa.

'Shall we put the wine on the table at the back of the room?' asked Anna, her hands free once again. 'They have stacked the cartons of bottles there ... and the glasses,' she said, gesturing.

'I think that is a splendid idea, my dear,' said the Contessa, turning to look at the wall of cartons, each emblazoned with the Capezzani-Batelli logo and the legend, *Vino della Villa Batelli,* in large letters. 'Splendid, everyone...

269

Well done to you all!' she said, applauding softly. 'They will shortly be letting the audience into the auditorium to take their seats,' she continued, glancing down at her watch. COGOL concerts always commenced at seven-thirty. 'I had better go and see how everyone is doing in the green room. It is already just past seven o'clock...'

She retraced her steps through the foyer, which was already starting to fill with concert-goers. She recognized one or two and smiled acknowledgement at others, before once again entering the auditorium. Halfway down the aisle she paused, taking in the effect of the simple set of chairs, table and brocade-draped screen. She thought how charming it all looked, basking in Tito's lighting.

'You would have been so proud of everyone, my darling,' she muttered as her hand unconsciously went to the gold locket around her neck.

For the second time in as many minutes, she had been returned to her past and the things she had lost. The wine reminded her of the disaster of their life out at the villa and the locket was her most precious reminder of her husband. Both had left a void in her, which her music almost – but not quite – filled.

Time marches on and so must we, she determined, patting the locket once more and then renewing her progress backstage towards the green room.

39

The green room was a large room located just behind the stage area, containing some chairs and three small tables, together with a single, full-length mirror, which was mounted on the wall next to the door.

Renata di Senno had balanced her vanity mirror on one of the small tables and was attending to last-minute adjustments to her make-up. At the same time, she kept one eye on Julietta Camore, who was pacing up and down, holding her score of *Lucia* in front of her. Every few steps she cast a furtive glance at COGOL's principal soprano. The barely controlled animosity that had been simmering between the two for months had now almost reached boiling point. As far as Julietta was concerned, the business of the *O don fatale* aria had seen to that.

Maria Santini, her ample form tastefully encased in a flowing gown of dark, iridescent navy blue, was sitting in one of the corners, her eyes closed. She was swaying backwards and forwards gently as she hummed her way through Dalila's aria. She wore a matching pair of enamelled, drop earrings, which swayed regally from front to back as she did so. None of the other COGOL members knew anything of the previous day's crisis of confidence in her top-floor apartment.

Riccardo Fossi looked every inch the male centre-spread in his bow tie and evening suit, which was such a snug fit that it looked as if it had been sprayed on, accenting all the right curves and bulges. In fact, as he crossed to the bottles of water that the Contessa had thoughtfully placed on the second table, Renata had been so distracted by the vision in her mirror that she had had to use a tissue to wipe away the ragged line of mascara that had missed her bottom eyelid by a mile.

'Do you want some?' he asked as he opened one of the water bottles.

Amilcare Luchetti, who had seated his substantial bulk precariously on one of the chairs next to the table, raised a hand in refusal. His jaw was moving as he kept his glance firmly on the score of Verdi's *Simon Boccanegra*, his eyes half closed.

He must be silently mouthing his way through 'Il Lacerato Spirito'. *You'd think that after the number of times he's sung it that wouldn't be necessary,* thought Fossi unkindly. *Never mind about the spirit; it's that evening suit that's going to be badly lacerated if he gets any fatter!*

Fossi had very little time for those of his sex whom he regarded as not being as perfectly built as he was. He turned away from the table and strolled back across the room. What he did not see was that Amilcare Luchetti quickly popped a handful of cashew nuts into his mouth and started chewing them gently. He had secreted the packet on his lap, under the discreet cover of his open score, and the enjoyment of its contents was what had caused him to half close his eyes.

'Good evening, everyone. Where shall I sit? Anywhere?' asked a voice that spoke Italian with the accent of someone newly arrived in the country. Yvonne Buckingham literally bounced into the subdued atmosphere of the green room and almost collided with Riccardo Fossi as he returned from the water table. Automatically he reached out, took her in his arms and steadied her. Renata saw this unintended intimacy in her make-up mirror and immediately had to face her old spectres of jealousy and anger. As if to

272

emphasize the point, her hand, suddenly freed from her concentration, slipped and traced a line of deep red where it should not have been. Whilst never taking her glare from the alarming image in her mirror, once again she was obliged to fumble with a tissue, this time to remove the red lipstick from her front teeth.

'Good evening, Miss Buckingham,' said Fossi in perfect English, his teeth flashing white as his smile broadened. 'I was beginning to think that you might not be joining us this evening,' he continued, every inch the *roué*.

Prior to the appearance of Miss Buckingham he had been eyeing Renata's back, exposed as it was by her very low-cut evening gown; he had also been fantasising on the promising shape of her breasts, raised as they were by the wiring in the gown's built-in support.

'And may I say how charming you look this evening,' he continued seductively, in response to the sensual pleasure of touching Yvonne's alabaster skin. He flicked a glance down and realized that her breasts were certainly not in need of any wiring support. Then he released his supporting grip and took her hand in his before kissing it.

'How kind you are,' the young lady replied, 'but I really do need the practice in Italian.' He smiled and bowed slightly. 'Do we sit anywhere?' she continued, switching to Italian.

'Anywhere at all,' replied Fossi, who was about to escort her to one of the empty chairs when Renata suddenly turned in her seat.

'Riccardo, would you be a darling and open this for me please. It seems to be stuck.'

Fossi crossed the room to Renata's table, but he paid more attention to where Yvonne Buckingham had settled herself. Before he could make a comment to the effect that the lid of the jar had not been stuck at all, the Contessa entered the room.

'*Toi Toi Toi,* everyone,' she said. 'The auditorium is filling nicely and we must soon commence. Remember to enjoy yourselves and just think of the music.' As she spoke, she moved around the room touching each of her angels in turn on the arm or shoulder. It was almost like a pontifical blessing, an acknowledgement that they had all done their best and that the ultimate outcome of that evening's performance was now well and truly in the lap of the gods. 'We have some very important people with us tonig –' The Contessa suddenly stopped as she drew level with Yvonne Buckingham.

'Good evening, Contessa,' said the young English Rose, smiling.

The Contessa smiled back; Fossi also smiled; Renata banged the box of tissues down on the table with unnecessary force.

'My goodness... How *lovely* you look, my dear,' said the Contessa, 'and what a ... lovely dress.' She had not missed the fact that the diaphanous gown did not leave too much to the imagination. Neither could she remember such vivid slashes of highlights in the young woman's hair from the previous evening's rehearsal. 'Charming,' she said as she reached out to pat her newest recruit's shoulder and then thought better of it, taking her hand instead. 'I hope you enjoy your first concert with us,' she concluded, smiling warmly into Yvonne's eyes as she did so. With experience, this young lady would learn about the proper dress code to be observed for a COGOL concert.

'And now I must go and prepare myself at the piano,' announced the Contessa as she completed her circuit of the room and found herself once more at the door. 'Another ten minutes and then we must start,' she said and turned to leave. Then she stopped and turned back into the room. 'Where is Gregorio?' she asked, looking at everybody.

'He will be here directly,' said Tito Viale, who had shed

the work clothes he had worn to set the lights and now appeared looking very dapper in the regulation evening suit. 'He telephoned me a few minutes ago and said that he was held up – a traffic jam or something.' Viale did not say that Marinetti had sounded extremely stressed and had spoken in short, almost incoherent phrases. He also did not say that Marinetti had asked – insisted – that Tito help him with an exchange of something before the concert began. At that moment in the conversation, a car horn had blared repeatedly at Marinetti's end and had obscured what had been said. Marinetti had hung up.

'As long as he is all right,' said the Contessa, concern showing on her face.

40

The first half of the concert had gone extremely well. The singing had been beautiful and the Contessa's solo contribution at the piano – her own Liszt-like fantasy on themes from the '*Intermezzo*' and 'Easter Hymn' in Mascagni's *Cavalleria Rusticana* had also been well received. Her angels were enjoying their well-deserved refreshments in the green room and the Contessa was pressing the flesh in the salon.

'A good concert again. I hope the Contessa is pleased?' asked *Signor* Orsini. 'I'm sure that the Contessa has met *Signor* Bruschetti – the manager of the *Teatro del Giglio*?'

She had.

'When are you going to present one of your concerts at the theatre?' he asked. 'Oh … it's quite all right; Orsini and I often work together. There is no bad blood between us…'

'Well done, *cara*, it is going very well and there are many favourable comments,' said Luigi, appearing at her side and kissing his mother on the cheek.

'Luigi dear, how smart you look in your evening suit,' she replied and in her turn, she kissed her son on his cheek. There was no hint of embarrassment about either action; it was merely a gesture of mutual support and affection. 'My dear, I want you to meet *Signor* Bruschetti from the *Teatro del Giglio*… And, of course, *Signor* Orsini you already know.'

Pleasantries were exchanged, which gave the Contessa time to wonder when her son was going to find a com-

276

panion to accompany him to these splendid occasions. She fully realized that she would not be there forever.

'So ... would the Contessa consider mounting a concert at my theatre?' continued *Signor* Bruschetti.

The Contessa inclined her head slightly in understanding. 'It is, indeed, strange that you should raise the subject, *Signor* Bruschetti. Very recently I have been considering the possibility of COGOL working with a group of instrumentalists on a concert. It is just an idea at present, but who knows...?' They continued chatting for another couple of minutes. Suddenly catching sight of Nicola Dolci shimmering in silver under the chandelier in the middle of the salon and surrounded by several admirers, the Contessa's attention was drawn to the two Australian backpackers who were standing on the edge of the crowd, talking to Roberta from the Tourist Information Office. 'Would you excuse me, please, gentlemen? I have just seen some people I simply have to talk to. I will see you shortly,' she concluded, patting Luigi on his arm before picking her way through the crowd in the salon, waving at Nicola as she went.

By the time the Contessa had worked her way through the throng, Roberta had disappeared to speak to some other friends and the two young visitors were left finishing off their plates of the delicious canapés provided by *Café Alma Arte*. 'Hello! How are you both?' she asked as she stood in front of Jez and Victoria, both of whom had nearly emptied their plates. The crumbs left behind amply testified to the amount of food they had eaten. 'Are you enjoying yourselves?'

'Hello... Yeah, just fine, thanks. The music's not bad. Never really been to one of these classical concerts before,' said Jez, whose mouth just happened to be almost empty when the Contessa appeared. 'The food's great, too.'

'Hi,' added Victoria, who had just swallowed her mouthful. 'Thanks ever so much, but we're right down the front and they've been giving us funny looks. We feel a bit uncomfortable.'

The Contessa wasn't at all sure what that meant, but surmised it had something to do with the casual way in which they were dressed. Jeans, T-shirt and a tie-dyed top were hardly the usual dress code. The *Lucchese* could be sticklers for protocol at times.

'What?' she asked.

'I don't think we're dressed well enough for them,' said Jez. 'We didn't pack our evening wear 'cos we never thought we'd be invited to anything so grand,' he continued, almost apologetically, a laugh hidden in the end of his sentence.

'Nonsense, my dears!' said the Contessa kindly. 'You are both here as my special guests – to enjoy the music and that is the important thing. It doesn't really matter what the rest of them think,' she continued, her eyes sparkling their defiance. 'I must circulate for a while… It's important to speak to everyone, you understand. Wait for me here at the end of the interval. The three of us will make a grand, slow progress down the aisle to your seats.'

At the same time that the Contessa was talking to the two backpackers in the salon, Gregorio Marinetti was on the stage struggling with the screen. Before the concert he had only just made it to the *istituto* in the nick of time. He had been preceded into the green room by a very strong smell of *Aqua di Parma* eau de toilette – his 'spray *de jour*', as Renata had sarcastically remarked a couple of rehearsals before. He had followed the fragrance into the room and because he seemed totally preoccupied and distracted, he had largely ignored everyone. Riccardo Fossi had been about to make a suitably cutting remark about this, but before he could do so, Marinetti had deposited a large carrier bag on the floor and had left the room without a word to anyone, almost as quickly as he had entered it a few moments before. Out of curiosity, Fossi had peeped into Marinetti's bag and poked at the contents with the fountain pen he always carried ready for any autograph hunters.

'We could be in for an interesting concert,' he had muttered as he stood up and put the pen back in his inside jacket pocket. 'A lot of cloth and some bubble wrap. Really! The things people carry about with them…'

Marinetti's contribution to the first half of the concert had gone well enough, but there were some barely disguised looks of concern amongst the other singers during the *Martha* quartet, as well as during the more taxing one from *Rigoletto.*

'I hope he pulls himself together before his *Toreador Song*,' muttered Fossi just before the interval, 'otherwise he could find himself on the horns of a dilemma, if he forgets himself.'

There had been no response to his pun.

Whilst Julietta Camore and Maria Santini sang the 'Flower Duet' from Delibes's *Lakmé,* which was the last item on the programme before the interval, back in the green room, Yvonne Buckingham had relaxed somewhat and was laughing, engaged in a conversation with Amilcare Luchetti. Renata di Senno was also engaged in a conversation, but one that seemed far more earnest and animated. She had gone into a rugby-like scrum with Riccardo Fossi. In the lavatory, Gregorio Marinetti had cornered Tito Viale and was insistent that he help him.

'It is a matter of life and death,' Marinetti had said, not totally untruthfully, 'and you have to help me. That's why I phoned you. We have to exchange the screen on the stage for the other one – the hospital one propped up in the wings. I can't do it quickly enough on my own.'

'What is so important about an old screen that y –'

'Trust me, you would not believe me if I told you … which I cannot do,' continued Marinetti, his voice a rasping whisper. 'If we both do it, nobody will think anything of it; it is just like changing the scenery. It has to be repositioned for the second act anyway … and if we throw that piece of cloth over the hospital screen in its new position, everything will look perfectly normal and natural.'

'Well … if you are sure that –'

'At the interval, which should be somewhere around a quarter past eight, I have to…' He stopped in mid-sentence. 'The exchange has to be done during the interval,' he repeated, 'then you have to help me carry the bloody thing to the back entrance.' Marinetti was sweating quite pro-fusely and he had not yet sung his first solo.

'But why does it have to go to the ba –'

'Will you help me … pleeease?' Marinetti sounded as desperate as he had begun to look. *And just stop asking bloody questions*, he thought behind the pained expression on his face.

Tito Viale stood looking at Gregorio for what seemed an eternity. 'Okay,' he said as he turned on the tap to wash his hands.

The interval had barely commenced before Gregorio strode across the stage towards the screen.

'Come on,' he hissed at Tito Viale, who was a couple of paces behind him.

They were no more than halfway across the stage when a mobile phone rang. The sound of the ringtone was barely muffled by the fabric of the trouser pocket in which it lay.

'Whose is that?' snapped Gregorio. He knew it wasn't his.

'Sorry, Gregorio, I have to take this… It is Letizia; some-thing could be wrong with the kids.'

'Oh, for fuck's sake, Tito; get your priorities right for

a change!' shouted Gregorio, without thinking. There was the faintest of echoes from the auditorium, but as Marinetti was relieved to note, most of the audience had already adjourned to the refreshments in the salon. 'Wait... Can't you phone her back?' he hissed in Viale's direction, but the henpecked husband had already disappeared, on his way to the privacy of the passageway outside the green room.

'Shit! Well, sod you then,' muttered Gregorio to himself angrily. 'I'll do the bloody thing myself.'

He retraced his steps to the wings, collected the hospital screen and marched back across the stage to place it in position for the second half. It stood in line with the von Hohenwald screen and much further downstage of it. He had no sooner opened the hospital screen and blanched at the truly hideous fabric which covered it, than a voice called to him with some considerable authority from the floor level behind him.

'*Signor* Marinetti!'

Gregorio wheeled around and stared out into the auditorium's interval lighting.

'*Signor* Marinetti!' repeated the voice.

Gregorio looked down in the direction from which it had come. Then the blood in his veins froze.

'A pleasant evening of music, so far,' said Inspector Michele Conti. 'May I introduce my wife?'

Marinetti had no idea what the inspector said next as he was far too busy trying to open the hospital screen to its furthest extent, before this annoying policeman saw around it and noticed the dangerous object further upstage.

'The pattern on that fabric does seem a little out of character with the rest of the setting,' Marinetti heard the inspector saying.

'Er ... yes ... well ... we can throw something over it,' mumbled Marinetti.

'I'm back,' said Tito Viale from the other side of the

screen. The situation had deteriorated to something out of the plot of a baroque opera. Marinetti found himself caught between the law on one side and the presence of emasculated manhood on the other.

'Please don't let us keep you from your task,' called up the inspector. 'I can see you have to prepare for the second half. Thank you once again. Goodbye, *Signor* Marinetti.'

Gregorio let the inspector and his wife walk almost to the top of the aisle before he turned to Tito. 'Get the cloth off the other screen,' he hissed, 'quickly.'

'That's a very ugly piece of furniture,' said Tito Viale as he handed the length of blue brocade to Gregorio. 'I wouldn't give you two euros for it.'

So much you know, thought Marinetti as he hid the offending pattern of the hospital screen under the brocade. He stood back to admire his handiwork, which was not as well arranged as he would have done it in the shop, but it would do. 'Right!' he snapped. 'Let's take the other one away, and we need to be very careful with it. I've brought cloths and wrappings in a bag – they're in the green room. I'll pick them up on the way to the back door,' he said, looking at his watch. It was just before 8.25 p.m.

41

The second half of the concert was going to start with Gregorio Marinetti's rendition of the 'Toreador Song' from Bizet's *Carmen*. The Contessa always stuck to her principle that her angels should sing whatever solos they themselves selected, but over the last week, she had begun to regret this.

Despite a concerted effort executed in the best diplomatic way, she had failed to dissuade Gregorio from settling on this particular aria. It was, after all, one of his party pieces, but she felt that he needed to broaden his repertoire and sing something new. There was also the festering problem of Maria Santini's association with Bizet's masterpiece; an association that was very definitely best avoided at the moment. As an alternative she had suggested Barnaba's lilting aria from *La Giaconda*, but to no avail. In fact, she had become more than just a little concerned when he had seemed to ignore her and had acted as if he had neither heard her nor understood what it was she was trying to accomplish.

Oh dear, she had thought as they drank their tea during a break in rehearsal, *I hope I haven't pushed him too far; he seems to be a long, long way away. Perhaps he is too preoccupied with his problems to understand.* The Contessa did not know the accuracy of her supposition. *And I just cannot tell him the reason why I would like him to choose something else,* she continued to think, the smile on her face hiding what she felt about the awkwardness of the situation. *That would be most improper. I'm sure that Maria would not like the matter discussed openly.*

Eventually, the Contessa had thought of a simple solution: she rearranged the items in the second half, to give Maria Santini a long break from the stage, so that she could stay in the green room and out of earshot during the singing of something which, the Contessa feared, might just cause the reappearance of her earlier problems. Seeing that one of the two highlights in the second half was a lengthy excerpt from the first act of *Hänsel und Gretel*, in which Maria was going to sing the important role of the mother, keeping her well away from anything that might rekindle the destructive thoughts of her imagined trauma was of the utmost importance. As it was, the Contessa was only too aware that they had to survive the possible after-effect on Maria's nervous system of her rendition of Dalila's famous aria earlier in the programme.

And so it was that, with Maria Santini safely ensconced in the green room and Tito Viale's additional lighting correctly set, Gregorio Marinetti was to be found pacing slowly up and down in the wings, waiting for his cue to enter as the self-centred, egocentric bullfighter: characteristics which were largely true to life in Marinetti's case. There was, however, something different about him – he looked taller and, for the first time in days, he was smiling to himself as he hummed his way softly through the music.

'*In bocca al lupo*,' said Yvonne Buckingham, leaning up close to his ear to offer him the traditional Italian wish for a good performance. 'Back in England we would say "Break a leg",' she added, smiling.

'In Italy we reply "*Crepi il lupo*",' answered Marinetti.

Yvonne Buckingham's knowledge of Italian, good as it was, had not yet grown to encompass the peculiarities of certain colloquialisms. She looked mystified, as she had heard the whispered reply as 'Crap *il lupo*'.

'It means, I wish it could die,' he whispered, 'and it comes from the story of *Cappuccetto Rosso*.'

'Oh, I understand,' said Buckingham, smiling and folding her hands behind her back. 'We call that Little Red Riding Hood.'

Whether by intention or not, she had presented Marinetti with a largely exposed pair of firm, well-formed breasts. She had obviously not yet deduced that his preference lay elsewhere.

'Please excuse me, but I must focus my thoughts ... on the aria,' he said as he turned away from her and continued his pacing.

'Are you looking forward to your solo?' purred a voice behind her, almost from the curve of her shoulder. It was so unexpected that it caused her to start.

'Oh! Who's that?' she said, jumping slightly. This action caused her breasts to bounce – something which was not lost on Riccardo Fossi, who stood a good head taller than she did.

'It is only I ... Riccardo,' continued the voice, its practised silkiness folding itself around her.

'You gave me a fright,' she said.

'That was not my intention,' he replied, putting a reassuring hand on her shoulder.

'I really enjoyed your aria from *Tosca*,' replied Yvonne, whispering to him over her shoulder. From the auditorium, the sounds of the returning audience indicated the end of the interval.

'"*E lucevan le stelle*" – the out-pouring of one so in love ... so ... overcome with *desire*...' he paused to let the stress he had put on the last word sink in.

'It is a very moving melody ... full of pathos. I could hear the passion in your voice,' she replied.

Fossi was encouraged by her response. His hand moved a little higher up her shoulder. 'The aria you are going to sing is also full of romantic yearning ... of urgency. It is a beautiful aria, like "*E lucevan le stelle*"; it is also about love. So emotional...' Fossi was getting into his stride. He hoped that Renata would not appear and spoil his progress. He thought that highly unlikely as they had already had one heated conversation in the green room and she was now sulking. He had been in this position before and knew how to handle both her and the situation, which did not necessarily mean he had to rein in his ambition in other directions – it simply required good judgement and a certain amount of cool manipulation.

Yvonne Buckingham, who, it should be said, harboured no objections to the presence of a hand on her petite shoulder, now turned her head to see Fossi's handsome face looming over it.

'It is very beautiful. I hope that I can do it justice,' she replied, turning to look ahead once again, towards where Marinetti was still pacing, humming quietly to himself. He reached the furthest point of his pacing and turned, and slowly approached them again. As he did so, Yvonne Buckingham's mouth dropped open. On his left-hand side, clearly visible under the unbuttoned evening jacket and running from the inside of his thigh to well over halfway up to his waist, was a large bulge. Despite her lack of years, Yvonne Buckingham, the delicate English Rose, was no stranger to that part of the male anatomy that usually gave rise to a protuberance of this nature. But she had never seen one quite as large as this.

'Would you throw yourself into the Arno for the sake of love?' whispered Fossi, paying the approaching Marinetti no attention.

'Good God!' replied Buckingham.

'Are you a religious person?' asked Fossi, innocently

pursuing his familiar path towards ultimate female conquest.

'Is that for real?' she continued, lapsing into English.

'It is a story of young love meeting a little parental opposition. Such a situation often arises in Italy,' continued Fossi, who had switched to English. 'It is quite common.'

'It must be the sunshine and red wine that does it,' she continued in awe.

'It is the hot blood of the Italians,' replied Fossi.

And there must be quite a lot of it, to fill that, thought Yvonne. She was prevented from saying so out loud by the sudden appearance of the Contessa, who had safely deposited the two Australians in their seats. She was now ready to commence the second half of the programme.

'Are we ready to start again? Gregorio, you're first. Then you and Tito in the *Bohème* duet.' She nodded at Tito Viale, who had just joined the group. 'And are you ready for your debut, my dear?' she continued, smiling encouragingly at the English Rose. '"*O mio babino, caro*" is one of their real favourites. They'll love it ... especially when it is sung by someone who looks as pretty as you do this evening,' she continued, avoiding looking at the exposed cleavage.

Riccardo Fossi had managed to remove his hand before the Contessa could catch sight of it and was now busy clearing his throat.

'If the Contessa is ready then I too am prepared,' announced Gregorio Marinetti as he reached the little knot of COGOL artistes. He seemed to have grown a little and had a decided spring in his step.

'Goodness ... yes, then let us perform,' she answered, somewhat taken aback by the sudden transformation in Marinetti's demeanour and outlook. 'I will play the introduction and then you are on ... as usual,' she said as she turned to resume her place at the piano.

'Absolutely as usual,' he replied, beaming.

The Contessa was about to leave the cover of the wings when she suddenly stopped, turned and retraced her steps. Fossi removed his hand from the English Rose's appealing shoulder for the second time that evening and was, once again, clearing his throat.

'I almost forgot to remind you about the change in our running order for this half ... as we discussed at last night's rehearsal,' whispered the Contessa. 'After the *Bohème* we perform the *Cosi* trio. Yvonne, my dear, that's you, Julietta and Amilcare. Riccardo, you won't forget to make sure that everyone is ready in the wings in good time, will you?'

'Please consider the matter already accomplished,' he replied gallantly. Yvonne Buckingham found both his close proximity and the sensation of being enfolded in the warmth of his voice not unpleasant.

'Good, my angels, then let us proceed,' concluded the Contessa as she once again turned and started to walk towards the stage. As she did so, her mind dwelt for a second on the words of the Trio from Mozart's *Cosi fan Tutte* – '*Soave sia il vento*': May the breeze blow gently and may everything be calm. She smiled to herself as she walked into the glare of the stage lights. *That is not a bad wish to make,* she savoured.

As the Contessa crossed to the front of the stage to descend the steps to floor level and resume her place behind the keyboard, she was greeted by a crescendo of applause from the appreciative audience. She was helped down the short flight of steps by Luigi, who was standing waiting for her. This was a tradition of many years standing and it had become a bond, which drew the two of them together. The Contessa knew that she could never share her son's world of medical practice, but he was more than welcome to share in her precious world of music.

'They will applaud even louder for your solo,' whispered

Fossi, his hand once again in the preamble-to-seduction position.

'They are enjoying our efforts. Listen to that,' whispered Marinetti, who was standing in front of Yvonne Buckingham, waiting to make his entrance. As he spoke, he smiled at Fossi and Buckingham. It occurred to the former that in the last few minutes, Marinetti had probably said more than he had in the past two weeks of rehearsals. The latter was trying very hard not to look down Marinetti's front.

'I feel that this performance is going to be one of my better ones.'

Neither Fossi nor Buckingham had any idea of just how powerful the presence of well over 250,000 euros, in tightly bound bundles of 500-euro notes, could be on a previously depressed and tormented soul, even if those bundles, in the interests of a secure hiding place, had been shoved into a trouser pocket for safekeeping.

42

'You would have approved,' said Penelope, *La Contessa* di Capezzani-Batelli. She was standing in the comfort of her music room looking up at the oil painting of her late husband. 'I'm sure that you were there, listening.' She reached up and gently touched the heavy gilded frame. For a split second, she thought that she saw the lips curve into a subtle smile under their captive layer of darkened varnish, but her reverie was interrupted by a soft growling. She turned around and bent down to pat the tussled head of Carlo Quinto, who was sitting on his favourite chair, propped up against a cushion.

'Yes, I know you've been a good boy,' she said softly, 'and I'm sorry that I had to leave you with Elizabeth, but there was far too much to do and you would have become very bored.'

The real reason for leaving him at home had been far less charitable: previous attempts to include him in the activities surrounding her concert arrangements had ended in near disaster. People did not take kindly to a bad-tempered, growling dog getting in their way.

'Anyway, I'm sure that Elizabeth looked after you very well,' she continued, talking to him as if he were a child.

Carlo returned her gaze with one of deep affection, which, as sincere as it was, barely hid the feeling of rejection he had felt when he had realized that he and the belligerent domestic were destined to be at daggers – or, in his case, fangs – drawn for what seemed an eternity. He yapped twice

and started wagging his tail against the cushion. With each
swipe, the faintest suggestion of a cloud of dust rose gently
into the air.

'Mummy's home now and is very tired after her concert
… but not too tired to forget to bring you something.' She
crossed to the settee and picked up her sling bag, from
which she retrieved a small bundle. 'You're going to like
these,' she continued as she unwrapped the paper napkins
that contained several slices of salami. 'These were left over
and I knew someone who would like them.'

Carlo yapped again and wagged his tail more enthusias-
tically as his little nostrils filled with the delicious aroma.

'And now Mummy is going to sit down and have a rest. It
has been a tiring day, but everything went very well. All our
efforts have been handsomely rewarded.'

From the comfort of the settee, she watched as Carlo
noisily made short work of his treat, then he trotted over
to her and climbed up, putting his forepaws on her
knees. He seemed to be smiling, showing flecks of salami
wedged between his teeth. She laughed and patted him
again.

'You silly boy,' she whispered, smiling. But as she did
so, she thought of something else – something of more
profound significance. Just as the dog had shown how
much he depended on her for love and affection, so she,
herself, had become the virtual mother of her angels
through their involvement in COGOL. She thought of
Maria Santini, of Tito Viale and their unhappy existences,
of Julietta Camore and the barely concealed antagonism
that seemed to have suddenly blown up between her and
Renata. She thought also of Gregorio Marinetti and his
sudden recovery from the depression and gloom that
seemed to have stalked him for the past few weeks. Then
there was Yvonne Buckingham, who might well fall victim to
the handsome Riccardo Fossi; Amilcare Luchetti and his

ever-increasing girth. And her own Luigi – when would he find someone?

'I've brought yourself the *cherry*...' said Elizabeth, bursting into the music room, carrying a tray on which stood a cut crystal decanter and two sherry glasses. 'If the *conceit* was a good one, yourself will be wantin' the usual tipple to celebrate,' she said, putting the tray down with a rattle of crystal on the low table, which stood in front of the settee. The Contessa patted the seat next to where she was sitting.

'Dear Elizabeth ... thoughtful, as ever,' she replied. 'Would you like to pour ... and why don't you pour one for yourself as well?'